About the Author

Harper A. Burge resides in Plano, Texas with her husband and four children. She graduated from UC Berkeley with a degree in Earth and Planetary Science. Her hobbies include reading, sewing, and exploring the world with her family.

THE ROAD THIEVES

Harper A. Burge

THE ROAD THIEVES

Vanguard Press

A CIP catalogue record for this title is
available from the British Library.

ISBN 978-1-80016-586-1

This is a work of fiction. Names, characters, businesses, places, events and
incidents are either the products of the author's imagination or used in a
fictitious manner. Any resemblance to actual persons, living or dead, or
actual events is purely coincidental.

Vanguard Press is an imprint of
Pegasus Elliot Mackenzie Publishers Ltd.
www.pegasuspublishers.com

First Published in 2024

Vanguard Press
Sheraton House Castle Park
Cambridge England

Printed & Bound in Great Britain

This book is dedicated to my family:
Henry, Atticus, Finley, Odette, and Viggo.

Acknowledgements

Thank you to all my friends and family for supporting me in my writing journey. Thank you to my husband, Henry, who read every chapter back to me multiple times with patience and a smile. Thank you to my children, whose excitement and suggestions made this possible. Thank you to my parents, who were instrumental in bringing this book to life. Thank you to my friend, Caroline, my trial reader and fellow fantasy enthusiast. Thank you to Cika Misha, who encouraged me to write, Memory Eternal.

PROLOGUE

O, Lo, old road,
The bane of my weary being,
The path, the way,
The yield of your works.
Open thy arms,
Take me in,
Show me the truth of my destiny.

- The Ancient Archives, Vol II, Book 1

"Quickly, Hedona, we must leave now." The old man wiped his brow. He was much too old for this sort of a journey, but he knew the babe's life depended on it. His limbs ached, and the weight of his cloak fell heavy on his shoulders. It was a journey he knew he would not survive.

"Ahh!" Hedona screamed from her bed. Her sheets were wet with blood and sweat. She was half naked, lying indecently, but Master Luka ignored the fact. This was not a time for dignity.

"Quiet now, Hedona. You must get up. It is time. Now." Master Luka gestured to the serving maids to help Hedona walk. He grabbed a candle — one only. There was a need for silence. There was a need for secrecy. One candle would be all they could spare to navigate the dark palace halls at this hour.

Hedona struggled, her face wrinkled in pain, but she got up. One foot at a time she made it off the bed, blood leaking between her legs. Master Luka knew it would make the perfect trail, they would be easily followed, but he hoped, nay he prayed fervently to the god of lost cause, that time was on their side.

They slowly made their way down the dark damp hallways of the palace. Master Luka knew the ins and outs like he knew his own body. He had lived here since he was a child, knew the palace secrets, knew which routes were least used. He used this knowledge now, creeping through the shadows and unused corridors, until finally the air became colder, crisper, and he could feel the dark night wind approaching.

"Almost there now, Hedona. Stay with us." Master Luka tried to remain calm, but he knew his voice quavered with fear. This was only the beginning of their journey. He looked back at Hedona, blood dripping down her chin where she bit her lip, staving off the screams that wanted out. He hurried on.

The wind was whipping at his face now, they only needed to make it to the end of the corridor where he had to trust Master Kevnon had left a horse and cart. The serving girls would ride with Hedona, he would drive the cart. He shivered; nervous his old bones would not be able to complete the task.

"You there!" A guard turned the corner, the gold and green of the royal household. Master Luka hoped he was the only one.

"Move aside, guard." Master Luka nodded in the direction he wanted the guard to go, but the man did not move. He said a silent prayer of thanksgiving to the god of good, that the cart was there, ready with blankets, packs, and a sturdy looking mare, saddled and with an extra oat bag. He motioned toward Hedona and the serving girls to get in the cart. He wished they would move faster.

"What are you doing with that woman?" The guard had his hand on the hilt of his sword, poised to fight if needed. Master Luka sighed; he was already tired. He stepped out, now in the open air of the night and looked around. No other guards. But the man was looking directly at Hedona.

"She is ill, and we are taking her to a healer. Move aside. I will not tell you again." Master Luka tried to muster up his strength, but he knew he must look a poor comparison to the young and fit guard.

"She is not ill. I know her, she is Hedona, the King's concubine. I recognize her." He drew his sword. "By royal decree, no one is to leave the palace. Turn back now and I will escort you to your rooms. If you—" But the guard never got a chance to finish.

The force of Master Luka's power ripped into the man and threw him back against the stone of the palace. He heard the crack of skull on rock and sighed. Yes, he was too old for this. The magic took too much strength out of him. He wouldn't have much left for the journey. He hoped it would be enough.

Hedona let out a stifled howl as the serving girls lowered her into the cart and covered her with blankets. Master Luka got on top of the horse, not without effort, as his legs shook beneath him, his muscles not used to this much attention. He kicked the horse into gear, and the sorry pack began moving toward the palace gate. Once they got to the forest, he would be able to breathe.

The gates were approaching quickly, guarded by ten of the royal guard. They wore the same gold and green as the guard Master Luka had just faced, and the similitude of them all made it easier for Master Luka to accept their fate. He took a deep inward breath and blew out, the guards one by one fainting, before they could question why a cart driven by a Master was leaving the palace at midnight.

Master Luka wavered, holding tightly to the reins while his head swam, and his vision blurred. He would not fall off his horse, not yet. He resigned to keep going, even as he felt the life quickly draining from his body. This much magic, this quickly, and at his age, would have consequences. But consequences were for the future, and here and now Master Luka could think only of getting Hedona to safety.

"Lubella, quick." He told the serving girl as she jumped off the cart and began to crank the wheel, lifting the heavy iron gate. He chose Lubella for her strength alone, hoping she would be able to fulfill this one task. He was relieved beyond measure when she agreed. A normal girl would not be able to turn the heavy wooden contraption that now creaked as the gate rose inch by inch.

Master Luka looked over his shoulder to see a cluster of guards running toward them — archers. They took up position in a line, kneeling and notching their arrows. *Oh doom!* Master Luka thought as the gate was barely above the horse's head. He looked over at Lubella, horror in her eyes as they both realized she would be a sacrifice.

"Go," she said as a tear ran down her cheek. Master Luka was once again grateful he had chosen her.

He slowly steered the cart forward ducking down as he passed beneath, the cold shadow weighing heavy on his back. He heard one guard's command as the first volley of arrows was loosed. They hissed from behind, one sticking in the back of the cart, just as it completed its journey under the gate. He looked to Lubella then, as an arrow came whooshing in the air to land in her eye, then three more in her chest. She fell quickly, releasing the wooden wheel, and the gate slammed shut behind them. Master Luka did not look back, but kicked the horse, willing it to full speed.

He prayed now — prayed hard and sincerely to every god he could think of, for a swift and speedy journey through the Forests of Venit Vox. He saw the line of trees up ahead, and knew at least that the guards who would be giving chase, would not follow them in there. Ten more seconds and they would be safe behind the tree line. His breathing became shallow. Five more seconds. His head was throbbing with pain. Almost there. The horse whinnied and bucked, refusing to enter the forest.

"Come on now, filly. It will be OK. We need to go in." Master Luka could feel the tension in the horse, the muscles taught with fear. He lay a soothing hand on the mare's neck and said a quick incantation, soothing the horse, as it finally stepped forward and into the Venit Vox. Master Luka breathed a sigh of relief even as his legs went numb. He tried wiggling his toes, willing his blood to flow as pins and needles ran down his lower limbs.

Finally, he looked back at Hedona, who had gone quiet. The blankets were soaked in blood, and the remaining serving girl looked horrified.

"Is she alive?" Master Luka asked, fear rising in his core.

"Yes, Master, but barely. I fear she must give birth soon." The girl looked questioningly at him. Master Luka could not remember her name.

"So be it. But we will need to continue forward." The young girl nodded, as she opened a nearby pack filled with midwifery instruments.

The next few hours were a blur. Master Luka used all his remaining strength to move them forward to the border. He remained vigilant, as he knew the forests to be plagued with monsters. He could feel the horse's fear, but occasionally stroked and spoke lowly to keep her moving. Several times he thought he heard something in the brush, but when he glanced to the side nothing appeared.

Hedona was panting, her ragged breathing was only broken by occasional deep moaning. She was paler than death itself, and judging by the blood on the sheets, it was a miracle that death had not yet claimed her. He could feel that sinister god stalking nearby, but maybe at least it was keeping the beasts away. Out of every bad there is good, or so he had been taught.

After what seemed a lifetime, the baby finally ripped free of Hedona's womb, with a high-pitched shriek that resonated through the forest. Moments later they crossed the border, coming finally to the small cottage Master Luka had hoped would be the birthplace of the babe.

He stopped the cart and came hobbling around to help the girl, Hedona, and the baby, who continued to wail with the piercing cries only capable of someone so small.

A tall man emerged from the cottage, and rushed over to help. He was followed by a portly woman with blankets and a ladle of water. The man grabbed Hedona, as the woman poured the water into her mouth, but it only dribbled down the sides.

"My baby—" Hedona tried to speak.

"Hush, hush," said the portly woman, stroking Hedona's feverish forehead. "The baby is fine, you will see, but first let's get you inside to rest." The man carried her quickly into the cottage where a fire was waiting. Master Luka and the serving girl followed.

The cottage was warm and quaint. Herbs hung from the ceiling and the smell combined with the musk of the forest floor was almost overwhelming. The man pulled a chair for Master Luka to sit, who was grateful, as he collapsed down into it.

"Were you followed?" He asked, glancing to the now boarded up door.

"Not since we entered The Venit Vox." Master Luka found breathing difficult. The man and portly woman glanced at each other. He could read the concern on their faces.

"Well, be grateful you didn't find any trouble in the forest, there are creatures abound, especially at night." The man said, looking only slightly relieved.

"Hedona was wailing loud enough to scare any monster away. Although, I was surprised no creature was attracted to the blood." Master Luka's legs were quickly becoming numb again. The feeling now moving up his arms as well.

"Yes, well it is a blessing." The man said taking a deep breath and standing to stoke the fire. The portly woman was bending over Hedona, the serving girl adjacent trying to quiet the baby. Hedona seemed to be having some sort of spasm as her body shivered uncontrollably.

"The baby—" She tried to speak again but could barely summon the words from her pale blue lips. "The baby — call him Annakkor. S*trength.*" Hedona let out a final shudder as her arm fell lifeless to the ground.

"She is gone." The portly woman said quietly. She pulled the sheet over Hedona's head and gathered herbs to rest over her body. The room lay quiet, as the serving girl finally got the baby to sleep.

"Montoc. Get the goats milk, the baby will be hungry when she wakes." The portly woman ordered the man. He quickly unbolted the door, leaving the cottage.

"*She*?" Asked Master Luka in shock. "The baby. It is a *girl*?" Master Luka felt the darkness take hold of him. The woman looked deeply into his eyes and gave him a solemn nod.

"Then it was all for naught," he mumbled to himself, the last of his strength failing. The numbness overtook his body, all resistance failing as his heart gave out and he collapsed to his death.

The portly woman sighed and looked at the serving girl, who stood trembling in fear at the sight of two dead bodies.

"We shall call her Annassa, instead, the female form of the name, and hope that she has the *strength* to live."

Part 1

8 YEARS LATER

Chapter 1

VOLYA

The darkness calls
To all the thieves,
Sleeping in their beds,
Their dreams are dark,
They hear the hark,
Of demons in their heads.

- Poems from the Deep, Verse 127

The small boy wove expertly through the marketplace. Though he was only ten, his feet were quick, and his hands were light. His pockets jangled with stolen coin and an apple bulged out of a burlap sack hanging on his left — a delicacy. It was a lucky day.

By the time he reached his favorite spot in the town, the sun was beginning to set. He crouched on the parapet of the old, ruined library, overlooking the city. *Thessola was beautiful,* he thought to himself. Especially as the sun hit the buildings glittering off the tall spires and lighting up below with colors. Thessola was far enough westward in Akkadia, that the city still thrived, unaffected by the ongoing wars with Sudonia to the East. But Volya didn't have to worry about that anyway. He was hardly yet a young man, although much older than his years belied.

He bit into the apple, the juices running down his chin. The sweetness thrilled him, there could hardly be anything better in the whole world.

"Volya!" His name echoed off the ruined walls, reaching him at the heights. He gave a weary sigh and rolled his eyes. Hardly a moment of peace. He quickly ate the remainder of the apple — core and all — making sure he wouldn't have to share with his band of brothers who now called on him. He hopped down the walls lightly, barely a hitch in his step, as he dropped softly onto the crumbled street.

"What do you want?" Volya asked his older band brother, not masking his annoyance. The response was a fist to the stomach. Volya bent over coughing.

"You little shit." Puntar spat at Volya. "Where is the money, you were supposed to come straight to the den."

"Dammit, Puntar. That hurt." Volya straightened only to be punched in the stomach again, this time causing him to fall on the rough-cut stone.

"Is that an apple I smell, you little shit?" Puntar growled his ugly face down at Volya, but Volya only winked at him. That got him a nice kick in the shin.

"Geez. OK, here is the money, Puntar," Volya said handing him a fistful of coins. "But leave me alone." Volya stood slowly wiping the dirt from his torn clothing. It would take a lot more than a bully like Puntar to sour Volya's day. He learned long ago that life was made of a series of decisions. Everything could be taken but not the freedom to decide. That he had for himself. And he had decided that while he was still alive he would enjoy life. It wasn't always easy, but at least it was his decision and no one else's.

Puntar snarled but turned, pocketing the money with one hand and yanking Volya by the sleeve with the other. Volya stumbled forward, following the gang.

"Here." Mara, handed him a small torn piece of bread. "We already ate back at the den, so there isn't anything left." Volya grabbed the small piece and ate it quickly before Puntar could take it away.

"Thanks." He said, smiling at Mara. She was only a year older than him, but she had stepped in as a mother figure to Volya when his parents died. That was before he came to Thessola, but they escaped *The Great Purge* together, traveling as far away as they could get. It was a different life, and one he hardly remembered. He had been only four.

By the time they got back to the den, it was dark. The boarded up empty warehouse they called home lay on the outskirts of Thessola, near the docks, but not too close to the dangerous gangs that roamed that area. Their band of brothers was made up mostly of kids —

street urchins, pickpockets, orphans — an odd assortment of the city's next generation of poor.

After they entered the den, Volya went to his spot tucked in the back corner. He had fought hard for this spot, where the boards opened up to a little nook of its own. Volya could just barely squeeze into it, but it was comfortable, with the extra rags he lay down for a cushion. He had even nailed a little shelf where he kept his knife at night while he was sleeping. He didn't have many other possessions, and those he did, he would never trust to leave out around the rest of the group. Instead, he kept them in his small burlap sack, which he used as a pillow while he slept.

He didn't have much in that sack. A couple of mementoes he stole away from the home where he was born. The home that had been burned to the ground on that awful fall day, six years ago. He tried not to think about it too much. His parent's faces were a blur to him, their memory fading with each passing year.

He sighed and looked around. Most of the kids were going to sleep now, knowing they had to be up early to hit the morning markets. He saw Puntar in the opposite corner by the fire, taking over far too much heat and space, already snoring. Volya scowled. Puntar was not only ugly but fat, a characteristic none of the other urchins shared. Volya wondered just how much of the money Puntar kept to himself for hot buns and other delicacies. His mouth watered at the thought. But today he had had an apple, and the sweet memory of it made him smile. He decided to dwell on that as his eyes grew heavy, and he quickly faded into sleep.

The next morning Volya was up early. A few of the younger kids were on kitchen duty and made a somewhat filling although incredibly bland porridge. Volya grabbed a bowl and guzzled it down as quick as he could. He grabbed his sack and quickly tied up his worn and faded brown boots, carelessly whistling a tune on the way out the door.

"Shut up, Volya!" Someone yelled from a pile of rags on the floor.

"Early bird catches the fruit!" Volya shouted back with a smile on his face as he stepped into the crisp morning air.

"The saying is, 'early bird catches the worm', you idiot," the same kid growled back through the planks. Volya grinned.

Volya strutted confidently down the road. He had a feeling it would be another good day. As he turned the corner, his foot caught on something, and he unceremoniously tumbled to the dirt and pebbled street. His face felt bruised and when he brought his fingers to his cheek, they came back wet with blood.

He looked up to see what had caused his stumble, only to find Puntar glaring down at him with a devilish grin. He leaned back against the wall, arms crossed, and foot still out. Volya rose to meet him, but Puntar shoved him back to the ground.

"This is a reminder to bring me my money straight. Don't forget today, or I'll give you a lot worse of a beating." Puntar spat on the ground next to Volya, then turned and headed back toward the den.

Volya sighed, and stood up, grabbing the sack that rolled off him and tying it tighter to his side. He would continue to ignore Puntar, but one of these days that kid had better get what was coming to him. Volya clenched his fists in frustration and made his way toward the market.

It was a busy morning, as were all mornings in the city center. The market brought a diverse crowd, sailors from across the Western seas, fur traders from the northern Muscovite mountain ranges, and even merchants from across the marshlands. Buyers and sellers participated in the shouting and bargaining routine that was commonplace in all market squares, but here the market was so packed, it was easy to slip in and out, a quick hand here, light fingers there. It was almost second nature for Volya to distract with one hand, and grab with the other. Too bad thieving was an illegitimate profession, Volya could make quite the career out of it.

"Excuse me, miss." He tapped a wealthy looking woman on the elbow, giving her his most chaste looking smile.

She appeared slightly taken aback, even with his virtuous expression. She cringed against his touch, her ruffled white frock and matching parasol repelling against his grimy fingers.

"You look lost, can I offer you directions?" Volya asked, still smiling innocently.

"No, boy, get away." The woman frowned, shooing him off, then turned toward a stand selling hand-sewn coin purses. Volya quickly moved in the other direction.

He didn't stop until he was safely hidden in a dark alley. Only then did he uncurl his fingers around the object he had skillfully grabbed from the woman's purse. Even in the dim light the object glowed, the beautiful rubies, emeralds, and sapphires lighting his eyes, which had gone wide looking at the treasure he now possessed.

The brooch was as large as a royal coin, the many dazzling jewels coming together to form a beautiful and exotic bird. He had never seen, let alone held, something so precious or extravagant. He wasn't sure where he would hide it, but he was sure of one thing — there was no way he would let Puntar get his hands on his new treasure.

The rest of his day passed in the same manner. When the crowd pressed around him, it was easy to grab a few coins here and there, and when the surge of people began to ebb, a quick help with directions made his own purse flow.

He returned that night to the den, once again exhausted but in good spirits. His treasure was heavy in his boot, and he felt the weight of it as he handed Puntar the coins he had collected during the day.

"Is that all?" Puntar asked, his lip curled up in annoyance. He sat behind a rotting wooden desk, in a rocking chair that no longer rocked. His office, he called it.

"It's five marks in total, Puntar. I'd say that's a pretty good day." Volya tilted his head and raised his eyebrows in a look of bored annoyance.

Puntar slowly stood from the rickety wooden chair. Before Volya could react, Puntar wrapped his hand around Volya's neck and slammed his head on the desk. It smelled of mildew and piss.

"Last week it was seven marks. Yesterday you brought me close to nothing. You're acting like a bloody shit thief, Volya, and I'm not buying it." Puntar's dirty nails dug into Volya's neck. He could feel the blood dripping down, but Puntar was older and stronger, and Volya could not break free of his grip. He clenched his teeth, biting back remarks that would only get him in more trouble.

"Hey! Everyone! Listen up." The whole of the den had already quieted at the commotion, but now even those who had been dozing were brought to attention. "I'm sick and tired of this little shit's attitude. I feed you, I cloth you, I give you shelter. And you repay me with five gods-pissing marks."

Puntar jumped ungracefully over the table, still holding Volya down. He grabbed Volya by the hair and threw him to the floor, kicking him in the stomach with a strong boot. Volya gasped for air, buckling to the side. Puntar brought his fist down hard on the side of Volya's face, and Volya was hit anew with a blinding pain. That would leave a nasty black eye.

"This is what happens when you treat me with disrespect!" Puntar shouted, as he kicked Volya again, this time bringing bile up his throat. He was thankful he hadn't yet eaten.

"Quibly, strip him. Gogo, get me the whip." Puntar cracked his neck and stretched his arms in preparation for the beating he was about to give.

Volya wanted to fight back, he wanted to with all his might, but the blows to his stomach had been too debilitating. Instead, he tried to retreat into himself, find a safe spot in his mind where the pain couldn't reach him. But as Quibly started to remove his clothing, he remembered the brooch in his boot. That would not end well.

At the same time his thoughts went to the brooch, Quibly pulled off his boot causing the jeweled treasure to clink gracefully to the floor. The room was in stunned silence already, and as the brooch bounced lightly the clang resounded off the walls. Puntar slowly looked at Volya, death written in his eyes.

"What is that?" Puntar asked slowly and frighteningly calm. Volya didn't answer but only glared back with equal parts defiance and anger out of his one working eye.

"This belongs to me." The hate in Puntar's eyes began to gleam with greed, distorting his features into an even crueler and ugly expression.

"Tie him up, leave him naked until morning. Give him time to reflect on the pain he is about to endure." Puntar grabbed the brooch from the ground, pocketing it. "I am going out. No one is to tend to him unless they want the same punishment." Puntar looked around in a circle making sure everyone understood.

"*You,* you little shit," he said looking down at Volya still hunched on the ground, "you better hope the gods have some mercy on you, because when dawn comes I sure won't. I will have you begging for your life and crying like a baby. I can't wait to see how much blood there is inside that puny little body." And without another word Puntar left into the night.

Chapter 2

NASSA

The lion and the faun lie down in harmony,
But the darkness comes,
Flowing with power,
Coursing through purple veins,
The lion devours its prey,
Now truly as one,
Fuel for the fire.

- An excerpt from The Fables of Fillander

Nassa woke with a start. She had been having the same dream again. Running through the forest, demons flocking, sucking at her soul. Shaking, she prayed to the gods for relief and tried to calm herself. She reached across her bed and opened the hatch that secured her window closed. She looked out at the dark forests, the hint of blue and orange in the sky, signaling dawn was near. The woods didn't spook her, but the demons lurking within did.

A piece of straw in her mattress poked through into her side, and she pulled it out, throwing it to the floor. She looked around her small modest bedroom, dirt floors, straw bed, and small chest against the far wall. Her eyes came to rest on the two small figurines her Papa had whittled for her.

It had been on her eighth nameday only a few weeks back. She had never possessed a toy before, not that she had thought she ever would. She often played in the forests around their small farm, making fairy circles, and flower crowns, imagining herself in a world full of wonder and magic.

That nameday, after she had finished her usual chores — checking the traps, boiling water, tending the garden, and feeding the chickens — she had entered the cottage to find her Papa waiting for her. Marny had baked an oil cake and placed it on the long, rough-hewn table.

Nassa gasped in delight. "For me?" she exclaimed, her mouth already sweating in anticipation of the sweet delight.

Marny laughed and Papa's eyes lit up with tenderness. "Yes, of course, Nassa, dear. It is your nameday after all."

Nassa ran to the table and stood at her chair, waiting for Papa and Marny to sit before she did so herself. As soon as they did, she plopped herself in her chair, unable to mask her delight. Marny handed her a fork and she looked quickly to them both. Papa nodded and she dug in, the smile now in her eyes.

"There is something else I have for you, dear." Papa said. Nassa looked up surprised.

"Something else?" Nassa questioned expectantly. This was unmistakably already the best nameday she ever had.

Papa brought forth from his pocket the two small figurines and placed them in front of Nassa. She stilled, lowering her fork and picking up the two figures. One was a beautiful woman, her long flowing hair wrapping around her, cloaking her. On her head was a crown of flowers, the kind Nassa could only pretend to make in the forest. She ran a thumb across the woman's face, the details beyond exquisite. The other figure was a man on a horse. The horse was bucking on its hind legs as the man raised a sword toward the heavens. The wood appeared to move in the wind, as the prince — as she would think of him — prepared to ride off on an adventure.

"They are beautiful." Nassa managed to breathe out. "Oh, Papa, thank you!" And she stood from her chair rushing toward her Papa and kissing him on the cheek. She gave Marny a hug for good measure as well. But she couldn't mistake the look of concern in both their eyes.

Nassa lay back in her straw bed as the memory faded with the darkness of night. Whether it was due to the happy recollection, or the rising sun, her mood changed quickly from apprehensive to content.

She got out of bed, her bare feet touching the cold dirt floor beneath her toes. She stretched, but was awake instantly in the ways that only children are. Pulling off her worn nightgown, she changed into her tunic and brown trousers. She had sewn all her own clothes just as Marny had taught her, but she dreamed her tunic was a beautiful flowing frock with rose epaulets and gold trim. She twirled around her room at the thought, curtsying to her invisible prince. Nassa giggled, then shook herself out of the revery. Looking down she found only the drab burlap fabric, rough against her skin. *Oh well,* she thought, these were much more practical for chores.

She left her tiny room and went down the hallway to the kitchens. No one was there, of course, Marny and Papa had their own set of duties, but they had left a steaming pot of malted oats over the fire, and she generously helped herself.

After breaking her fast, she went outside to feed the chickens. She was surprised to find Papa waiting there for her. With winter approaching, he was generally off hunting, trying to obtain as much meat as possible to cure for the cold months ahead.

"Nassa, dear, feed the chickens quick, I will wait here, there are some things we need to discuss." Papa sat on a bench outside the coop while Nassa obediently obliged him. When she was finished, she came to sit next to him on the bench. There was a long moment of silence, but Nassa would wait for Papa to break it.

"It has been two weeks now since your eighth nameday, and I'm afraid I can't put this off for much longer." He finally said. Nassa nodded. She knew in the eyes of the villagers; her eighth nameday marked her as a young woman. But she didn't feel any older.

"It is important you know where you came from, there may be changes taking place in your body soon." Papa twitched uncomfortably in his chair.

"Is this something maybe Marny should tell me?" Nassa asked, trying not to laugh at her Papa's awkwardness.

"No, dear, this is for me to tell you. But it isn't what you think." Papa ran his hand through his hair and shook his head, trying to find the right words.

"You are not from here, Nassa." He said uneasily.

Nassa knew, of course, that Papa wasn't really her father. She knew she had been found in the woods as a baby, but Papa and Marny had cared for her since she could remember, and whoever had abandoned her was no true parent of hers.

"Papa, I know this, of course. But you and Marny, you are all I need." Nassa put her hand on his, comforting her Papa.

"Nassa, it is not as we've said, Marny and I. We did not find you in the woods when you were a baby. You were brought to us as a child of Sudonia. Back during the start of the *Great Purge*." Papa looked down at

Nassa with concern. Nassa let his story sink in, connecting the pieces.

Although she did not attend school, Papa and Marny instructed her the best they could. They taught her to read, and to write, and even bought a few history books for her to study. It was illegal in Akkadia to learn much about Sudonia, but Nassa, like most children had been taught the recent histories of the warring nations. Sudonia had dark magic. Akkadia did not.

"You mean I may have magic inside me? I don't think so, Papa." Nassa felt for her poor Papa. How long had he been worrying about her turning eight, the year they say the magic shows itself for girls. A celebration in Sudonia, but here in Akkadia, magic was a death sentence. Had he been nervous and dreading this since she was a baby?

"I have been observing you for signs since your nameday. It is true, there has been nothing. But maybe you are just a late bloomer." Papa took a deep breath. "There are some tests we can do, tests to see if the magic is inside you."

"And what will happen if I do have magic, Papa?" Nassa asked, the seriousness of the conversation finally hitting her. Tears welled in her eyes.

"You know the law, Nassa." Papa said, shaking his head.

Nassa did know the law. She had seen it carried out only once, in the nearest town, which was half a day's ride by mule. The poor boy had screamed as they burned him alive. He had been only ten, the age most boys showed their magic.

Nassa didn't respond, but only nodded. Papa turned and held her hands, bending down to her eye level.

"We will go into the woods today, Nassa. I will test you there." Again, Nassa only nodded.

Papa had allowed Nassa to continue with her chores, hoping she would come to terms with what was ahead. No wonder her dreams had been dark that night, she thought. Her good mood receded as quickly as it had come.

She finished her chores in a blur, going through the motions, not thinking of what she was doing. She tried to feel inside her for any magic living within. But she felt nothing.

She had always wondered at her story. That she had been found in the woods as a baby. It made much more sense, that she had come from Sudonia. But she preferred it the other way. A mythical creature, born out of the forests, taken by fairy elves for a changeling but making it out of their grasps unhurt. Sudonia meant the enemy. Sudonia meant war. Sudonia meant dark magic. And it may very well be coursing through her blood.

When the time came, she went quickly into the forest and found Papa once again waiting for her. She always felt maybe there was something different about her, and now it terrified her. She prayed to every god she could think of, that her blood was pure.

"Nassa, come here." Papa motioned for her to stand on a log next to him. "Magic can generate itself in several different ways. Most mages have an affinity with certain natural elements. You are still young so it is probably not strong, but focusing on the elements should bring out the magic. Just as learning a language, it takes time to become fluent, but a dictionary will help." Nassa was surprised to hear that he knew so much about it. She also did not like the way he talked, as if it was obvious she would have the magic inside.

"Stand here, I'm going to hand you a series of objects. They will help to focus your energy." Papa showed her a candle, a twig, and a small vial of liquid. She took the candle and stood as told.

"Now close your eyes and think only of the candle." She did so. She breathed deeply, feeling the weight of the candle in her palm, trying to imagine it was a part of her. She could feel her heart beating, imagining the candle flickering along to the rhythm in her chest. Sweat began to trickle down her forehead and she squeezed her jaw, struggling.

"Now let it go." She let go of the candle, unsure what was supposed to happen, and it dropped to the floor. Papa ran over and stomped out the flame. He took a long sigh of relief as he walked back to her side.

Nassa sat on the log, already tired after her first effort, confused and scared. She looked up at her Papa, wanting to get up and hug him, wanting him to hold her and tell her everything would be OK, that she was safe.

But she wasn't sure everything would be OK, or that she would be safe. She stood up, determined anew to act strong. Papa reached out, handing her the stick.

"Now, again, close your eyes and think only of the stick." Once again, she did so. This time she focused on how the stick felt. She moved her thumb over the notches and dimples in the surface of the wood, willing it to obey her. She felt all her muscles going taught with the effort, trying to concentrate on the stick as an extension of her arm. Once again she felt the sweat dripping down her forehead, but this time a sense of calm began to overtake her, and she smiled.

"Now let it go." Her Papa commanded. The twig fell softly to the forest floor. Her Papa let out another sigh of relief. Nassa was unsure whether she felt relief or surprise, but she couldn't suppress a vague feeling of disappointment. She knew that was crazy, having magic would only get her killed.

"And now, Nassa, my dear, close your eyes and think only of the vial of water." Once again, she did as told. But this time, she could hear a note of hope in her Papa's voice.

She still was unsure exactly what she was supposed to be focusing on, so instead she tried to erase her mind completely and only think of the water. As she inhaled and exhaled, she imagined the ebb and flow of water. She relaxed her body, allowing for it to behave in a fluid like manner, trying to free herself from the confines of her mind. She took a deep breath trying to inhale the liquid, making them as one.

"Now let it go." Nassa hesitated, then turned her palm slowly upside down, letting the vial slip away. It dropped slowly, turning in the air and then hitting the corner of the log as it shattered into thousands of pieces.

Papa ran his hands through his hair, clearly relieved.

"Now, for the last test. This one is a little different, because I do not have an object for you to hold." Nassa looked at him quizzically as he went on. "Stand up straight, feel the wind stirring in the trees?" He asked her.

Nassa closed her eyes, feeling the breeze in the air, hearing the birds chirping in the branches. She nodded to Papa.

"OK good. Now, hold on to that feeling. Feel the wind. Now open your hands, yes like that, and push your palms forward." Papa's voice shook slightly with fear at the last part of his sentence.

Nassa did as she was told. She inhaled and it felt the world was inhaling into her lungs. She opened her palms and pushed. She opened her eyes, looking around. Nothing had changed. Nothing had happened. She was safe after all.

Papa wiped at a tear; he had become quite attached to Nassa after all these years.

"Ah, Nassa, come here. All will be well." Papa put his arm around her, pulling her in close and leading them both back to the safety of the cottage.

Chapter 3

VOLYA

The demon groans,
The thief, he moans,
The demon turns his tread.
But then a wail,
The demon pale,
A knife stuck in his head.

- Poems from the Deep, Verse 133.

It was still dark out, but Volya knew dawn was fast approaching. He had barely slept, instead left to shiver in the cold damp surroundings. His naked body was pale and pimpled from the night air, without even socks to warm his feet. His eye was swollen shut and his body still throbbed in pain. But he was angry, and the heat of his rage at least kept him alive.

Puntar was a vile creature, but he had messed with the wrong kid. Volya was not sure how he would take revenge, but he was certain he would. He knew Puntar planned to beat him mostly to death once he returned, but Volya was not afraid. There was nothing left Puntar could take from him.

Before long, dawn came, the light from the rising sun sending splinters of light through the wooden slats of the den. No one had helped Volya, although Mara had looked at him remorsefully. They all had the sense not to cross Puntar, but at least they also had the sense not to jeer at Volya. Volya, although young, was still a formidable foe, with his light hands and quick wit.

He braced himself as the others awoke, waiting to hear Puntar come barreling in, but instead only heard the others readying themselves for the day. More porridge was served, even a few small loaves of bread for the lucky ones who got there first. But no one offered any food to Volya. He didn't hold it against them, most of them were weak and scared from the beginning, he couldn't imagine them having courage now. Not against Puntar. Nevertheless, he glared them down with his one good eye as they walked by, most refusing to make eye contact back.

Mara was the only one who spoke with him, although discreetly. She looked around first and talked quietly, bending down, pretending to do up her laces in case anyone was ready to tell Puntar for a quick favor.

"I'm going out to see where he is. I will try to get back first and warn you when he is on his way. I think I may have a plan." Mara pretended to stretch and then moved quickly on and out the door.

She had saved him once before when their village was raided at the end of *The Great Purge*. They had lived in one of the outlying villages, in the border towns of Sudonia. Raids weren't unheard of in those parts — the towns were so close to the border, it was often hard to distinguish which town belonged to which nation. With the war front so close, raiding and violence were a part of life on the border, but this was different. This time they were dressed in the gold and green of the Royal Guard. This time there was no mercy.

They came silently with their magic words and dark intentions. Volya had watched his parents suffer. His mother screamed out, begging him to hide, after they had cut his father's throat with a dull knife. But Volya could not move, he was frozen with horror. He watched as the soldiers one by one got on top of her, his strong mother screaming in pain, flailing her limbs in hopeless struggle. After, they had taken her to the fires with the others, chaining her limbs and throwing her in. It was then Mara had found him, yanking him away and forcing him to run. Somehow, impossibly, they had escaped. And now here they were years later, in a city on the far side of Akkadia, far away from the terrors Sudonia imposed.

But not all terrors came from Sudonia. And although Volya was no longer afraid, he was angry — angry that he had escaped one evil only to find that it was inescapable. Suffering knew no borders.

Volya inhaled deeply, he didn't like to dwell on the past. What's done is done, he could no more get his old life back than he could bring his parents back from the dead. He wouldn't let their sacrifice be in vain. Mara said she had a plan, so he would place his faith in her.

Warmth slowly flowed back in his limbs as the warm sun began to beat down on the den. Although it was nearing winter, Thessola remained warm as always. The morning grew into midday, and still no sign of Puntar or Mara. Volya knew he should count each extra second as a blessing, but he couldn't help restlessly thinking how badly he wanted some clothes to wear and food to eat. His annoyance grew with the pain in his tied-up limbs.

He looked around the den, most of the others were out, making their rounds and doing varying tasks and duties assigned to them. Two of the youngest among the brothers and sisters of the den sat playing dice by the door, on guard duty.

"Psst. Hey, you!" Volya snapped at them.

"We aren't supposed to talk to you, Volya," the younger one said, only to get a hard nudge in the arm by the other.

"Shut up, Petey." The older boy chastised.

"What's up your arse, Dinby? I'm just sayin' we can't talk to him, I'm not *talkin'* to him," Petey said guilt-free.

"Yeah, but you sayin' that *is* talkin' to him, you dimwit," Dinby said, peeved.

"Shut up, both of you," Volya said, rolling his eyes. "Pretty soon I'm gonna be in charge around here and both of you will be thanking the gods that you helped me out." Petey and Dinby looked over to him suspiciously.

"How you reckon your goin' to escape?" Dinby asked skeptically.

"And how you goin' to throw down Puntar? He got you real bad yesterday. You just sat there like a dummy doll." Petey added without mercy.

"I have a plan," Volya answered back, trying to sound confident.

"Well, we better be hearin' that plan before we makin' any decisions. Plus, what's in it for us?" Dinby said with a note of avarice.

Before Volya could answer, there was a loud bang on the wooden door. It was followed by four short quick knocks — a friend not an enemy.

Petey opened the door and Mara rushed in. Volya knew Puntar must be close behind. He hoped Mara really did have a plan, he sure didn't intend on being whipped and beaten by that ugly cretin.

Mara hurried in, sprinting across the room to the nook where Volya slept. She grabbed his spare tunic and then rustled through a few neighboring rags for a suitable pair of trousers. She got up and sped quickly toward Volya, falling to her knees and furiously untying his hands and legs.

"Here, get dressed." She threw him the clothes. Volya rubbed his wrists then began to dress. It was funny to him how great a comfort it was to be clothed.

"Is this part of the plan?" He asked her, eyebrows raised, and remaining calm, true to his nature, while putting on his clothing.

"There has been a change of plan. Come on, follow me." She didn't wait for him to finish donning the tunic before she rushed back out as quick as she came.

Volya gave Dinby a wink with his good eye and ruffled Petey's hair as he followed Mara out the door. They both looked at him with mouths open, unsure if they should stop him or applaud him. He knew if Puntar came back, they would be in big trouble, but he hoped Mara's plan factored in as little bloodshed as possible.

He followed her as she wove her way through alleyways and streets, his still bare feet caking with mud and dust. His body still ached, but luckily he was young and agile, and kept a good pace. The lower city, dirty and overcrowded, soon gave way to the paved walkways and larger storefronts, an indication they were heading toward the city center.

Volya enjoyed the feel of his muscles in use, his body stretching out after being cramped in the confines from the night before. He felt like he could run forever but just as he was having this thought, Mara stopped. They found themselves in a dark alley, one of the many that would open up into the main city square. She turned to him, raising her finger to her lips, signaling him to be quiet, although he could already hear the roar of a crowd ahead.

They slowly turned the corner to be greeted with quite the spectacle. The square was bulging wall to wall with a zealous crowd. Guards stood throughout trying to keep the peace as those surrounding yelled and threw objects and old food toward the middle of the square. And there in the center of the raised dais was a young man badly beaten, now with a rope around his neck, ready to be hanged. Puntar.

A woman stood to the side with the judge and executioner, clearly she was the injured party. Her stark white attire stood out against the dirty crowd, and Volya recognized her as the woman from whom he had stolen the brooch. Volya couldn't help but feel relieved at the fate he had narrowly missed, yet he was disappointed he wouldn't bring Puntar down himself.

The judge turned to the crowd, ready to speak, and the crowd finally grew silent. Tension pulsed through the air, as death lingered close by, awaiting to take its prize.

"Residents of Thessola!" He shouted, "This man was caught stealing. By law he is sentenced to death!" He looked to the woman, who nodded. The executioner pulled the lever, causing Puntar to fall, snapping his neck and killing him.

Volya gave Mara a sideways look. She grinned back at him.

"What now?" Mara asked.

"I guess it's time for a change in leadership," Volya smirked.

Chapter 4

NASSA

The path decided,
Never leads,
The direction want to steer.
When thought provoked,
The temper stoked,
The way no longer clear.

- The Ancient Archives, Vol II, Book 3

Nassa sat on a bench outside the cottage watching the steam of her breath. The seasons were beginning to turn, the air becoming frigid, although the snow did not yet stick. She pulled her mantle around her tightly.

Papa hadn't talked about magic again since that day he had tested her several weeks ago. Nassa thought about it often though. She was relieved she didn't have the magic inside her, and yet she felt something was not quite right. Her papa had nodded off her origins a little too quickly, and when she asked Marny, all she received was a hush and a 'not to worry, we don't need to speak on it — you are Akkadian now, that's all that matters'. But she was worried. They had lied to her. The mother she had thought abandoned her, maybe hadn't really done so at all. And she hadn't ever thought much about her father. But maybe she should. All she knew now was that she was a refugee of *The Great Purge*. She didn't know much about *The Great Purge,* except that for two years the wicked king of Sudonia had killed all the little children. But she must have somehow escaped. Could her parents still be alive? It didn't seem likely. Had any other children survived? She tried to hold back the anger growing inside her. Marny and Papa owed her more of an explanation. They only seemed to care that Nassa had no magic. Her feelings were hurt.

Nassa knew she shouldn't ask around about Sudonia. It was treason to even wear the green and gold colors of the magical state. But she was curious. She decided she would approach Marny one last time. If she still didn't get any answers, well she would just try and move on.

Nassa went about her morning as usual, a chill taking hold even though the sun still peaked through in intervals. She decided the best time to approach Marny would be during her afternoon tea, when she was done with her daytime duties but before she began to ready for dinner.

The day dragged on impossibly slow. Nassa moved through her morning chores but found focusing very difficult. Her mind wandered often as her chores passed and the day inched forward. When the sun was overhead, her stomach began to growl, confirming it was time to break for a meal. She ran down the lane toward the cottage, away from the chicken shed, where she had been sweeping out the droppings. The sun beat lightly down on her now, and she enjoyed the warmth, knowing it wouldn't last too much longer this season.

She was surprised when she came around the bend to see a horse and cart parked adjacent to the cottage. It wasn't often they got visitors, especially ones she did not know, and the mare she saw now was none she had ever seen before. She approached it cautiously, sticking out her hand to show her benignancy. Even so, the mare started, and Nassa noticed the lash marks across its flank; this creature was not used to a gentle hand.

"Nassa." Nassa started, mimicking the creature next to her. She turned to find Papa waiting in the doorway.

"Papa! You startled me!" She smiled meekly and walked toward the cottage. Papa's face was unreadable, but he put a hand out and patted Nassa on the head as she walked through the door.

"Nassa, I'd like you to meet an old friend of mine. We served together in the war when we were younger."

"Voltred, this is my daughter, Nassa. Nassa, Voltred," Papa gestured to the man and Nassa reluctantly approached him stopping short to give him a small curtsey.

He was dressed in a style not suited for this part of the world. His belt was made of gilded silver, a treasure which Nassa had never seen. He wore a thin sword at his side which he gripped now as he looked down at Nassa.

"Montoc, you never told me what a beauty your *daughter* was." Voltred looked Nassa over with a gaze that made her spine shiver. The way he said 'daughter' made her uncomfortable.

"And what good does beauty do? She is a hard worker and a fine girl, but even so, young for all that. Come now, let us share a pint and talk of the old days when we served," Papa gestured for Nassa to leave, and she quickly accommodated the request.

Nassa ran out of the cottage and back down the lane toward the stables. There maybe she would find Toc, the stable boy, who could share some bread since it didn't appear she would be getting any afternoon snack from the cottage today. As she approached the stable, she tried to shake off the lingering feeling of unease the stranger had given her. Something about him made her insides crawl. And where had Marny been?

Toc ran out, interrupting her thoughts. He was ten, not much older than herself, and as lively as they could come. Sometimes Nassa thought he would never run out of energy. He seemed to bound more than walk, and to see him on a horse was a sight to behold. She knew there was supposed to be no magic left in Akkadia, but if there had been, Nassa was certain there were remnants in Toc, his mastery over the beasts was too impressive to be real.

"Nassa! Come quick!" Toc grabbed her hand, forcing Nassa to run alongside.

"What is it, Toc? I was hoping to share some bread!" Nassa's stomach growled again in agreement.

"No time for that now! Lady has foaled!" And Toc continued to pull her toward the stable, much to her stomach's protests.

Toc brought her to the large birthing stall and signaled for her to be quiet while pulling her inside. Nassa gasped at the beautiful sight as she entered. Lady was licking her foal clean, nuzzling the creature, encouraging him to stand as she did so.

Nassa felt a surge of warmth as true happiness took over at the sight of the natural bonding.

"Oh, Toc! It is an amazing sight to behold!" Nassa whispered with joy. Toc gave her a sideways look, grinning from ear to ear.

"Come on, let's go." He led her out, still holding her hand. Once back outside, he continued to lead her, running along the stables until they reached the stall where he lived. Although meant for a horse, the stall had been transformed into a small living quarter when Alago had found Toc on the side of the road as a child.

Alago, the stablemaster, happened upon Toc when he was just five. Toc had told Alago his parents died of the Marsh-flu, and old Alago couldn't help himself, as it was his kind nature to care for the world's creatures.

He had taken him in as a stable hand and had vouched for him ever since.

Nassa and Toc had become quick friends, as there were no other children nearby. Although they both were very busy with their daily chores, they still managed to find some time to play. Toc had also nurtured Nassa's own love of animals and in turn Nassa had taught Toc about the herbs and plants of the forest. Although life was laborious, they were happy.

Toc led Nassa into his stall, only then letting go of her hand. Nassa sat as Toc continued to pace around the small room, never able to sit fully still. He grabbed a cloth and unfolded it to reveal a fresh loaf of bread, clearly one that Marny had made and brought over fresh this morning. Nassa's mouth watered.

Toc took out his belt knife and cut them each a slice, handing a thick piece to Nassa, who devoured it whole heartedly.

"Papa has a visitor today," she told Toc while still chewing a mouthful.

"Who is it?" Toc asked with indifference while ripping off a large chunk with his teeth.

"His name is Voltred, I think they fought together in the war."

"Which war? Why is he here?" Toc asked distractedly as he practiced a new fighting stance jumping off the wall.

"Has there ever been more than one war? The war with Sudonia, obviously. What are you doing?" Nassa looked at him with eyebrows raised as he continued to jump and roll around.

"I'm practicing. Alago has been teaching me new fighting moves in our spare time. It's Hildish fighting, that's where Alago is from, Hildlerland, you know." Toc continued to move about spastically. Nassa couldn't see how this style of fighting would do much except to make your opponent laugh.

"Anyway," she continued. "I am not sure why he is here. I couldn't read whether Papa was nostalgic or weary toward his presence. I, however, did not like him." Nassa wrinkled her nose.

"You can stay here with me while he's here." Toc tried out another move but instead ran into his small desk, falling to the floor. "Ouch!" He exclaimed clutching his side.

"Looks like the table beat you," Nassa said trying not to laugh. They looked at each other then, a rare moment of stillness for Toc, and then both broke out in a fitful round of giggles.

"Marny wouldn't let me stay here," Nassa said once she regained control. "But it's OK, I am safe in my room. And I doubt Marny, or Papa would ever let a bad stranger in," Nassa said with a resolve she didn't quite feel.

Toc jumped to his feet, "Well time to go then, out with you!" He grabbed her off the cot she had been sitting on and shooed her out.

"Hey!" Nassa exclaimed at the quick force out. "I haven't finished my bread!" Toc tossed it to her. Then continued to push her out.

"I've got lots of work to do with that foal, and you being here is too great a distraction! Come tomorrow — early, Marny said she'd bring some cheese! And you can update me on your night with this stranger!" Toc widened his eyes in mock fright. Nassa stuck her tongue out at him then turned to go find Marny.

After searching for an hour, Nassa found Marny seated on a bench in the forest, not far off from where Papa had tested her. Nassa knew it to be part of Marny's mushroom hunting route but was surprised to find her there at this time of day.

"Marny?" Nassa questioned as she quietly approached taking a seat next to Marny on the bench. She rubbed her hands together to keep warm. The cold didn't seem to bother Marny.

"Ah, dear girl." Marny put her arm around Nassa, bringing her in close and sighing. Nassa was reluctant to bring up her questions, she could tell Marny was in a thoughtful sort of mood.

"What is the matter, Marny?" Nassa asked, slightly concerned. Marny looked as though she had been crying.

"Oh, nothing to worry about now, my dear." Marny smiled and gave her a reassuring pat.

"Does it have to do with Papa's visitor?" Nassa nestled into Marny's side.

"Nothing gets past you does it, sweet girl? Yes, it has to do with him. Was just surprised to see him so soon is all. Time passes too quickly." Marny stroked Nassa's hair.

Nassa desperately wanted to ask more about her birthing parents, but knew now was not the right time.

"Is he a bad man, Marny?" Nassa asked instead.

"Only time will tell, sweet girl. Come let us head back to the house, the day has gone too quick. It is time to ready supper. Tonight you will help me." Marny stood up and Nassa followed along.

Chapter 5

VOLYA

Though Darkness falls,
Concealing hope,
The sky is black with nigh',
He climbs the walls,
Bright with enthralls,
He sees with his trained eye.

- Tales of a Thief by Pickering Fool

Volya took a deep breath. He felt free up here in the night sky. The sun was no longer beating down, and the air felt fresher from the cool breeze as the land slowly cooled to the air. It hadn't been difficult to rise to power over the band of brothers. Once Puntar had hanged, he gathered as many as he could find to stand behind him. He promised he would take less, and give more, supporting the brothers and sisters and not stealing what they had earned, like Puntar so often did. Most pledged loyalty to him, although there were still a few who were not happy someone so young had gained leadership.

Dinby and Petey were content to follow him, although he knew from experience they would be just as willing to betray him for a favor. Although he led the brothers, he knew it was a volatile situation, anything could happen. Luckily, most of the kids didn't want to lead, and since Volya was the best thief in the band, he hadn't received much resistance.

He surveyed the city from his favorite perch. It had become quite his evening routine to come up here to the top of the library after a day's work. He liked to see what he gathered. And it felt good to be up where the breeze reached, away from the swollen humidity of the city. Even though winter was approaching, Thessola would see no break from the heat.

Thessola stretched wide in all directions, almost as far as Volya could see. The golden domes of the palace sprawled out on the far hill, the forests expanding out beyond. Volya thought what it would be like to live inside that giant palace, living in luxurious silk clothing and spreading his feet on thick rugs, lushly hand woven. He chuckled to himself, though he was young, he was still the king of his small world. With that thought, he began jumping down from the heights, knowing that it was time to join back with his band.

When he got back to the den, he slammed the door open. He liked to make an entrance, let everyone know their leader was home. A few eyes looked up as he walked through the door, a couple of the youngers rushing to him with a bowl of pickled broth.

"Gogo, where are you?" Volya shouted.

Gogo rolled his eyes and slowly got up. He was one of the harder ones to come to Volya's side. A brute by nature, and older than Volya, he didn't have the brains to lead, but generally preferred to follow someone who used his more sadistic talents. To Gogo, Volya was far too green and far too kind.

Gogo didn't respond, but slowly sauntered over to Volya, making no effort to conceal his contempt. He stood in front of Volya, raising his eyebrows in a lazy questioning.

"Gogo, bring that table here and a chair. We are having a meeting." Volya waited a few long seconds, unsure if Gogo would follow his commands, but soon he turned moving to grab one of the long tables, picking it up easily, and moving it where Volya designated. Volya continued to direct Gogo until all the long tables were rearranged in a rough square.

"OK everyone! Listen up!" Volya shouted. "We are having our first meeting!" He was met with a few annoyed grumbles but most of the band of brothers and sisters slowly got up and began moving toward the various seats placed around the square of tables.

"I witnessed something today! Something I found very interesting!" Volya began.

"What? Twokey shit in the street again!" Someone heckled, causing a roar of laughter.

"Shut up, Foba! You want my knife in you so soon?" Twokey stood up holding his knife in the air with anger.

"Foba, shut your fat mouth," Volya shouted, but couldn't help from laughing as well. "We all know Twokey can't handle the spice markets." Another roar of laughter, but Foba and Twokey both sat down, Foba looking amused, Twokey still simmering.

"Like I said," Volya continued. "I saw something very interesting today." Volya paused for dramatic effect and jumped on top of one of the tables. He began pacing in the rough rectangular circle, stepping over plates, bowls, hands and knives. A few of the brothers threw things at him, but he continued to pace thoughtfully.

"Us, band of brothers, see, I think we are the greatest in the world. But we have no order. Our leadership is weak." Someone threw a knife at Volya, and he caught it midair. "Well, not all that weak." he gave a tiny bow and winked. The kids all laughed again. He was creating quite the spectacle.

"I thought, *hmm, what do normal leaders do?* So, I snuck into the High Council." He said this nonchalantly, though in truth when he had snuck into the legislature building outside the palace earlier this morning, it had been no easy task.

"Liar!" someone shouted from below.

"You know what they do in these council meetings? They put their tables in a square like this,"

Volya gestured to their surroundings. "And they talk about things and vote."

He took another dramatic pause. "That's it boys and girls, all these high-level bureaucratic idiots do is sit around and talk. Then vote. Then rule all our piss shit little lives!" Some of the kids started banging on the table, enjoying this display of oration.

"Well, I thought to myself, *Volya, this seems easy*. And then I had an idea. Can anyone guess what it was?" He stopped pacing and turned to his audience, arms sprawled, waiting.

"You thought it was about time you took your head out your ass?" Foba shouted, clearly confident from his earlier crowd pleaser. This too brought loud amusement from the room.

"I thought, why aren't we in charge? Sure we are young, but we are fierce!" More loud banging. "Boys — and girls — I think it is time we join *The Guild of Thieves*!" The room broke out into a frenzy of banging, laughing, and incredulity.

"Volya, are you insane?" Quilby rose, silencing the room. Of all their band of brothers, Quilby was the one Volya had to keep the closest eye on. He was cunning this one, and had been Puntar's second. "*The Guild of Thieves* is for real, grown men. You are a little piss shit toddler to them. *The Guild of Thieves* runs a legitimate business. The only thing you have legitimate, is your *il-legitimacy*, you bastard." Quilby sat down with a thump, followed by many shouts of agreement.

"Brothers and sisters, look around you. We live in a shithole. We can't go two blocks without one of us getting punched in the face by a gang member. They only leave us alone here because we aren't worth shit." Volya kicked someone's glass on the table across the room. It shattered with resounding effect.

"What the hells, Volya!" Volya ignored the brother.

"We *can* be great. We are quick, we are smart, we are older than our young years! Dingby, you watched your parents die by fire! Twokey, you gut a man at age five! Come on, boys! Let's pull together, we can really make something of ourselves!" There was more banging of agreement and some reluctant nodding.

"Tomorrow, *The Guild of Thieves* will meet. I will go and petition them. Gogo, you are coming with me. Twokey, you as well. Mara, you will be in charge here. And that's that!" Volya hopped down as the room broke into excited arguments and frustrated sighs.

"What about the vote, Volya! Aren't you trying to follow those bureaucratic shitheads?" Mara stood up and shouted. Volya shot her a look of extreme annoyance.

"A vote, is it? Fine." Volya turned and stood back on the table.

"All in favor of petitioning *The Guild*, raise your hand." About twenty of the Youngers raised their hands.

"All in favor of staying put here and living like pigs?" About twenty more raised their hands.

"Decided then, we petition *The Guild*!" Volya jumped back down off the table.

"It was a tie!" someone shouted across the room.

"Well, I didn't say the vote would be fair." And with that Volya grabbed another bowl of pickled broth, inwardly smiling. If he played his cards right, in a few years' time they would be eating spiced meat and fresh bread instead.

Chapter 6

NASSA

O Fate,
Your tainted eyes watch me,
Can I resist your tempting glare?
With weariness I strain,
But time is fast approaching,
The hour has come,
I cannot falter now.

- The Ancient Archives, Vol II, Book 3

Nassa and Marny made their way slowly back to the cottage. Nassa could feel Marny's feet dragging, and wondered what it was that made her so reluctant. A feeling of dread came over her, but she nudged it off not wanting to upset Marny further. *Who was this strange man, Voltred?*

When they got back to the cottage, neither Papa nor Voltred were there. Marny and Nassa began silently preparing dinner. Nassa put a fire on the stove, boiling water for the pheasant they would poach, whose feathers she had earlier plucked. Marny began chopping potatoes, fennel, and chicory root from the garden. It would be a feast tonight then, in honor of the mysterious guest.

An hour or so later, Marny told Nassa to wash up while she finished preparing the meal. Nassa went outside to the small well that stood in the center of the yard. She pumped some water and brought it to her hands and face, rinsing off the flour and seasoning stuck to her hands. She turned to the sound of footsteps coming down the lane and ran quickly back into the cottage as her Papa and Voltred came around the bend. Once inside her room she shut the door, heart pounding, the same feeling of dread lingering.

Marny had laid out a dress for her on her cot. It was the red dress with lace on the sleeves and hem, the nicest dress she owned. Marny and her had gone into town to pick out the fabric for her nameday celebration. It was the most luxurious material she had ever seen, and she was thrilled the whole time sewing it. But looking at the dress now filled her with terror. Why did Marny want her to wear this dress tonight? Again, she shivered to think who this man was to require such formality.

Obediently, ignoring her intuition, she slipped the dress on and brushed out her unruly hair. She closed her eyes and took a deep breath. She could hear the voices in the other room, and knew they were waiting on her.

She walked down the small hall into the dining area. The three grownups were waiting there — Marny, Papa, and Voltred — all silent and staring, looking directly at her. She felt like a prize at the fair. It made her extremely uncomfortable.

"Ah, Nassa." Voltred walked slowly toward her with predatory eyes. Nassa could see Marny look toward Papa, concern written across her brow. "You are the spitting image of your mother." Voltred bent down, grabbing Nassa's hand, kissing it. *How did he know what my mother looked like,* Nassa thought with a start. Nassa wanted to pull away, but didn't want to be rude and disappoint Papa and Marny. Instead, her body tensed, and she clenched her jaw.

Voltred laughed.

"A little fight in this one I see," he said turning to Papa with a wolfish grin. Papa did not return the smile.

"Did you know my mother?" Nassa asked, shocked from his previous comment. She had never heard anything about her mother before recently, and curiosity began to overtake her fear. Maybe she would finally have some questions answered.

"Of course," Voltred said without elaborating. Nassa was confused and frustrated, but determined to know more.

"How?" She asked rather bluntly, but she couldn't help herself.

"You'll have plenty of time for questions later, Nassa. Now us men are hungry! Let us eat while it is still hot!" Voltred said holding his tummy in mock hunger.

Nassa was still not sure who this man was to demand Marny in such an ill-mannered way. And she didn't want to wait until later, besides, her hunger had disappeared with the unanswered questions.

Marny brought out the poached pheasant pie, and began serving. They all waited until Papa took the first bite before digging in, but Nassa could only pick lightly and push the food around on her plate. Her stomach was in knots and her emotions were running high. She waited patiently, hoping to soon be given answers.

Since her eighth nameday, so much had happened. She knew with eight passing years, she was beginning to grow up, everyone now expecting so much of her. But she still felt like a child, and there was so much she didn't understand. Still, she held her tongue and waited patiently for dinner to end.

After dinner, Papa rearranged the chairs in front of the fire and brought out two smoking pipes for him and his guest. Marny brought out the lute and handed it to Nassa.

"Play us a song, Nassa," she instructed.

Nassa reluctantly grabbed the lute and began plucking the strings, tuning the instrument. She didn't want to play for this man. Her music was beautiful, and she felt he would taint it.

Nevertheless, she began to obediently play. She started slow at first, weaving her anxieties into the tune, until the music filled her, and she was able to let go of all fear, giving in to the sweet melody. Her fingers moved expertly along the strings, creating a captivating crescendo, which ebbed and swelled until at last she could no longer play, emotions rushing forward, and she abruptly stopped.

The room was silent, hardly anyone could breathe whenever she played. And she hadn't even sung. The effect her singing brought was intoxicating. She did not want to share it with this mysterious and frightening stranger.

"That was miraculous!" Voltred exclaimed as everyone was shaken out of their reverie. "I will look forward to hearing that often." He chuckled to himself again in that predacious way. Nassa was unable to understand his meaning.

"Will you be visiting often then?" Nassa asked sheepishly, trying to hide her dread at the only logical explanation to his hearing her play more often.

"Oh, gods, I hope I won't have to!" Voltred smiled, though his eyes remained dark. Papa coughed uncomfortably.

"Montoc, are you sure you have you tested the girl?" Voltred asked, turning to Papa, and ignoring Nassa, who stilled nervously. She assumed this topic was strictly off limits. A secret between her and Papa only.

"Yes. There is no magic," Papa said stiffly.

"Ah, so then, even more like your mother. But your father must be in there somewhere! No?" Voltred fixed a piercing stare on her, as if he was trying to look deep within her. Nassa felt ill.

"Voltred, she did not know her mother nor her father. She is nothing like either. She is a good and hardworking girl. Enough said on the matter. Come let the ladies go to their rest and we shall continue to reminisce the war." Papa shifted awkwardly, motioning for Marny to bring Nassa to bed.

Marny quickly stood, grabbing the lute off Nassa's lap, and brought her swiftly to her room. As they walked down the hall she could still hear Papa and Voltred talking.

"You know, Montoc, *reminisce*, is really not the right word. The war is still very much going on." Nassa could hear a deep drag of his smoking pipe.

"There is no need to scare the ladies. They do not need to be a part of it," Papa spoke back, rather harshly.

"We both know there is a very good chance that they will be a part of it regardless. It is no longer safe here for her, she is still too close to the border. You knew I would come once she turned eight." Marny quickly shuffled Nassa into her room, closing the door and cutting off the conversation from their ears.

Nassa went to her trunk and pulled out a worn nightgown. She got dressed for the night and sat down on her bed, with her comb, brushing out her hair and plaiting it into a long braid.

"Marny, what do they mean it is no longer safe here? It seems like everyone wants me to grow up, but no one will tell me any straight answers. What is happening, Marny?" Nassa looked to her with pleading eyes.

"Oh Nassa, my dear." Marny spoke quietly and sat down next to Nassa on the bed. "I know you overheard them just now. And I know you are confused about this strange man coming among us. Tomorrow he will be gone, and I will explain everything much better. Tonight you need some rest. It has been a long day for us all." Marny got up and went to the door. Nassa wanted to cry out in frustration.

"I beg you, please tell me at least one thing, Marny. Who is this man and how does he know my birth parents? Are my parents still alive?" Nassa gave her a look of absolute misery.

Marny took a deep breath. Nassa could tell Marny did not want to answer her questions.

"Nassa, your mother died in childbirth. Before she died she asked me to name you Annassa. Annassa means *strength*. I want you to remember that, Nassa. You have a strength deep inside you, it is your namesake." Marny squeezed her eyes shut.

"And why has this man come now?" Nassa asked, as a piece of her heart broke knowing her birth mother was dead.

"He is your uncle, sweet girl." Marny smiled back at her, but Nassa could see the defeat and anguish in Marny's eyes.

Chapter 7

VOLYA

The demons chopping,
Never stopping,
Bodies thrown astray,

The heat severe,
With screams to hear,
Bodies prone to flay.

- Poems from the Deep, Verse 142

Volya slept fitfully, thoughts of the meeting filling his brain, causing him to toss and turn restlessly. It was an excited sort of restlessness, plans and lists of things to do filling him up, keeping his body active with the sheer ambition of it all.

When dawn finally came, he was awake with a jump, quickly washing and dressing. The meeting of *The Guild of Thieves* would not be until the late afternoon, but he had some work to do before then, anyway.

He made his daily rounds across the city, making sure all his band of brothers and sisters were in position on their assigned corners and alleyways, giving the younger and newer members little tips along the way so as not to get found out, or worse, caught by the city patrol.

Around midday he got the impression he was being followed. He wove his way through the streets of the mid-city merchant district until he was back in the lower levels and close to the den. He hoped he had shook whoever was following him off, but even though he never saw anyone, the hairs on the back of his neck continued to erect themselves in warning.

He decided not to go back to the den, not wanting to give whoever it was any reason to know exactly where he lived. He pulled quickly into a dark alley, hoping that the mysterious person would pass him by. But he saw nothing.

He knew at least it was not the city patrol. They were far too stupid and clunky to creep around unseen. This must be someone who knew exactly what they were doing.

Time slipped by, but Volya waited in the dark alley, fingers ready to pull out his dagger if needed. But no one suspicious ever walked by. The sun was getting lower, and his stomach was starting to grumble, so he decided brashly he would come out of hiding. If this person wanted him killed or robbed, they already could have easily overtaken him unseen in the dark alley.

Stepping into the lowering sunlight, he blinked a few times and looked around. He was on a relatively secluded street, and nothing unusual seemed to be in place. There was a small group of beggars on the far corner, and a stray dog looking for scraps in a heap of trash across the way. He scanned the tops of the lower ramshackle buildings but saw no indication of anyone hiding on the roofs. His fear quickly dissipated, and he made his way back to the den.

He swung open the door with his usual dramatic flare, a few youngsters rushing to him with a cup of rusty looking water. He shooed them away.

"Where's Mara?" He asked the room before he spied her sitting with her back turned playing dice with a few of the brothers.

"What is it, Volya?" Mara turned to look at him questioningly.

"I need to speak with you." Volya waved her over and went to stand in a quiet corner. Mara followed him, slightly annoyed to leave her game.

"What, Volya? I was about to win!" Mara put her hands on her hips. Even though Volya was now in charge, Mara still retained an air of older-sister like authority.

"Today, around the markets, I think someone was following me." Volya spoke in a low whisper.

"Did you catch a look at who it was?" Mara asked, now intrigued.

"Nope. I waited a while tucked away, but nothing. Anyway, you are in charge while I'm gone. Just keep an eye out for anything unusual." Mara nodded and Volya stalked off to ready himself for the meeting.

He donned his nicest tunic and pants, though the linen had greyed, there were hardly any holes or frayed edges. He grabbed a rough rag and attempted to put some shine in his boots, before lacing them up. From his small bag of things, he pulled out a rough brush he had stolen from the stables a few blocks away. Although meant for brushing an animal, he used it to slick back his thick dark hair, the natural grease of it providing the perfect pomade. He was ready.

"Gogo, Twokey!" he shouted. "Let's go." He didn't attempt to tell them to dress their best. He knew they only had the clothes on their backs.

He chose to bring Gogo in case he needed the strength and as a test of loyalty. Twokey he chose, since he was quick with a blade, but also to pacify him. He had been getting out of hand lately, and Volya thought giving him a little extra attention may sooth his ego.

Gogo grumbled and slowly followed, Twokey jumped up eagerly, a knife in each hand.

"Easy, Twokey. Strap 'em down, we don't need to use them yet," Volya said, amusement in his tone. Twokey strapped a dagger to each arm. Two more swung from his belt loop. Volya sauntered toward the door, Gogo and Twokey flanking each side.

"We will be back after supper!" Volya shouted back as they made their way out of the den with cool calm.

The other brothers and sisters watched them leave but kept silent, even Quilby, who sat in the corner, feet up on the table, sharpening his knife.

The sun was almost down now, the heat of the day beginning to dissipate. Volya enjoyed the slight breeze at his back that pushed him forward. It wasn't a long walk to Thieves Hall. Volya hoped to enter sometime in the middle of the meeting. He had been scoping out these parts for the last several weeks, and knew the best way to go to slip past a few posted guards.

Thieves Hall was in the center of the roughest part of town. Near the docks, the fishy smell lingered here, but also the suffocating air that could only be found in slums where bodies were forced to live too close together. Not for the first time Volya was happy their den was on the outskirts.

They managed to slip past the outer two peripheral layers of guards without questioning. As they approached closer, however, they were stopped outside the large warehouse that was The Hall of Thieves.

"You there?" the sentry said. He really was not much of a sentry; he had one missing eye and several missing teeth. Nevertheless, Volya didn't dare underestimate the man's darker talents.

"We are here for the meeting," Volya said, standing up tall trying to look older than his ten years. The man just laughed, but he let them in anyway. *Well, that was easy,* Volya thought to himself. Perhaps they underestimated *him*, then.

Volya led Gogo and Twokey down the hall, through the reception area and before the doors that entered into the chamber. He could already hear loud voices coming from inside. He was happy at this moment that he had picked Gogo and Twokey, neither of them appearing in the least intimidated by their surroundings.

Volya opened the door himself, and was immediately met by shouting and laughing, the room filled with the roughest kind of men. They walked down the center aisle, approaching the dais, where the twelve leaders of thieves sat presiding. No one seemed to notice them, nor care.

When they got to the front of the room standing below the dais, Volya shouted out.

"Hello!" He shouted and waved his hands. "Sir!" The leaders continued to ignore him.

Volya nodded to Twokey, who immediately withdrew all four blades, sending them flying and missing the four men in front of them by inches, impaling the back of each man's chair. The room quieted and the men before them turned to look finally at Volya.

"Go home to mommy," the man in the center said looking peeved and dismissing Volya with a wave. He was tall and brutal looking, a scar inset deeply across his brow. His hair was greying and slicked back, similar to Volya's own. His voice was rough, but he retained an air of aristocracy in his graceful and upright movements, even among thieves. It was clear this man was their leader, Rasmere.

"Rasmere Blogovdan. I come to petition our band be let in to *The Guild of Thieves*." Volya spoke as loudly as he could, using his deepest voice, and mustering up as much authority as he could find within.

A raucous laughter filled the room. Volya tried not to show his aggravation. Rasmere, however, remained quiet.

"And why would we," Rasmere gestured to the room. "Allow a bunch of little children into our guild? This is not a nursing chamber." He stared Volya down with a piercing gaze. Volya was not intimidated, but tried instead to memorize that look, hoping to copy it and use it on his own unruly band.

"We are not children. We may be small, but small can be good. We can go unnoticed, we can easily get information, pick a few prized trinkets. Gogo here, he can kill a man with his hands. Twokey, here, he can knife down a man twice his size." Volya stared unblinkingly at Rasmere with an air of defiance.

"And you — ?" He asked Volya questioningly.

"Volya." He stated his name and took a slight bow, eyes still locked on Rasmere's.

"And you, Volya, what can you do?"

"Anything," Volya said with unflinching confidence. Rasmere upturned his lips in a tight smile.

"Anything else to say for yourself?" Rasmere sized up this young boy in front of him.

Volya leaned in close. "One day, Sir, I promise you," he gave a wicked smile. "I will be seated right where you are." Volya attempted Rasmere's own piercing gaze.

Rasmere paused, considering this child in front of him. An unnatural heat swelled around Volya. He was unsure if it was in his imagination or if it was his nerves getting the better of him. He clenched his jaw and pushed it away. Rasmere narrowed his eyes, a slight smile on his lips.

"We will accept your petition." Rasmere concluded, leaning back in his chair.

"You can't be serious," the grizzly man seated next to Rasmere spoke, irritation in his tone.

"I think I may have some use for this one. But that in mind," he turned to Volya, "you will not find any wet nurses here. Dismissed." And he flicked his hand, shooing Volya and his brothers off.

They quickly turned and walked out the way they came. The one-eyed guard at the front looked surprised to see them all in one piece as they came out of the building. Volya tried to keep his face hard and emotionless, but once they were a few blocks away, he allowed himself a wild grin.

"Does this mean we are members of *The Guild*?" Twokey asked him with excitement.

"No, not yet. But they have accepted our petition. Now they will send us a test, then take a vote. Just like those stupid shitheads in the capital building. I told you all grownups are the same." Volya chuckled to himself.

They rushed back to the den, eager to let the brothers and sisters know the news. They would become legitimate now. The band could start making some real coin, maybe even getting some lush bedding, more clothing, and food. Volya was thrilled at the minor victory that had seemed too easy.

When they turned the corner, Volya stopped abruptly. Something was out of place. The door to the den creaked on its hinges, someone had left it unlocked. As he got closer, he noticed a small stream of blood leaking across the threshold.

Chapter 8

NASSA

In wait they hide,
The giant's bone-crunching steps encroaching,
Swiftly they harnessed their power,
But no power could stop the one who was coming.

- The Ancient Archives, Vol I, Book 1

Nassa woke with a start. Something was wrong. She could feel it in her soul. Her heart was pounding violently, her muscles tense, ready to run if necessary. She didn't remember having any bad dreams, she thought as she rubbed her eyes. But then she remembered what Marny had told her.

Despite the shocking news of her mother's death and Voltred being her uncle, she had fallen asleep quickly, drained of all emotion. Now she woke with a start to the sun leaking eerily through her shuttered window.

She had bolted her door shut that night, wanting to feel extra secure, and now was grateful for doing so. She jumped out of bed, dressing quickly, the cottage feeling unnaturally quiet. She unlocked her door and made her way out and down the hall. No one was in the kitchens or common rooms, although there was water bubbling at a rapid boil over the fire.

She continued past the common room toward Marny and Papa's sleeping quarters. Her breath caught as anxiety filled her. *Where was everyone?* She thought to herself. She told herself to calm down, it was just so much news to handle at once, but she still felt apprehensive.

When she arrived in front of Marny and Papa's door, she slowly opened it, the old wood squeaking on the metal hinges. No one was inside. The bed was made, and the room appeared tidy, just as it did every morning. Afterall, Marny believed a tidy house started with a tidy room. Nassa sighed, they must be out doing their chores. She started to close the door but paused. There was a piece of paper sticking out from under the bed.

She kneeled down slowly and grabbed the rough paper. Unfolding it carefully, she read the letter, written in Marny's hand. Although it bore no name, she knew it was meant for her.

I'm so sorry. We should have told you more. Do not trust him, your uncle. Master Perigreen will have the answers. Tell him Master Luka sent you long ago. Balrigard Monastary. Destroy this note.

The feeling of dread rushed back and Nassa felt lightheaded. She scrambled to her feet and began running to the front of the house. She tore the note to pieces as she ran, throwing it into the fire, where the water still furiously boiled. She burst through the cottage door but found nothing unusual in the front yard. She looked around expecting something, yet nothing happened.

The cart that Voltred had rode was gone. Marny had said he was leaving today, but never said her and Papa would be leaving too. She didn't know where to turn.

She decided to run to the stables. She would see if Papa's horse was still there, and if Toc or Alago knew where they had gone. She couldn't help the uneasy feeling that she had been abandoned.

She couldn't see the stables from the cottage, the dense forests blocked it from her view. She ran along the path from the cottage to the stables, knowing once she got around the final bend, it would come into view. Before she made it that far, she could smell the fire. Panic rose within her growing from a seed into a boil.

The creek ran beside the stable, so she took a shortcut off the path toward the water. If there was danger of a fire, she would rather be close to the saving element. Branches and fallen twigs scraped at her ankles as she ran, but she continued faster and faster until, at last, she could see the stables.

The sight before her made bile rise. The stables were roaring with flames. Marny and Papa's horses were tethered to the posts kicking and whinnying, trying desperately to break their tie with the reins as the flames threatened to consume them.

All fear subsided and she dashed to the beautiful beasts. She could feel the burn of flame against her skin and tore a piece off the hem of her skirt, wrapping it around her mouth and nose, to better breathe.

"Easy, boy." She stroked the kicking horse as she approached, trying to calm him as she untied the reins on first the one and then the other, both who quickly ran off in a panic.

"Is anyone in there!" She shouted, though her voice was lost in the roaring flames. There was no response, but she couldn't just sit by and watch the stables burn. Alago or Toc could be in there. Papa and Marny could be in there too. She took a deep breath, then kicked in the flaming door.

The world around her turned into a blazing inferno. She imagined this is what the hells looked like. The heat was unbearable, her skin felt as though it was melting. She continued forward anyway, headstrong as always.

A scream pierced the air. It was not human, but that of an animal. She ran to the compartment where Toc's horse had just foaled, jumping over fallen timber and smoking remains of the stable.

"Toc!" She shouted. He was trying desperately to kick down the stall, but it appeared stuck. He looked at her as she shouted, a wild panic in his eyes. She could hear the horses screaming with anguish. She looked around desperately, finding nothing. Her muscles clenched as she willed with her whole body, soul, and mind, for the door to open. To her complete and utter surprise, the door shattered with Toc's next kick. She was left looking stunned; her mouth open wide. There was a power she had never felt before coursing through her veins.

Toc ran into the stall and came out carrying the baby foal. There were tears dripping down his face, trails running through the ash marks.

"What about Lady?" Nassa asked, trying to run into the stall herself. Toc grabbed her arm and shook his head. He was too distraught to tell her that Lady was dead.

"We need to get out of here!" Toc shouted over the flames.

She knew if they did not hurry, it would be too late. But she couldn't leave anyone behind. "Where is Alago? Have you seen Marny or Papa?"

Looking closer into Toc's eyes, she could see the true anguish. The tears hadn't just been for the horse. Nassa felt sick.

"What happened, Toc?" Nassa yelled, fear and confusion in her voice.

"I don't know! I was asleep in my stall when I smelled the smoke. I tried to get to them but the stall… it wouldn't open! Nassa, I'm — I'm sorry." Toc was crying, his voice cracking with despair.

"Where are they!" she demanded.

"Nassa, it's too late. They didn't make it." Nassa heard the words but didn't listen. She ran like she had never run before, tearing open stalls and searching for her parents who had raised her, loved her, and cared for her all these years.

When she reached the end of the stables she stopped. The final stall was mostly burned down, if it had been locked, she could no longer tell. Nassa kicked it in. The charred remains fell, exposing the inside of the stall.

Lying in a heap near the back corner, were Marny, Papa, and Alago, all charred and blackened. Their flesh lay in crispy clumps, exposing bone and sinew. Flames still roared around them.

"Nassa! We have to go! Now!" Toc ran up behind her yelling. He grabbed her arm, trying desperately to rip her away from the horrible scene, but she could not tear her eyes away from the devastation before her.

Anger, pain, and utter despair welled up inside her. She clenched her hands into fists, feeling the fire burn within her. She grabbed her face, tearing at her hair, hitting herself, full of torment and heartbreak, and screamed. The world around her exploded into flames, washing over her, Toc, and consuming everything in their surroundings.

Chapter 9

VOLYA

Creeping, crawling,
Never falling,
The thief moves in the night.

The darkness hides,
The thief, he glides,
Always out of sight.

- Tales of a Thief by Pickering Fool

Volya swore under his breath. He ran the remaining few yards to the front to the den. *The fools.* He thought. He pushed open the door but was met with resistance. He couldn't budge the rotting wood more than a few inches open. It wasn't even enough to peek inside. He pulled out his knife, ready if he should need it, and continued to push at the door.

Twokey and Gogo finally caught up with him, and together the three were able to pry open the door. When they entered, they saw what had been blocking their entrance. Two of the littles, bloodied and stiff with death.

Volya had seen his fair share of death, but what met him now was even worse. This was his den, his band of brothers. He was supposed to be their leader, but he had failed. And failed horribly.

Before him was a scene of gore and sport. Someone had enjoyed what they had done. He ran through the whole den, looking in all the corners, and everywhere he went he saw and smelled more death. Someone had killed them all. He searched the faces of the children, they all seemed much younger in death than they had in life. An innocence that was lost to them all, was once again written on their faces. This he thought at least was a consolation. Maybe in death one's purity could be restored. Maybe, where they were now, they could be kids again.

He cursed as he finally found the face he had been dreading to find — Mara. She looked like a rag doll, slumped against the back wall, head lolling to the side and eyes wide open. There was blood leaking from her mouth, and a slash mark across her neck. She had been beautiful, Volya realized with a start. He had never looked at her that way before but seeing her in death he saw how true it was. She would have become a lovely woman one day. Now that future had been snatched away.

Mara was the only one among them who knew of Volya's past. Now there was nothing tying him to his old life, his old roots. The last connection was severed, all family was officially lost to him. The thought was depressing yet freeing at the same time. He would weep for them all, but not now. Now he would stash away this ball of pain deep inside, just as he'd always done. He had the power to decide. He would decide now to put away the pain.

"Volya! — " Gogo's shout was cut off in a gurgling grunt. He turned to look where Gogo and Twokey had been waiting by the door. Two large men stood behind them each with a bloody knife still held where they had slit both his remaining brothers' throats. Gogo and Twokey slumped to the ground.

The men moved to the side as Rasmere walked through the door, followed by Quilby. Volya cursed himself for not noticing sooner that Quilby's face hadn't been among the dead. He could feel the anger rising inside.

"Quilby, you bastard. You did this." Volya walked toward Quilby, knife in hand, ready to fight. Rasmere nodded his head in Volya's direction. The two men came stalking forward, danger in their eyes. Volya, flung his knife, striking one in the forehead. The man went down with a thump. Rasmere smiled.

The other henchman rushed toward him too quickly and grabbed Volya by the arms. Volya kicked and struggled, but the man's grip was too strong.

"Volya, Volya, calm down." Rasmere spoke slowly and softly, as if nothing unusual was going on, as if they weren't surrounded by death. "Don't forget. You asked for this." He gestured to the room.

"I did not!" Volya shouted, emotion taking over. "I never said to murder all my band!"

"You wanted to join *The Guild*." Rasmere spoke as if it was the most obvious thing in the world. "I told you there would be a test. If you are to be raised in *The Guild*, we needed to know your loyalty."

"And what about him!" Volya pointed to Quilby.

"He wanted to join *The Guild*, too. And this was his test, though don't worry, killing children is only for a certain kind of guild member." Rasmere chuckled, immune to the evil in the actions before him.

"You were following me earlier, weren't you!" Volya clenched his jaw trying to push his anger down. The pieces of the puzzle were coming together.

"No, not me, but one of my followers, yes. We needed to know when you left for the meeting. We've been watching you since you spoke so openly about wanting to join. You really shouldn't be so conspicuous." Rasmere patronized.

"But how did you kill them all? Many of them know how to fight back. How else could they have survived so long." Volya asked with despair.

"It isn't so hard to kill children in their sleep." Rasmere spoke softly, musing.

Volya tensed against the henchman, wanting with all his soul to get to Quilby who smirked in front of him. "How?" He asked with teeth clenched.

"Quilby gave them some sleeping solution with dinner. Don't worry, they did not suffer too much." Rasmere smiled.

"But so many. You have wasted all their lives!" Volya couldn't keep the anger out of his voice this time. It boiled deep within.

"We both know most of these ruffians would have been dead by age fifteen, Volya." Rasmere sighed and rose his eyebrows in annoyance as if it were transparent to all but Volya.

"They were my family." Volya spoke with sorrow, sagging his head in defeat. He had lost this battle.

"We are your family now, Volya." Rasmere stated with confidence.

"But why kill them all? Why spare me." Volya did not understand why they all had to die.

"They would have held you back. You will see this in due time, and you will come to agree. As for why we spare you, well, you have a power inside you, Volya. I recognize this, and soon you will feel it too. Do you remember where you come from?" Rasmere looked deep into his eyes. Out of the corner of his eye, Volya saw Quilby jerk his head and noticed his confused look.

Volya was just as confused by this statement. He didn't feel any power within. He knew as a refugee of *The Great Purge,* it was a possibility, but it was a slim chance. His mother and father had both been powerless. Mara had asked him about it on his tenth nameday, the age magic shows in boys, but there was no change, so he had shrugged it off.

He knew that magic was a dangerous thing in Akkadia, deathly so. Was Rasmere talking of a different kind of power? He couldn't help but be tempted by his words. He met Rasmere's eyes and slowly nodded.

"So will you come with us now, Volya, and quit whining. My impression was that you were stronger than this. I told you once already, we've no nursemaids in *The Guild*." Rasmere sounded annoyed.

"Yes. But first, I want him dead," Volya said, pointing at Quilby.

"Very well." Rasmere gave Volya a piercing look and nodded.

"Hey, wait!" Quilby protested, but before he could continue, the henchmen released Volya and grabbed Quilby, pulling him to his chest from behind and wrapping his hand around Quilby's weaselly mouth. His protests became muffled.

Volya stood there unsure what to do. He knew this was a changing moment for him. One of those momentous times in life where you had to decide who you wanted to be. He had one once before, when Mara and he ran from *The Great Purge*. But Mara was dead, along with everyone he knew. He recognized this moment for what it was. He needed to decide right now who he would become. He met Rasmere's gaze and once again nodded.

"You do it," Rasmere said.

Volya tightened his grip on his knife. He took a step toward Quilby. He looked him straight in the eye. He could see the horror and fear reflected in Quilby's expression. He could feel Quilby begging for mercy with his pleading stare.

"This is for betraying us." Volya bent down and stabbed his knife across the backs of Quilby's knees. He kept his eyes fixed on Quilby as the henchman stepped back, releasing Quilby and causing him to crumple to the floor. Quilby clutched his legs in pain, moaning. Volya moved in closer.

"This is for my brothers and sisters." He kept his eyes fixed on Quilby as he struck him again, this time stabbing him in the stomach. Quilby let out a shriek and started to whimper and thrash.

Volya took his time, staring Quilby down to his very core.

"And this," Volya smiled viciously. "Is for Mara." And he plunged the knife into Quilby's neck. Quilby's eyes widened, the terror still clear in his face, as warm blood spilled in a pool around him while his life bled out.

"Good. That's done then. Come with me." Rasmere turned and walked out of the den. Volya followed.

Once they were outside, Rasmere turned to his henchman "Burn it," he told the man with no emotion. He continued on and Volya followed, the henchman staying behind.

Volya looked back only once to see his home going up in flames. The home he had lived in since he was a young boy. The home that had molded him into the tough kid he was today. He pushed away any sad feelings; emotions, he was quickly learning, only served to complicate things. He shrugged off all thoughts of the lost and turned, only looking forward.

Chapter 10

NASSA

Again they come.
Light fades to night.
There is no stopping the force.

Flee, young one.
Flee — now.
Your fate approaches with teeth bared.

\- The Ancient Archives, Vol II, Book 3

Nassa stood amidst the blazing inferno. This was a different flame from the chaotic anarchy of the fires that lit up the stable. This was a pure flame, a clean flame, a flame born of her soul. This flame did not burn her, nor did it destroy. It pushed back the wild fires, dismantling their power in a burst of smothering energy before surging back into Nassa's very core.

Nassa fell to her knees panting. She took in huge gulps of air, her lungs desperately filling up with the unsullied air, no longer choking with black smoke. She was crying now, uncontrollable sobs. She felt a hand on her shoulder, and looked up, relieved to see it was Toc, unharmed by her uncontaminated power. She looked around her then, and what she saw was astonishing.

The flames were gone, and so were the stables. Where the outbuildings had stood, there was now only a rough scar burned into the ground, as if a small star had somehow fallen from the heavens.

Her parent's bodies, and that of Alago, were a pile of ash. She strode over to where they had lain and pleaded with gods of death, that theirs be judged worthy of the heavens. It scared her, looking down at the pile, realizing that what had been people full of life and soul, able to communicate, love, and nurture could so quickly be reduced to a meaningless pile of dust. It made her own mortality seem so very fragile. She sat there in silence for a long time.

She didn't understand what was happening to her. Papa had tested her, and she had no magic. But this, this somehow felt right. Deep down she knew something was there waiting to be unleashed. Finally, it had all come out. But why so late? And what was she to do now? She didn't know how to use her power, and even if she did, it was a death sentence. She would have to keep it hidden. She would have to suppress it at all costs. She looked back to the scene in front of her, still shocked at the sight of it.

The tears flowed on their own accord now, she barely even noticed them except for the cool sensation where the wind stung the wetness on her cheeks. Toc stood next to her, the same expression of agony and despair, anger and fear, written on his face. Next to him lay the small colt, alive, but in need of care.

"What now?" Nassa asked him. She felt so lost. A gripping panic was beginning to take hold. Toc looked just as helpless.

She stood slowly and took Toc's hand. She led him down to the river where they took their time washing and scrubbing in silence. Nassa went into the forest and foraged for some healing herbs. Toc had burns on his hands and face, he would never look quite the same. She ground a poultice from the garlic reed and hems bane seed and lathered it on Toc's wounds. It would at least soothe the pain, if not heal the scars.

When they were finished, they returned to the scene and slowly surveyed the damage. There were no longer any bodies to bury. The ashes were too fine a dust to collect. They would blow away with the wind, scattering Nassa's beloved family across their land.

When they both felt they could no longer look, they walked slowly back to the cottage.

"It's just you and me now, Toc," Nassa told him with a sad smile. "I think we will start by cleaning up the mess."

Toc followed her to a shed in the side yard, where they grabbed shovels and hoes. Nassa grabbed a few seeds and sacks of potting soil from the potting shed as well. They made their way back to the fire site.

"Nassa, I won't tell anybody, I promise. You know about—" Nassa cut him off.

"I know, Toc. Thank you." She looked at him and his face was full of fear. Fear *for* her or fear *of* her, she wasn't certain.

They worked all day in silence combing the ground, removing any scraps of metal or wood left from the fire, although barely anything had survived Nassa's burst of power. Neither Nassa or Toc spoke about it again. Nassa was silently grateful Toc didn't ask any questions; she wouldn't know how to answer anyway. She wanted to pretend the whole thing never happened, although deep down she knew she would have to deal with the consequences eventually.

As the sun was going down, they finally felt the cleanup was as good as it would get. They surveyed the site where the stable had been, now a blank spot in the earth, as if it had been abruptly erased from all memory.

Nassa grabbed the potting soil and seeds and went close to the place where Marny, Papa, and Alago had burned. She dug with her bare hands, fingernails cracking and dirt soaking into her blistered palms. She took her time carefully planting the flowers, Corinthians, Marny's favorite. They would bloom every spring.

When she was finished, she wept, using her tears to water the soil. Toc gave her space, but when she rose, he went to her, hugging her and trying to offer comfort, although he had tears of his own wetting her hair.

It was getting dark, so they walked back to the cottage. Nassa planned to make some broth for them both. She knew they wouldn't be able to stomach much more.

Rounding the corner to the cottage, the sound of a whinny made Nassa stop in her tracks. Her heart began to beat furiously once again. As they made it to the front of the cottage, Nassa recognized the horse and cart that stood waiting.

"Nassa, my dear." Voltred jumped down from the horse and came striding over to her. She tensed but resisted the urge to cringe away from her uncle. "I'm so sorry for this tragedy that has befallen." Nassa didn't think he looked very sorry.

"How do you know what happened?" Nassa asked suspiciously remembering the stall that wouldn't open. *Why had they all been together in there? Why wouldn't the stall open?* She thought as she stood strong and met his eye with defiance.

"Local boy, was running over some turnips when he spotted the fire. Came running into town. Luckily, I hadn't gotten very far on my journey home yet." He again met her with a wicked smile. Nassa wanted to cut it off his face. She stared at him without responding.

"Well, since I am your next of kin, you are to come and live with me." Voltred turned and jumped back on the horse. Nassa stood in shock, dumbfounded with horror.

"Surely, I can stay here and run the farm?" Nassa asked, a plead in her voice. She knew it wouldn't be possible.

"Surely you cannot," Voltred spoke back. "Go get your things and put them in the cart. I have already lost enough time." He spoke in a manner that demanded no questions.

Nassa couldn't move. She did not want to go with this uncle of hers but saw no choice.

"What about Toc?" Nassa asked. Toc stood next to her, unmoving. He appeared to be in some kind of stupor. Nassa wished he would snap out of it and protect her, take her away somewhere far from here where she could escape all this mess.

"What about Toc?" Voltred asked in turn.

"Can he come with us? And his colt as well, it will grow to be a respectable stallion." Nassa supplicated.

Voltred stared at the boy for a minute before answering.

"Very well. But it's no easy work I have in store for you, boy." Voltred scowled as though it was a compromise he was unwilling to give. Toc nodded solemnly.

Nassa wanted to cry again, but she mustered up the courage to be strong. She didn't want her uncle to have the satisfaction of seeing her act like a child. She was grateful at least that he hadn't seen her powers. There was no telling what he would do to her then. She knew he would have to burn her by law; whether or not he kept with the law was the question. If only Marny and Papa were still here.

Nassa ran into the cottage and into her room. She grabbed her small leather satchel and stuffed her few clothes and possessions in. She grabbed the figurines she had received from her nameday and wrapped them in her softest wool mantle to keep them from breaking. She looked around her room once and sighed, wiping a tear that escaped down her cheek, then left the only home she had ever known, as the first true snow of the season began to fall.

Part 2

10 YEARS LATER

Chapter 11

NASSA

Hear me, Oh angels,
Watch over me,
Protect me from demons,
Who come in the night.

My eyes are heavy,
My body needs sleep,
Hear me, Oh angles,
Take my soul with thee.

- Prayer of a Child from the Hildish Translation

Nassa woke. She hadn't dreamt that night, she hadn't
dreamt at all in years. By the time she went to bed at the
end of each day, she was so exhausted from her busy
work, she practically fell on her cot.

Her rooms were in the Northern tower of Voltred's
manor. When she first arrived ten years ago, the
looming fortress had terrified her. It had taken two

weeks to arrive by horse and cart from her old cottage. Two miserable and torturous weeks. She tried not to think about that dark time.

The castle was built of stone, dark and stained by soot and moss over the hundreds of years since coming into existence. The four towers poked through the dense forests, but light never seemed to touch the place, it was always somehow entombed in shadow. Ivy had crept up the sides of the fortress over the years, reaching like spindly fingers toward the sky.

Although Voltred seemed wealthy enough to Nassa, running the estate was clearly not his priority and much of it had decayed. Over the years, Nassa had tried to amend for this, taking on much of the cleaning and repairs, yet no matter how hard she tried, the manor was still in a state of dismal deterioration.

Her room in the northern tower had frightened her when she first moved into the space. But now it had become her home, she had lived here longer than anywhere else, after all. She had a lock on her door, and a thick blanket to keep warm from the wind, which crept in through her broken shutters. She had painted a few frescos on the wall to cheer her up and had done her best to make the space more hospitable with the little resources she was given. She was no longer afraid of the spiders and their webs, the mice scuttling to and fro, or the stray bird that happened in through the broken shutters. It was as good a home now as she could ever hope for.

When she first came to live among Voltred and his family, her thoughts were plagued with uncertainty and dangers. Back then she had thought often of her parent's deaths and the unusual circumstances. She looked at Voltred suspiciously, wondering if he could possibly have been responsible for the fire and the three adults mysteriously stuck in the back stall together.

Over the years, her worries had diminished with her strenuous yet familiar routine. The horrible treatment she had expected had not come. She assumed from Voltred's attitude that the household would have been abusive toward her, but no one had bothered or touched her. However, there was still an air of eerie mystery, she was never fully able to shrug off. And she couldn't negate the dark stories she heard from some of the household staff. And although no one touched her, the years of neglect and lack of love were abuse enough.

She had tried once to run away. Not long after she had come, she had remembered the words in Marny's note *I'm so sorry. We should have told you more. Do not trust him, your uncle. Master Perigreen will have the answers. Tell him Master Luka sent you long ago. Balrigard Monastary. Destroy this note.*

She knew nothing of Balrigard Monastary or its whereabouts. She had left early in the morning, hoping to get to the nearest town on the outskirts of Thessola City by nightfall. She traveled on foot, for she did not want to be accused of stealing a horse. When she finally made it to the town, she went to the nearest inn, hoping to get answers as to which direction the monastery was in.

"Excuse me, ma'am." She remembered asking the barkeep. The old haggard woman had just stared back at her, pockmarks scarring both cheeks, her yellow teeth scowling.

"Where might I find Balrigard Monastary?" Nassa pleaded.

The woman laughed. "Balrigard Monastary? Are you serious, girl? You better be leaving quick and asking no more questions about such places if you know what's good for you!" She grabbed a rag and turned back to her work, wiping down the counters.

Nassa had left the inn disheartened. She had walked among the dirt streets of the town, not sure where to turn before deciding on the local blacksmith. She guessed he must have news of the comings and goings of the town, welding materials for traveler's horses and carts would be part of his trade.

When she reached the blacksmith's forge, she had to shout over the noise of hammering metal.

"Excuse me, sir," Nassa had called out. "Do you happen to know where Balrigard Monastary is?"

The man had stopped hammering and looked up, staring Nassa down. He was a brute of a man, balding with his years, but he had kind eyes.

"What do you want with Balrigard Monastary, girl?" he answered back with a thick accent that Nassa didn't recognize.

"I need to go there; it is an errand for my mother."
Nassa had lied hoping it wouldn't be too obvious, but
feeling optimistic that this man could help her.

"Well, you best tell your mother that it is an
impossible task. And she should know better at that."
The man had looked Nassa over with concern.

"Why is that, sir?" Nassa asked with desperation.

"Well, Balrigard Monastary is across the border in
Sudonia, lass. Not only is it too far and too dangerous
from here to be walking, but you'd have to cross the war
front. You best run home and be safe." He looked out at
the dwindling light and then back at her anxiously. "Do
you have somewhere to stay the night?"

Nassa shook her head, tears beginning to stream
down her cheeks.

"You can stay here, just one night. Then go back
wherever you came from first thing tomorrow with the
dawn. I'd keep all thoughts of Balrigard Monastary out
of your little head." The man had sighed, but set her up
with a wool blanket by the fire. Nassa had fallen asleep
comfortably but had lost all hope in escaping her new life.

She hadn't been punished like she had expected
when she had returned the next day. But a few weeks
later, Toc had told her of an old Blacksmith who had
been hanged in the nearby town for inscrutable reasons.
Nassa had been sick that night. She had never even
learned his name.

She sat up in bed, wanting to keep the past behind her. It was supposed to be a happy day after all. She was in no hurry as it was not quite dawn, she still had a few minutes before she would need to be dressed and downstairs. She kept better track of the seasons than the days, but today she had woken early, knowing it was her eighteenth nameday. There would be no celebration, so she would take this time to leisurely wake, a luxury in itself.

When the time came, she moved to her chest of drawers, donning her usual working attire and aprons. She twirled around, in good spirits, then unlocked her door and skipped her way down the spiraling stairs, through numerous corridors, down two more flights, and into the kitchens.

She hummed to herself as she entered through the swing door, the smell of cinnamon and fresh dough lingering in the air.

"Good morning, Ari." Nassa smiled to the cook and continued to hum. She grabbed a bun from a nearby basket and began to retreat as quick as she came.

"Nassa! Get back here!" Ari, the cook waved her wooden spoon at Nassa in mock anger. Nassa retreated from the doorway backward than spun toward the plump cook. She looked at her questionably.

"Now just where do you think you are going with that bun?" Ari scolded. Nassa just shrugged, trying to hide a guilty smile. Nassa knew Ari was just teasing her, the cook was slow to warm but Nassa had managed to quickly charm her. Nassa had managed to charm most of the staff. It was the family that she tried to avoid most.

"Ari, you know very well I have many chores to do." Nassa scolded Ari back.

"Yes, yes. But I think you are forgetting something important." Ari shot her a look of faux rebuke but couldn't help the smile in her eyes.

"And what is that?" Nassa asked, no idea where this conversation was going.

"Come out of the pantry, would you Toc?" Ari shouted behind her toward the pantries.

Toc came running out, holding a plate with a kitchen rag drawn over it, a huge grin across his face. In the past ten years, Toc had grown into a young man. But where Nassa had grown charming, regal, and beautiful, Toc had grown tall and gangly. The burn scars that still marked his face and arms had not faded over the years, but to Nassa they were the marks of courage.

"Happy nameday!" Ari and Toc shouted together.

"For me?" Nassa beamed in delight, not able to hide her smile. She quickly regained her composure and put her hands on her hips. "I hope you two weren't up all night doing something silly." She rose her eyebrows at them but continued to beam. Toc came over, giving her a kiss on the cheek and handing her the plate. She took off the kitchen rag and found a delicious and still steaming hot *plaviçi,* a traditional cinnamon and nutmeg cake, rolled with layers of whipped sugar and egg whites — Nassa's favorite.

"It's beautiful!" Nassa beamed, taking a deep whiff of the mouthwatering scent. "It is almost too perfect to eat!"

"Oh, don't be foolish, girl. Eat up!" Ari hit her softly with her spoon, encouraging her.

"But you two better help me! I couldn't possibly eat it all alone!" Nassa put the delicacy on the counter, and the three of them dug in graciously, giggling all the while. It was rare to have a moment to themselves.

"What's this?" The three of them turned as Lord Voltred walked in, followed by his eldest son, Brutav. The two of them scowled, as if any form of celebration was an annoyance.

"Pardon, sir," Ari stammered, bowing. "It's just the girl's nameday and we thought we would—"

"Thinking is not your job, Ari," Voltred spoke. He grabbed the rest of the cake, throwing it in the trash with disgust. "We've been at the table waiting to break our fast. I do not like to wait, Ari."

"Yes, sir. Forgive me. It won't happen again." Ari bowed and Voltred and Brutav turned to leave the room.

"Nassa," Voltred turned back to Nassa. "Join us."

Nassa bowed and followed them out of the room. It was rare that she broke her fast with the family. Her days were generally filled with chores from sunup to sundown, and she usually just grabbed something quickly from the kitchens whenever she got a chance. The attention made her nervous.

Nassa came to sit at the dark mahogany dining table with Voltred and his three sons — Brutav, Maldrig, and

Temid. Voltred's wife had died during childbirth with their final son, and Temid had remained a weakling all his life. He preferred the solace of books, and Nassa often envied the time he was able to spend languidly in the library. Maldrig followed mostly in his father's footsteps, reserved yet with a domineering air. He was still somewhat of a mystery to Nassa. Brutav, the eldest, was also the cruelest. It wasn't unusual to find a serving maid bruised or crying from Brutav's unwanted attentions.

Nassa sat quietly as Toc served the family half boiled eggs, buns with cinnamon crusting, walnuts foraged from the nearby walnut grove, and an array of elder fruits. She smiled up at him, then looked worryingly across to Voltred, who caught her eye. He glared at her, then at Toc, and cleared his throat.

"I want to make an announcement," Voltred said standing up and grabbing his glass of morning port. The already quiet table stared up at him.

"Congratulations are in order. Nassa, as it is your nameday, I found it an appropriate occasion to share the good news." He smiled darkly down at Nassa.

Nassa had never quite forgotten what happened on that dread day ten years ago, although she tried to suppress the memory as much as she could. It was moments like this; however, she could feel something stirring inside her wanting out. She shivered the thought away.

"Nassa, Maldrig, please rise." Nassa's stomach dropped. A sudden fear took over. She was afraid she knew where this going.

"Congratulations, to the new couple. You shall be wed the weekend next." Voltred took a sip of his drink, his eyes meeting Nassa's over the cup, smirking.

Chapter 12

VOLYA

An arrow in his chest,
Will he ever rest?
In the dark and bleakest night,
The thief will learn his flight.

- Tales of a Thief by Pickering Fool

V olya stood at the edge of the bluff. They woke early that morning to travel to the cliffs of Wanmere, about an hour's ride south of Thessola. The massive cliffs lay along the southern coast of Akkadia, the jagged outcropping notorious for ruining ships. Now Volya stood looking out over the sea, ready for what came next.

He stared down at the dark and violent ocean. Powerful waves crashed against the rough-cut stone tens of meters below, trying desperately to beat through the rock face. Gazing out he could see white caps slicing apart the blue seas as far as the horizon. This was a violent body of water, powerful, and full of energy from the wind.

"Are you ready?" Rasmere asked him with a sideways glance.

"Aren't I always," Volya replied with a smug smile. He ran his fingers through his dark hair, slicking it back in the same style he had worn since he was ten. Now at twenty, he had grown tall and strong. The training had toned his body shaping him into a sizable creature. His boyish features had roughened over the years, and he stood now as a devilishly handsome and formidable foe.

Rasmere had personally been training Volya for the past ten years. When Volya had come to join *The Guild,* he thought it would be an opportunity to make something more of himself in the world. He thought he would learn secret insights into thieving and have access to things he would never have dreamt before. Maybe he would make some good coin, possibly steal from even the richest of Thessola.

Of course, there *was* that side of *The Guild.* Actually, most of *The Guild* did involve the underground world of crime and thieves. But what he had entered into was very different. He had joined a small and elite clandestine group. His imagination never could have prepared him for what he was now capable of.

Looking down at the dark waters he recalled when he first learned the truth of the world.

Volya still cringed to think of that day long ago and the horror at seeing all the dead children. However, he had a different outlook on it now. Rasmere had been right, they would have weighed him down.

Ten years ago, after they burned his old den, Rasmere took Volya back toward the docks. They entered The Hall of Thieves, Volya taking a deep breath against the sorrow and uncertainty he had felt. Rasmere led him through a series of rooms and halls before coming to a dark library. Books had filled the shelves, bottles and jars packed with unusual trinkets were stacked around the room.

Coming to one such trinket, Rasmere had pulled the jar forward with strain, causing a secret doorway to open to a spiraling staircase. The stairs led downward into the belly of the Hall. With Rasmere leading, Volya had followed down unsure where this next chapter of life would take him. Rasmere brought a candle with them, as there were none to light the way down the flight. When the stairs finally gave way, the sight was spectacular. Rasmere had breathed out, the flame of his small candle somehow filling the whole room with light.

The walls were gilded in gold and silver, pewter bowls lined the mahogany tables that were arrayed in columned lines throughout the room. The floors were covered in rich foreign rugs with exotic patterns. Volya had stood there mesmerized by the luxury.

"Come now, Volya," Rasmere had said, continuing onto the far side of the room where a large double door stood. Volya had followed, still shocked by the bounty in front of him.

They made it through the double doors in what was a very different sort of room. It was shaped like a pentagon, and where the hall before them had been extravagant, this area was bland. The floors were cold stone with no adornments and the walls were bare except for a single picture on each, each depicting one of the five elements.

"Do you know where we are, Volya?" Rasmere asked, sounding slightly excited. It had been the most emotion Volya had seen from the man.

"No," Volya responded curtly. At the time, Volya had felt apprehensive, but thinking about it now made him smile.

"We are in the bowels of The Hall of Thieves, Volya. This is where I live, and where you will live until your training is complete."

"In this room?" Volya looked around at the bare setting.

"No, Volya." Rasmere rolled his eyes. "We have many rooms down here. I will show you to yours once I test you."

"Test me?" Volya was slow to understand.

"Yes, Volya. This is a testing room." He gestured around to the elements.

"For magic?" Volya asked, dumbfounded.

"Volya, I'm getting tired of your asinine questions. Think before you talk." Rasmere gave him a pointed look.

Volya was about to respond but decided to keep quiet. Rasmere *had* said he had seen something special in him.

"Volya, you will go around to each wall. Place your hands against it, feel for power, then turn and I will test you."

"And if I have magic?" Volya asked feeling nervous but also doubtful.

"Then your training will begin." Rasmere looked deep into Volya's eyes.

"But magic is illegal." Volya challenged him.

"Everything we do is illegal, Volya." Rasmere had spoken with a matter-of-fact attitude.

"And if I don't have magic?" Volya asked afraid he may know the answer.

"Then we will part as friends." Rasmere gave Volya a vicious grin. Even as a ten-year-old, Volya had known they would not be parting as friends under those circumstances. More likely he would part as a corpse.

Volya nodded slowly to Rasmere and began moving to the closest wall. This one had a picture of a flame — the element of fire. He placed his hand on the image, trying to imagine flames coursing through his veins. He had no clue what it should feel like, only that focusing would probably help, but nothing in him seemed to change.

He turned around casually toward Rasmere, not sure what to expect. Fire hurled toward him, knocking him to the floor. He rolled frantically, beating away flames that scorched his tunic. He looked up at Rasmere with wild eyes. *Rasmere has fire magic*, he had thought with surprise, shock, and a bit of anger.

"No fire magic then," Rasmere said looking disappointed. Volya scrambled to his feet. Rasmere nodded for him to move to the next image.

Volya placed his hands on an image of water. When he turned around this time, he was more prepared for the flames that shot out at him, but all he could do was throw himself on the floor. No water magic either, then, he assumed. Rasmere just shook his head and nodded for him to move on.

The third image was what looked like a swish of air — wind power. Volya placed his hands on the image, trying once again to feel some sort of power, but he felt nothing. He was getting more nervous that he would need to start coming up with an exit strategy.

He turned slowly as a rush of fire came spiraling at him. This time however, the fire didn't reach him. He felt instead, a sudden surge, and saw to his amazement that the fire was being pushed back. He let out a whelp of excitement, but as he did so, the power failed, and he was once again knocked down to the ground in flames.

He had scrambled to his feet, excitement still writ on his face even as he patted out the fire.

"Did you see that?" He asked, feeling exhilarated.

"I did," Rasmere replied curtly. "You have very little control. We have a lot of work to do."

Volya had asked Rasmere about the remaining two images after that. The first was a tree — earth magic he explained. The second image was a strange looking symbol. Probably written in some ancient text, Volya had thought. When he asked Rasmere what it was, he simply said 'don't worry about that one, only those with royal blood can have that kind'. Volya didn't think much about it, especially because he knew he was no royal. It hadn't mattered, anyway. He had wind power. His training had started immediately after that.

Volya smiled to himself as he stared down from the precipice. Those days had been wild and uncontrollable as he came into his power. But he spent the last ten years training in every way possible. He had learned skills beyond his imagination. Now, here on the Cliffs of Wanmere, he was having his final test. He had come a long way.

He looked up at Rasmere, who stood waiting patiently. He gave him a mischievous smile, then jumped off the cliff.

Chapter 13

NASSA

Again the demons flock,
Crying out in the night — they charge,
Will this be their final assault?
Or only the first of many.

- The Ancient Archives, Vol I, Book 4

Nassa was in her room crying when Toc came and found her, once again ignoring her dawn chores. She had been in a state of misery ever since the meal with her cousins. News of the engagement had stunned her. She had turned ashen faced, then ran into her room where she cried uncontrollably.

No one had bothered her, or had demanded her presence, for that she was slightly thankful, but the weight of her future lay strong like a boulder on top of her chest. She knew Toc and Ari were starting to worry.

"Nassa, are you OK?" Toc asked.

She looked up at him, sweet and loyal Toc, whose face covered in burns was still a constant reminder of her past. She couldn't respond but instead threw her face back in her hands and continued to cry.

Toc sat down next to her and patted her on the back.

"Nassa, it's OK, it will be all right." Toc shushed her, pulling her close, and stroked her hair comfortingly. They sat that way for a long time, until Nassa finally pulled herself together and sat up.

"Oh, Nassa, I know it isn't what you wanted." Toc looked at her with a mix of pity and devastation. She knew it wasn't what he wanted either.

"It will be OK Toc. I am just shocked, that's all." She gave him a weak smile, trying now to reassure her loyal friend. "Maldrig might not be so bad."

Toc nodded, trying to be strong, but she could see the fear deep within his eyes.

"Anyway, I should get up and do some chores. I'm awfully behind," Nassa sighed and rose, it was already too late in the morning, she had squandered away precious time in self-pity, but she resolved herself now to be stronger and not neglect her duty any more. Her eyes still stung and felt puffy, but she didn't care.

She was stronger than this. She knew she was. She scowled at herself, in a moment of disgust, cursing herself for being so pitiable. She had been through a lot, but she would not become helpless. Afterall, her name was Annassa, *strength.*

"Remember when we were kids, Toc? You moved so quick back then; you never could sit still." Nassa wasn't looking for an answer, but times like these, when her anger peeked through, she would always find herself thinking of the past.

"Things are different now. The accident changed me, changed us both." Toc looked down at his feet, embarrassed to talk of that day.

"But you used to have more fight in you, Toc. You used to want to become a Hildish warrior!" Nassa couldn't help but sound angry. Toc looked ashamed but didn't reply. Nassa sighed.

"Never mind that, Toc, it doesn't matter any more. Come, let us get back to our duties." Nassa rubbed the remaining tears from her eyes and set off down the stairs. Could there be a way out of the wedding? She couldn't possibly imagine marrying Maldrig. She thought of the brave knight her Papa had whittled for her on her eighth nameday. She had always imagined she would marry some sort of hero like the statuette, but of course that was ridiculous. She was destined for a life of service, not a life of adventure.

She spent the rest of the morning doing her chores, really her life wasn't terribly different than it had been on her childhood farm. She still tended the animals and gardens, gathered herbs for the estate, and helped with the cooking in the kitchen when she was free.

She would go there, to the kitchens when she finished sweeping the stables. She would find peace there, with the savory smells of the noontime meal, and Ari's jolly demeanor permeating the air.

She pulled out the small dagger she kept lashed to her ankle and threw it at the makeshift target she had drawn on the stable wall long ago. The knife whizzed across the room and struck the middle, barely making a noise. Nassa smiled to herself. A perfect bullseye, like always. Toc had taught her a bit of fighting as a girl, but when she got a chance, she would watch her cousins practicing in the courtyard. She liked to come to the stables and practice on her own, and somehow her aim was always perfect.

"Nice throw." Nassa turned with a start to see Brutav leaning casually against the stable door, hands in his pockets and smirk across his face. He was handsome, her cousin, but there was a haughty air and something dark that lingered behind his every move.

Nassa's heart rate sped up. Brutav tended to make her uncomfortable.

"What do you want, Brutav?" Nassa asked, picking up her broom and continuing to sweep. She hoped he would see she was busy and move on.

"I wanted to congratulate you on the engagement. My brother, he can be cold, but I don't think you will find him *too* unpleasant." Brutav stalked slowly toward her, a predatory look in his eyes. Nassa froze.

"You are a beautiful girl, cousin." Brutav now stood too close, but Nassa had backed against the wall with nowhere to retreat. He brought his hand to her face and gently stroked his finger across her cheekbone. Nassa tensed at the touch, flinching away.

"Nassa, you don't need to be afraid of me," Brutav chuckled to himself. "I'm only here to help you."

"And how's that?" Nassa tried ducking under his arm, but he grabbed her by the shoulders and pinned her to the wall. He pushed his body up against hers and Nassa could feel the heat of his desire.

"Get off me!" Nassa screamed, but Brutav just laughed cruelly, and continued to pin her. She wasn't able to match his strength.

"Nassa, how innocent you are! There are things I can teach you about the marriage bed. I promise it will only help; I am gentle compared to my brother. It will be a kindness to ease you through this." Nassa started to thrash and struggle as Brutav began kissing her neck.

He grabbed the front of her tunic, ripping it halfway down the middle and exposing her breasts. He smiled hungrily and began to touch her, biting at her flesh. Tears began streaming down her cheeks as she continued to cry out, but she knew no one could hear her. The stables were too far removed from the manor. The distance from the house used to comfort her, but now it only served to betray her.

"Stop! Please!" she cried but Brutav brought one hand to her mouth, forcing her silent as he used his body to pin her and began lifting her tunic with his other hand. She closed her eyes in pain and fury wishing she hadn't thrown the dagger across the room. She wished she was stronger, but then, for the second time that day was reminded of her name — Annassa, *strength.*

She roared, extending her arms against Brutav with all her might, and *pushed* with her mind. He flew backwards, launching into the air and landing with a thump across the room. She heard the whinny of a horse nearby. Shocked and scared she looked at Brutav, who now appeared unconscious, a pool of blood forming beneath his head.

Nassa's eyes went wide. She grabbed her tunic closed and turned, running as fast as she could back to the castle and the safety of her rooms.

Chapter 14

VOLYA

Ha! The thief keeps no secrets,
Except in his heart,
And those are his deepest,
Which he'll never part.

To steal the thief's secrets,
A plan must be made,
A knife in the heart,
And a debt to be paid.

\- Tales of a Thief by Pickering Fool

Volya felt exhilarated. The wind whipped at his hair, he tried to keep his mouth closed, but found he was grinning too wide to control.

He soared over the seas, breathing the salty air in deeply. He didn't really fly as much as he controlled the winds. A little push this way, a little push there, and of course a large counterbalance of wind from below and behind. And as simple as that he was airborne.

He shouted out to the empty nothingness beyond, the seas stretching for years in front of him. He had never felt so free in his life. He toyed with the idea of staying out here forever, of never going back and returning to his training, well it wasn't training any longer, this was his final lesson. That made him smile even more if a wider grin were possible.

But he knew also that his power wouldn't last forever. For every action there was an opposite reaction, one of the first lessons he had learned. Although he had immense power stores, they would run out eventually. He would need a good night sleep to recharge, as if he had been running for days, his body would feel the consequences of using so much concentrated power. He could already feel the ache in his limbs.

With difficulty, he convinced himself to turn around and head back to the cliffs. He had a bit of a hard time rotating around, still getting used the push and pull mechanisms of shaping the wind to his will. But, eventually, he ungracefully started back the way he came.

Rasmere was waiting for him in the same spot. He had a smile on his face as well, but it didn't quite reach his eyes. Volya saw a flash of something — was it jealousy or pride? — but it left his face as quick as it came.

"Good work, Volya." Rasmere patted him on the back. Volya knew the compliment was more than

Rasmere usually gave. Volya grinned back rubbing the kinks out of his neck and stretching his shoulders.

"Like always, you will need to work on your control. You are too cocky, Volya." Rasmere shook his head, but Volya just laughed. He had grown a sort of fondness for the man, although he could be unbearably cruel at times. Volya liked to think Rasmere had a special place for him as well — at least most of the others in the gang seemed to resent the attention Volya got — but Rasmere was not one to share his feelings.

"Come on, Dominar," Volya put his arm around Rasmere, Rasmere shrugged him off — he hated when Volya did that — especially now that Volya was taller than him. "Let's go, I think you owe me a strong drink."

"What did I tell you about being cocky, Volya? It will be your downfall. And do not address me by my first name." Rasmere gave him a warning stare.

"Yes, Rasmere, sir!" He gave him a mock salute. "I thought maybe now that I'm done with my training, and we are equals and all, I could start calling you Dominar."

"You can never call me that. And we are not equals. I am still head of *The Guild*. Do not forget." Rasmere turned toward Volya, lighting his hands on fire, balls of flame held above his hands threateningly.

Volya put his hands up lazily. "OK, OK, I get it. Still my master and all, I won't forget." Rasmere turned and continued forward, Volya followed but didn't mistake the threat in his words. He may have to be a little more careful. But caution had never been his style.

They were back in the Hall of Thieves by dinner time. Volya could hear the loud boisterous crowd waiting inside, but when they entered through the doors, the Hall silenced. Rasmere was still very much in control here. They walked down the center aisle, Volya trailing Rasmere, now taking on a serious demeanor, complete with a threatening walk. He never let the other guild members see any weakness.

They made their way up the dais and sat at the head table, Rasmere taking the only throne-like seat, with Volya on his right. Rasmere waved to the crowd, and they erupted back into life, chatting and fighting now that they had permission of their leader.

They were served by one of the few women they had on rotation working the kitchens. She was a pretty one, Dina was her name, and Volya winked at her. She giggled and bent down close, teasing him as she poured him a large pint of ale. Volya watched her as she walked away, leaning back in his chair. She glanced back periodically at Volya as she left.

"Volya, stop flirting with the serving maids." Rasmere grabbed Volya's drink and downed it, Dina clearly forgot to fill Rasmere's cup with Volya distracting her. "Don't spoil my meal, I'm hungry."

Volya turned to the man on his other side, grabbing his drink and downing it as well, in imitation of Rasmere. The man looked up to complain, but realizing it was Volya, thought better of it.

"Dina! More drinks!" He shouted to her at the end of the dais, holding up his cup. She nodded with a flirty smile and left to the kitchens for more.

"I will take petitions today, Volya. I want you with me." While Volya had been in training he wasn't allowed to sit for petitions, this would be his first time. It should be an honor, but Volya thought the whole process sounded rather boring.

Dina came back with the pitcher, and Rasmere grabbed her by the wrist.

"You serve me first, woman," Rasmere spoke harshly, and Dina averted her eyes, becoming serious. She bowed and served Rasmere first, then Volya. "Wait for me in my rooms after lunch," she nodded and bowed again as she retreated.

"You ruin all the fun, Rasmere." Volya rolled his eyes as he drank his ale.

"The world is not for fun, Volya, it is for power. You should know that by now." Rasmere took on a cold demeanor, Volya had pushed him enough for one day.

"And what is power for, except for having a bit of fun?" Volya asked, annoyed.

"Don't push me, Volya," Rasmere spoke with barely hidden threat.

"Yes, master." Volya couldn't help the edge of defiance in his voice. He finished his drink.

They were served a traditional Thessolonian fish stew, and each had a thickly cut piece of course rice bread. The food was better than most in the slums, but still Volya couldn't help but scowl. He was *powerful* and yet he still was a sheep serving a master, still he ate peasant food and was told which woman he could bed. He was growing restless and annoyed more and more every day.

After the meal, the room cleared out except for those at the head table who would be taking petitions. Volya sat back in his chair, crossing his feet on the top of the table. He was on his fourth — or was it his fifth? — pint, and feeling a bit relaxed, although it would take him a whole barrel before he would become drunk, the magic resisting the effects of the drink.

He stayed that way through the first couple of petitions, as guards would one by one usher in folks who came to ask favors, in turn making deals with *The Guild* — many they would later regret. However, Volya ignored the proceedings as his thoughts wandered to the freedom he felt earlier while soaring above the seas. He sighed, wishing his lungs were filling with the thick ocean breeze.

"Volya?" Rasmere asked, looking at him expectantly.

"What?" He let his chair settle back in place, sitting upright. For the first time he noticed it was a woman standing in front of them.

"We would like to know your thoughts on the matter." Rasmere raised his eyebrows, clearly aware that Volya had no idea what they were referring to, but not wanting to help him either.

"Uh — well. Let me think." He twiddled his fingers trying to guess at what they may be talking about.

"It's obvious to me you are way too attractive to be married," Volya said glancing down at the large ring on her finger. "My first advice would be to leave your husband, come to my rooms, and I will show you what you are missing." Volya smiled devilishly at the young woman. Her cheeks turned a violent shade of red and she looked extremely offended.

"Well, I never—" The woman started as Volya laughed putting his hands up in defense.

"Beg pardon," Rasmere gave Volya an angry sideways glance. "My ward here has forgotten his manners. Volya, Lady Rothschild, would like some advice on what to do with her nephew, the one we were just talking about. Who is trying to take hold of her estate now that *her husband has passed.*" Rasmere clenched his jaw as he looked at Volya, clearly displeased.

"Yes, pardon, M'lady," Volya bowed his head and clutched his chest pretending to care deeply, "I am ever so sorry for your loss. I will gladly take care of your nephew."

"And if you do this thing, what will I owe you?" Mrs. Rothschild looked only at Rasmere, appearing still very perturbed.

"We will talk of payment later, Mrs. Rothschild. The time now does not seem appropriate considering your loss. Rest assured it will be taken care of." Rasmere stood, dismissing her as she turned and left quickly.

"Volya, you are a menace." Rasmere sat back down slowly.

"Ah, yes, but now we will be able to squeeze her of all she's worth! A menace or a genius, my dear Master Rasmere?" Rasmere pointedly ignored him as the next man was escorted down the aisle.

Rasmere leaned in close whispering in Volya's ear. "Be careful with this one, Volya. Let me do the talking. Now stand up." Rasmere rose to meet the man who now stood before them. Volya rose lazily looking bored. The man looked him up and down once then addressed Rasmere.

"Dominar Rasmere Blogdovan. Rasmere, my old friend." The man hugged — actually *hugged* — Rasmere. Volya stared shocked as Rasmere hugged him back. The man had used Rasmere's formal name. Not many were allowed to do that. Volya was slightly intrigued.

"All is well, Lord Voltred? How long has it been? Can it really have been eighteen years?" Rasmere asked the strange man. Volya instantly disliked him — there was something wrong with his manner, the air around him seemed to repel away.

"All is very well, Dominar. Yes, eighteen years, and we are still in our prime. We can finally resume the plan to—" He glanced to Volya, mistrustingly "To finish some old business."

"Is that so?" Rasmere rubbed his chin musing. Volya was completely lost on what they were talking about, but he didn't care. He did, however, feel very suspicious of this man.

"I came to announce the engagement of my son, Maldrig, and my niece, the Lady Annassa. My family will be attending Duke Farring's ball, where it will be publicly announced." Lord Voltred smirked.

"Aw, so the time has come. Has she been retested then?" Rasmere asked.

Voltred didn't answer but glanced once again to Volya and nodded in his direction. "Power?" Voltred asked Rasmere, referring to Volya.

"Of course, I only employ the best," Rasmere nodded back. Volya did not feel flattered. Instead, he felt like a prize. The taste did not settle well with him.

"Put him on it then," Voltred said. "Good to see you again Dominar. Now that she is of age, we will be in touch."

"Very well." Rasmere and Voltred hugged once more to Volya's continued disbelief, then Voltred left back down the aisle.

Once he was gone Rasmere dismissed the other men at the dais, but stopped Volya from leaving.

"Volya, a word?" Volya sat back down.

"What was that all about?" Volya asked Rasmere.

"Your real job starts today, Volya. First take care of that woman's nephew." Rasmere waved toward the door.

"Easy, what next?" Volya asked.

"You have sworn yourself to me Volya, with your own blood." Rasmere looked him in the eyes.

"Yes, I know." Volya still had a slight scar across his palm where he had spilled blood for the man, pledging his life.

"Now is the true test. There is a girl we have been watching for a long, long, time. This man, Voltred, is her uncle," Volya nodded. "She comes from Sudonia, and may be a powerful bargaining chip for us in the future. Or a great threat."

"And why is she so important?" Volya genuinely wondered.

"She has powerful blood. And is possibly powerful herself, though Lord Voltred didn't quite answer that question." Rasmere smiled to himself.

"But you don't want me to kill her?" Volya questioned. *The Guild of Thieves'* main job was to hunt and kill. People paid a hefty prize for an assassin, and even more when they wanted someone with magic to die. It wasn't easy to kill those with power. And when powerful people wanted someone dead — well it helped *The Guild* in more way than one. They were thieves and assassins, a little blackmail was the least of their crimes.

"Hold off for now, Volya. It might well come to that. There are a few things I must put into play first. This is good news indeed. Go to this ball and keep an eye out. Don't let anything happen to her yet. And Volya — no games. She is not yours to seduce." Rasmere nodded to Volya in dismissal.

Volya left the room intrigued. He took a deep breath contemplating the hypocrisy of his job and the lingering curiosity of who this girl could be.

Chapter 15

NASSA

The drums beat with vigor,
The armies approach,
Blood will pool and mix,
Devastation will reign.

What, ho! Behold,
A herald has come,
What can be the fate,
Of a desolate land?

- The Ancient Archives, Vol IV, Book 2

Nassa hid in the tower the rest of the day, then once again went to bed crying. She woke with a start in the early hours of the morning angry with herself and the world. This was not her. This was not the girl — or woman now — that she wanted to be. There were so many unknowns in her life, but since she couldn't control all that, she would try and control what she could — herself.

She barely had slept waiting for the door to slam open, and guards to take her away for what she had done to Brutav — but no one bothered her. She didn't understand anything that was going on. She didn't understand her power — the power she tried so hard to suppress but was slowly building up inside causing an almost unbearable amount of tension. She didn't understand who she was — a child of Sudonia, displaced, without a mother or father. She didn't understand why she had to marry her cousin — cold and distant Maldrig, always a scowl on his face. And she didn't understand what had happened the day before. Shame and anger warred inside her, she screamed, angry that she felt so much, angry that she knew so little. The glass on her bedside table shattered. Who was she kidding, she had no self-control.

She stared at the broken shards. That was her. Broken in so many pieces with no idea how to put it back together. Her life was in shards, a mysterious puzzle she had ignored far too long. The time had come for answers.

She slammed open her door in a rage, rushing down the spiraling staircase and heading toward the library. She would hope to find Voltred in his study. She made it to the main hall before she was grabbed hard by the elbow. Voltred was standing in an alcove, waiting.

"Nassa. I've been waiting for you." He yanked her by the arm and led her through the library into his study. The room was dark with old mahogany wood walls. Dusty books arranged themselves on the shelves and miniature alcoves dotted the space with bronze statues depicting dark scenes from ancient texts.

"Sit." Voltred commanded and threw her into a seat before taking his own on the other side of his large desk.

She sat glaring at him, forcing down the fear she felt creeping up.

"I am happy to see you this morning." Voltred glared back. He didn't look happy. "I've just returned from Thessola City, and I am proud to announce we will be going to court. It is time you were introduced as part of the family."

Nassa's stomach sunk.

"Have you seen Brutav lately?" She asked boldly, heart dropping in fear of his answer but needing to know. The anticipation of punishment was killing her.

"Of course. It appears he fell off his horse in the stable but is fairing just fine." He gave her a knowing look. Nassa hardly felt relieved. Why would Brutav lie? Or did Voltred know? Why would he pretend? She didn't know how to respond.

"But never mind that, we will deal with that all later." He looked down his nose at her. Was that a threat? "Now we must be getting ready for court. We go in two days' time. You will need new clothing. We can't have Maldrig's bride looking like… that." He waved a hand at her. She clenched her jaw.

"Is that all?" She asked, her blood still simmering.

"Yes, but do finish your chores in a timely matter, you have been very sloppy of late." Voltred bent his head down and began reading a letter. Nassa stared at him a moment, hating him more than ever. She stood up before she did something she would regret, and left the room.

She ran to the kitchens, heart pounding, where she found Ari and Toc. They seemed to be having a private conversation and jumped when they saw Nassa come in, her face fuming.

"Dear gods, girl!" Ari said. "What creature has nipped you in the ear?" she came to Nassa fussing, feeling her forehead for warmth. Nassa batted her off.

"Quit mothering me! I'm eighteen you know!" Nassa took out some of her fury on Ari, but immediately felt guilty. "I'm sorry, Ari. It's just a lot happening quickly that's all. I didn't mean to take it out on you." Nassa sat on a stool and put her face in her hands, letting out a moan.

"Oh, dear, it will be OK." Ari stroked her back, but Nassa could hear fear in her voice as well. She shook her head and shook off Ari.

"I'm fine!" she shouted again, standing up. "You and Toc have made me soft! Stop babying me! I am fine and I will be fine!" As she lost her temper a soft wind began swirling around the room. Toc's eyes went wide, and he ran to Nassa planting her back on the stool.

"Ari, bring her something to eat," Toc said, then whispered to Nassa. "Nassa, get a hold of yourself." Nassa looked up in his eyes, her loyal Toc, and felt suddenly grounded.

"You're right, Toc." She clenched her jaw and closed her eyes, forcing herself to concentrate and suppress the rising tide inside her. She stood up and grabbed the fresh roll Ari placed in front of her.

"I've got to get going on my chores," she told them, eyes down, and quickly left.

Nassa spent the rest of the morning buried in her work. Ever since she came to this place she had suppressed her memories. She didn't like to think about Montoc or Marny, but today of all days, their memories kept surfacing. They had been hiding something. They had been hiding her. But why? *Balrigard Monastary.* Her mind kept going to the place from Marny's note. But she couldn't travel there. Not to Sudonia. Not only was it dangerous, but she did not know the way. And although she was adept with forest botany, she was no hunter, no trails man, she would get lost, she would starve, she would die.

She squeezed her eyes shut, trying to block out the memories and the nagging voice inside her wanting answers. She was from Sudonia. She was powerful. Who were her parents? Who was she? She shook the thoughts away again. No, none of that mattered. She would suppress her power. She would marry her cousin. She would spend the rest of her life here, serving Maldrig, breeding for him. She wanted to vomit. But as frightening as that life sounded, finding out who she really was — what she really was — frightened her more.

"Nassa, there you are." Nassa jumped, almost falling off the step stool she stood on, dusting the books of the library. Temid caught her before she could hurt herself.

"Temid, you startled me." Nassa shook him off, standing tall. She tried not to look too bothered by his presence.

"I apologize." Temid gave her a slight bow then stared her down with his sunken eyes. Although Nassa was not close with any of the family, Temid she knew the very least. He was tall and sickly looking. His skin was pale, as though it had never seen the sun. Probably, it hadn't, he spent so much of his time cooped up here in the library.

"Can I help you with something?" Nassa asked, when Temid stood there unmoving.

"I saw Brutav this morning," Temid spoke slowly. Nassa tensed. Was she finally going to be in trouble? Would he strike her? "Rarely have I seen him so upset… it was… enjoyable."

Nassa was unsure how to respond to this. Everyone seemed to know she was involved and yet no one was willing to call her out on it.

"Is that all?" Nassa asked, not able to keep her voice from squeaking.

Temid nodded almost unnoticeably then turned leaving Nassa to stare after him. Was he trying to thank her for what she had done to Brutav? Maybe Temid wasn't so bad as the rest, after all.

By the time dinner came around, Nassa was physically and emotionally worn out. She thanked all the gods that the family didn't summon her to eat with them tonight, and instead she barely picked at her food as she sat in the cold stone hallway off the kitchen. Ari and Toc must have known better than to bother her tonight as well, and she passed the time alone.

When she got back to her rooms, her legs barely able to make the climb up the tower, she began crying at the sight in front of her. There were several gowns laying out across her cot. A reminder that soon they would go to court, and a new chapter in her life would begin.

Chapter 16

VOLYA

Slice, slice, scourge,
Slice, slice, scourge,
The blade is quick to act.

Wrestle and pound,
Wrestle and pound,
Death lingers as a fact.

- The Recitations of Hildish Fighting Scheme 3

Volya always assumed taking a life would be difficult, but in truth it turned out to be incredibly easy. Part of his training was to learn the finer arts of taking a life, and he had caught on rather exceptionally. Lady Rothschild's nephew really was a straightforward target — it would almost be too easy.

Volya had helped on these missions before, of course, but this was the first time going at it solo. He was not afraid though, not even a tiny bit bothered by the whole thing. In fact, he found it rather fun. And using his powers without a mentor standing over him telling him what to do was rather freeing.

He went first to Lady Rothschild's manor in the upper city to get more information. She shared a glass of wine with him — reluctantly at first — but even the young widow couldn't withstand his charms for too long.

He awoke the next morning, the embers of the fire still alight, and his arm asleep under Lady Rothschild indisposed form. He wiggled his arm awake, trying not to rouse her, as he left out the window, with no more information than he had started with — although if he was honest with himself he never really needed any information from her in the first place.

He made his way down to the middle city, where merchants were already awake in the early hours preparing for deals with far off lands. His mark was awake too — Volya spied on the young man through his open window as he shaved his face with a rough blade over a porcelain bowl of water.

Volya slipped in, his powers quieting his every step, and used that same razor blade to slit the man's throat. The water in the porcelain bowl ran red. The most obnoxious thing about the whole process was the amount of sticky blood. Volya really did hate getting sticky.

He disposed of the body in the riverbank, cleaned himself up, and made it back to Lady Rothschild's manor in time for lunch. When Volya told her the news, she eagerly took him back to the bedroom for Volya's favorite course — dessert.

Volya smirked to himself, finding the comedy in his day. Women were so predictable. Give them a little gift and some sweet words and they happily came to him. He took a deep drag of his cigar, he was back in The Guild Hall, enjoying a round of cards with some of the other thugs.

"Looks like I win again, boys." Volya put down his hand of cards, biting his cigar as he spoke.

"Volya, you prick." Folem pounded on the table angrily as Volya took all the money on the table.

"Not my fault you are shit at cards," Volya laughed, scooping the money into the pouch at his side.

Rasmere walked in at that point and Volya jumped up from his chair.

"Ah! Rasmere! I was just coming to look for you." Volya strode to where Rasmere stood in the doorway.

"And why am I surprised to see you here, Volya? Don't you have work to do?" Rasmere gave Volya an irritated look.

"Ah, Rasmere, such little faith. My work is already done!" Volya padded him on the back as they began walking down the hall to Rasmere's quarters.

"Well now, that was quick, even for you." Rasmere couldn't help but lift the corner of his mouth in a small smile.

"Now, now, my dear Rasmere. I'm quick only when I want to be," Volya winked.

"Volya, you are an arrogant pain, but even I must admit you have your uses." Rasmere shrugged Volya off as they entered his antechamber. He poured them both a glass of thick Thessolonian liquor and sat, gesturing for Volya to do the same.

"When I took you as a ward, *The Guild* had some very large doubts, you know?" Rasmere continued. "But, I must say you are not a total failure." Rasmere looked at his glass as he swirled, sniffed, and sipped the amber liquid.

"Failure! Ha!" Volya slapped his knee. "I am the best you ever had — and don't deny it! I have been told so many times after all!"

"Volya, would you just shut up." Rasmere looked annoyed by Volya's childish remarks. Volya at least had the sense to appear more serious.

"What is it you want, Rasmere?" Volya asked, sitting back in his chair and taking a swig of the liquor.

"You did well, Volya, but Lady Rothschild's nephew was very simple. This next task is much more complicated, and much more important." Rasmere looked down his nose at Volya. Volya hated that look. He found it condescending.

"Yes, yes, the girl," Volya waved his hand bored. He didn't understand how this girl could be such a threat. A girl? He could wrap her around his finger within five minutes. And a lady? Even easier! They always seemed eager to fall in bed when they got a whiff of danger.

"She is not just any girl, Volya." Rasmere raised his eyebrows. "She grew up in the country very sheltered, she is not like these city girls you call playthings. And she may be very powerful."

"A country girl with power, hm? Sounds rather boring to me." Volya took another sip.

"Volya, dammit!" Rasmere pounded his hand on the desk, causing Volya to jump. "I've said it before, and I will say it again — your arrogance will be your downfall! Do not underestimate this girl. I warn you."

"OK, OK! Understood." Volya ran his hands through his hair. "I will do my job well — I always do." Volya stood. "Is that all?" He was annoyed now. Didn't Rasmere understand he wasn't his ward any more? He was a full-fledged member of *The Guild* now that he had finished his training. He was getting incredibly sick of being spoken to like a child.

"Volya. You are very skilled — but you are not the best." Rasmere gave him a pointed stare and Volya clenched his jaw. "You need to learn to control your temper tantrums and take things more seriously. Sit down."

Volya remained standing. A small defiance, but he refused to take every order. They stared at each other for a long moment, but finally Volya looked away.

"I need to prepare for my next assignment," Volya spoke through clenched teeth.

"Very well. You are dismissed — but one last thing. I have put some new clothing and an invitation in your chambers. You will attend Duke Farring's ball as Viscount Halford of the Northern Baskar region."

"Viscount? That is a bit of a stretch is it not?" Volya snorted.

"I need you to be high up. None of these westerners have ever been to the North anyway." Rasmere didn't seem concerned by the insane social advancement. Volya smiled, being a Viscount for a night might be rather enjoyable.

"And what exactly am I looking for?" Volya asked, his mood improving.

"Her name is Lady Annassa. She is engaged to Lord Voltred's — the man you met — son, Maldrig. Be on the lookout for any intrigue or any contacts. Voltred has sheltered her, but you never know with these Sudonese — she may be part of an underground. Or, to your liking — she really may be an innocent country mouse. Time will tell."

"And her powers? Should I be as worried as you have said?" Volya rolled his eyes.

"She won't be using her powers in public, Volya. You should know better than anyone — it would be a death sentence." Rasmere rubbed his face in his hands. He looked tired, Volya noticed. For the first time Volya realized Rasmere was getting old.

Chapter 17

NASSA

A trumpet sounds,
Drowning the clang of swords,
A figure stands atop the hill.

Basked in light,
Cape flowing in the wind,
Can this mean the tide will change?

- The Ancient Archives, Vol IV, Book 3

Ari helped Nassa dress. Even though Voltred was a
Lord, it was easy to see by the state of his grounds that
he squandered his wealth away on things other than
maintenance and servants. He did employ a personal
valet and footman, a few stable masters, sword master,
tutor (although he was never available to Nassa), and a
few serving maids here and there, and of course Ari and
Toc. But Nassa seemed to pick up all the missing jobs
required of such a large estate.

Nassa would never have assumed she would have her own lady's maid. The thought was, in fact, preposterous. But she was to be the lady of the house, and she had read enough books to know that most ladies did have a ladies maid. She was happy though, that she had Ari to help her.

"Ari, that is too tight!" Nassa struggled against Ari, who was pulling her corset so tight, Nassa thought she might squeeze apart into a bottom half and a top half.

"Oh hush." Ari didn't seem bothered. "A lady needs to be presentable."

"I am not a lady!" Nassa huffed.

"You may not have the proper training, Nassa, but you are niece to a Lord, and therefore you are a Lady. There." Ari finished tying the corset and stood back to look at her work. Nassa felt like a prize colt. "Oh Nassa. I am worried for you. Your uncle has completely failed to teach you the way of the world."

"I will be fine, Ari." Nassa rolled her eyes. She was in a much better mood today. No one had bothered her since the incident, and she began having hope it would never be brought to attention.

"Hm." Ari put her hands on her hips. "The best advice I can give you is to just keep your mouth shut. These pretentious lords and ladies only like the sound of their own voices anyway."

"Ari!" Nassa's jaw dropped. Ari was stubborn, but she had never heard her outright rude.

"I apologize, milady." Ari bowed but had a smirk on her lips.

"Oh, Ari. Do not apologize to me. You are probably right." Nassa sat down on her cot. "I don't know how I am going to do this."

"Here, dear girl. I will teach you how to curtsy. A good curtsy and a closed mouth go a long way in court. Besides, you are pretty enough that none of it will matter." Ari gave her a smile.

"Oh, Ari. You are ridiculous. But anyway, let's see it." Nassa stood back up, smiling as well.

Ari spent the next hour trying to teach Nassa how to curtsy. By the end Nassa was able to roughly manage it.

"I look ridiculous," Nassa said.

"You look... fine. Tonight, I will light a candle for you, dear girl. All will be well. Now, we've spent too much time on this. Time to get dressed. Your uncle will be waiting." Ari began fussing around, dressing Nassa and setting her hair.

To say Nassa had butterflies in her stomach as she descended the stairs, was an understatement. It felt more like her nerves were boiling, waiting to spill over. Maybe she would just have a stroke and die, and all her problems would be solved.

She made it down the tower, past the servant's quarters, through the west wing and finally down to the kitchens.

"My gods, Nassa." Toc stood in the doorway mouth opened and eyes wide.

"What, Toc? Do I look that bad?" Nassa asked, concern knitting her brow.

"No, Nassa. Quite the opposite," Toc continued to stare.

"Close your mouth boy, before you start drooling." Ari hit Toc on the back of the head but laughed all the same.

"I must be going." Nassa took a deep breath. "Wish me luck!" She had to admit to herself, as much as she was dreading this affair, a part of her was excited to see the city. She had spent the majority of her life in the woods, and the thought of seeing something of the world was undeniably appealing.

"Good luck." Toc managed to squeak out, then began to busy himself.

Nassa slipped out the kitchens into the large front atrium. Here there were several rooms, including the unused ballroom and dismal dining room, breaking off before the front entry. She heard rough voices coming down the hallway that led to Brutav's main floor chambers. Although she knew she should hurry along, she couldn't help herself from tip toeing down the hallway and putting her ear to the cracked open door.

"I don't understand why she wasn't punished! Did you see what she did to me!" The anger in Brutav's voice made Nassa's heart drop.

"Brutav, my boy. Don't you see? This is why we left Sudonia! This will be our chance for revenge!" Nassa peaked through the door to see Voltred grabbing Brutav firmly by the arm.

"No, Father." Brutav ripped his arm out of Voltred's grip. "I don't see. All I see is that brat of a girl injures me, and no one does anything about it!"

Voltred slapped Brutav across the face. "Pull it together, you imbecile. Did you not see her power? Power you should by rights all possess!"

"So what, that's it? I just let it go? She should be punished, Father!" Brutav seethed.

"The time will come, son. But we need her breeding. We need her power. That will teach that arrogant brother of mine!" Voltred sounded too eager.

Nassa staggered back. So, they did know everything. And yet they were not going to punish her, but use her. She felt lightheaded but quickly tip toed back down the hallway to the entryway before she would be caught.

She was deep in thought as she waited for her uncle and cousins. There was a horse and carriage already waiting out front. Although it was early in the day, the ride to Thessola City would take several hours.

She started as Voltred, Maldrig, Brutav, and Temid approached, breaking up thoughts about her uncertain future. They passed her without thought or word, heading straight for the carriage.

"It isn't over between us." Brutav sneered at her under his breath as the others passed. Nassa couldn't hide the fear in her eyes. Brutav smiled at her wickedly before following the rest of the party out the door.

Chapter 18

VOLYA

The thief, he cares?
He never dares.
Who calms the night but him?

Without a thought,
A dream he caught,
However dark or dim.

- Tales of a Thief by Pickering Fool

Volya readied himself in his chambers. He slicked back his dark hair in the mirror but couldn't help the strand that fell out of place across his brow. The upper-class women tended to like that, though. It reminded them of his darker side, the side that wasn't quite as polished as it looked.

"Good evening, milady," he practiced his roguish smile in the mirror. "Viscount Halford at your pleasure." He nodded to himself and chuckled then turned to leave the room. Oh, this would be fun.

A carriage waited for him outside the Hall. A few neighborhood boys ran up, it was probably the fanciest thing they had ever encountered. Rarely would a horse and carriage grace the slums. He shooed the urchins away and climbed in, banging the top of the buggy as he did, so the driver would start their trek.

The journey up to Duke Farring's estate took quite some time. Volya noted he would have been able to span the distance from the docklands to the upper crust much quicker with his own powers. But Rasmere had insisted that a carriage was best for appearances. He leaned back against the plush fabric of the carriage bench, sighing deeply out of boredom. Volya was not one to enjoy sitting still.

Finally, he arrived at the duke's gates, which stood open for the festivities. The duke's estate resided up the hill, past where the congested city gave way to large roads and grand, gated estates. As the carriage made its way into the grounds, Volya looked out taking note of the imposing lawns and gardens on either side leading up to the palatial manor.

The estate was well taken care of. Volya wondered at the absurd amount of servants it must require maintaining such a resplendent home. The carriage rounded a large fountain in front of the manor, waiting in line to pull to the entrance, gravel crunching underneath. When it was his turn, a servant opened the door, head looking down, as Volya descended from the carriage.

He made his way through the grand marbled entry where a man stood, stopping each guest.

"Name?" The man asked in a distinctly western accent.

"Viscount Halford of Northern Baskar." Volya looked out in astonishment at the grand room. This was only the entryway to the larger ballrooms and dining rooms beyond, which the party would move through as the night progressed. The servant repeated Volya's 'name' to the room, giving introduction. Volya entered the party.

He grabbed a glass of champagne from a nearby tray as he began his rounds. He kept his eyes and ears out for references to Lord Voltred or Lady Annassa, but had not yet heard an announcement of any such titles. He was unsure what to look for. He knew of course what Lord Voltred looked like, but neither he nor Rasmere knew what to expect in regard to Lady Annassa. He did not worry though. He had plenty of time to do some reconnaissance work as well as have a little fun.

"By gods, man. I say, you hail from Baskar?" A portly little man stood at Volya's side. He was fat and pink, and had sweat running from his brow. He quickly remedied the situation by producing a small handkerchief and wiping his forehead.

Volya looked him up and down.

"That I do, sir?" Volya questioned.

"Duke Farring." The man gave Volya a pat on the back as if they were old chums.

"Your grace. Forgive me." Volya gave the duke a slight nod. Was this really Thessola's upper crust.

"No need for airs, son. Call me Plumpy. Everyone does." Duke Farring gave a hacking cough and took a large swig of his glass.

"Plumpy, who's your friend?" An elegant woman approached their conversation. She gave Volya a sly smile, looking him up and down and putting out her hand. Volya took it and gave her a slow kiss, looking her in the eyes. She gave him a knowing smile.

"My dear, this is Viscount Halford, did I get that right? Viscount, this is my dear wife, The Duchess Rubela." Volya couldn't help but smile, the pair could not be more ill-suited. "The Viscount hails from the Baskar region. Great hunting up there, I do say. Do you hunt much, Viscount?"

"One of my favorite pastimes." Volya grabbed another glass of champagne from a passing tray.

"Oh, no, old boy. Don't drink that." He grabbed the champagne from Volya's hand and motioned for a servant. "Get this man a glass of my finest Thessolonian whiskey." Duke Farring motioned his servant away.

"Tell me, Duke — Plumpy," Volya tried to hide his smirk. "What is your favorite game to hunt? Do you often make your way up to Baskar?"

"Oh heavens no. A bunch of heathens up there — no offense." Duke Farring gave Volya a big pat on the back with a laugh. "Every five years or so we put together a group, go hunt up the western coast, make our way up to Baskar for the foal season. Shoot a couple of those large, winged things you have up there. Jolly good fun it is. A right sport, I say." He finished off his glass just as the servant returned with more for both the Duke and Volya.

"Indeed." Volya took a sip of the whiskey. It was smooth and warm, truly one of the best he had ever tasted. "Delicious." He licked his lips but looked at the Duchess, who still stood watching him, her arm through her husbands. He winked at her. She smiled.

"I will let you two boys chat. I'm off to find the ladies. I hear Lord Voltred is bringing his niece, it is her first time at court so I must be sure to make all the right introductions. Always so fun to have a virgin among us," she nodded to Volya, giving him a sultry smile, as she withdrew her arm from her husband and walked away, hips swishing.

"Your wife, she is quite the refined woman." Volya sipped his drink as he watched her walk away.

"That she is, son! A real minx," the duke chuckled to himself. "Her and all those ladies. Always up to some mischief, I say."

"And who is this niece she speaks of?" Volya asked, trying to see if he could gather any information.

"Oh no one of consequence. Related to that awful Lord Voltred. Talk of a rut in the sand, that one sure is, I say. But enough of them, we men need to talk of better things. Say, what's the biggest creature you ever shot?" Duke Farring would be of little information then, Volya thought to himself.

The conversation went on for quite some time, Duke Farring always steering toward talk of his grand accomplishments. Volya thought it would be surprising to see him carrying a heavy bow without his heart failing, let alone kill half the things he had claimed to.

"Your grace, please excuse me, I see a fellow from my schooling days, I must say hello." Volya excused himself quickly before the duke could protest. He was exhausted by the droll man, he needed some fresh air, to feel the wind on his face. He made his way out on the large terrace overlooking the duke's manicured rose gardens and forests beyond.

He leaned on the railing with his elbows, his face in his hands, then stood taking a deep breath and blowing out slowly. The roses rustled beyond, and he smiled to himself. The night air felt good.

A noise came from behind him, and he turned suddenly. He hadn't seen the girl sitting on the bench to his side. Had she been there the whole time?

"Miss, are you cold? You seem to be shivering." Volya walked toward the young girl. She was frighteningly petit, her skin pale but smooth as porcelain. The front of her hair had been woven into braids on top of her head, while the back flowed freely in naturally smooth waves. She was beautiful, yet seemed too young and innocent to be in a place like this.

"I'm not cold, sir." She gave him a deadly stare. Volya laughed putting his hands up.

"I mean no harm, I assure you. I didn't even notice you out here until now. Are you hiding?" Volya looked at her questioningly, but she did not reply.

"Very well then. Not much of a talker. Who do you belong to? I didn't think they let children attend these things. You seem far too young." Volya sat down next to her. She moved farther down the bench away from him. He couldn't help but smile.

"I'm not a child. I'm a lady. And you seem *far* too sure of yourself. I believe *you* are the one hiding," she spoke in clipped tones, annoyed by his presence.

"Yes, you're right. I needed some fresh air; it's awfully stuffy in there." Volya chuckled.

"Well, I can't disagree with that." The girl confessed.

"Forgive me, lady-?" Volya questioned.

"Annassa."

Chapter 19

NASSA

A golden ray comes overhead,
A force, the sun,
Warmth spreading to every nook and crevice.
Power there is, in the heat,
In the advancing array of light.

- The Ancient Archives, Vol II, Book 2

Nassa and her cousins made it to the festivities without incident. Voltred remained quiet during the long journey, and therefore her cousins did as well. They had made a couple of quick stops along the way, but overall they had made it to Duke Farring's estate quickly.

Nassa was disappointed that the estate was on the Northern edge of Thessola and therefore they approached through the woods. She was unable to travel through the city, as she had hoped. She had been looking forward to seeing Thessola, but would have to make do with only glimpsing the lights out in the distance.

The estates were grander than anything she had ever seen. Compared with Voltred's dismal and dark manor, Duke Farring's home was bright and majestic. This is how things should be run, she thought to herself as she surveyed the expertly tended gardens.

They entered the party and were properly announced, but it was all too overwhelming. Hundreds of guests in smart form flitted to and from, socializing in ways she knew nothing about. She was approached by a group of women, one indicating she was the Duchess herself, but Nassa found herself quickly curtsying and running away to the terrace. She needed fresh air.

She was happy to see she was alone, but that only lasted a brief moment before a young man came striding out. He was dashingly handsome, with dark hair slicked back in a dangerous manner. His eyes were slightly sunken, but in a way that only highlighted his long lashes and piercing gaze. He seemed confident but there was something about him that made him stand out from the rest of the aristocracy. Nassa couldn't put her finger on it.

The man didn't appear to see her as he sighed, taking a deep breath, blowing out slowly. It made Nassa shudder, but not in an uncomfortable way. He seemed to finally notice her at that, and came to sit next to her, making small conversation.

Nassa was reluctant to talk with him, she had not fully recovered from the last time she was alone with a man — her cousin Brutav. But for whatever reason, she didn't feel afraid of this man next to her.

He seemed surprised when she introduced herself. And did she really look so young? She supposed the dated dress, collar coming up around her neck, made her look younger than her years.

"I am not a little girl you know. I'm eighteen." She looked up at him then, his deep stare made her blush. She was not happy about it.

"I must say that's surprising. I would have thought you were no more than fifteen." He gave her a half smile, one side of his mouth rising out of amusement. She looked away annoyed.

"And how old are you? You can't be much older than I." She stood up, standing tall while he remained sitting. She didn't like feeling so small.

"I'm twenty. But even though I'm only two years your senior, I imagine I've seen much more of life than you." The young man stood as well, leaning against the railing toward Nassa, too close for comfort.

"You never told me your name," she said, backing away.

"Viscount Halford of Northern Baskar, at your service." He gave a silly bow. "There's no need to be afraid of me, you can come closer, I won't bite." He smiled clearly amused by her naiveté.

"I'm not afraid of you, sir. I merely don't wish to be close to you," Nassa spoke with what she hoped was her most commanding voice. He looked amused which only made her angry.

"Nassa, there you are." Voltred made his way through the French doors and grabbed her elbow. "You are wanted for introductions." He gave Viscount Halford a slight nod then pulled Nassa back inside.

The remainder of the night Nassa followed Ari's instructions. She would slowly curtsy with each introduction and then remain silent. She shuddered every time she was presented as Maldrig's fiancée.

Nassa noted with some interest that Voltred did not seem well liked by his peers. That at least made her feel better — she wasn't the only one. However, by association, the other ladies seemed hostile to her as well. She didn't mind though; she wasn't here to make friends.

The party was eventually ushered into the dining hall. Several long tables had been laid out, each able to accommodate an absurd amount of people. She took her place in between Maldrig and Voltred.

She ate in silence as the servants brought course after course of rich foods. First figs wrapped in thinly sliced lamb, followed by southern whitefish in creamy lemon sauce, then there were the spring vegetables, sewn together with puff pastry drizzled with exotic oils. The main course of stuffed pheasant in wine sauce, was almost too much to bear. She was beyond stuffed and did not think she could possibly take another bite.

The young man from earlier, Viscount Halford, had been stealing glances at her throughout the evening. She could feel his stare from down the table, but when she looked up, he quickly glanced away.

Why was he so interested? She could feel the heat coming to her cheeks, but his attentions made her uneasy. She wanted to go back home, back to the somewhat safety of her tower and fall into a deep sleep.

She looked across from her where Brutav sat. Thoughts of safety quickly vanished. He stared at her, jaw clenched, as he jammed his knife repeatedly into his pheasant. Maybe she wasn't so anxious to return home after all. She looked down at her plate and moved the food around.

After dinner there was dancing. Nassa had no intention of partaking, but Voltred insisted she dance with her fiancée, Maldrig.

He didn't seem at all interested in her. He didn't speak with her through the whole dance, and barely even spared her a glance. Was this what their marriage was to be like? Maybe it wasn't the worst of things.

She sat back down, only to be approached by Brutav.

"Cousin. Let's dance." He held out his hand to her, giving her a menacing smile.

"I'd rather not, Brutav, my feet are already sore." She remained seated.

"I insist." Brutav grabbed her arm and pulled her up. Nassa had no choice but to comply.

Brutav led her rather forcefully on to the dance floor and held her too close. She struggled against him, but his grip was too tight.

"Unfortunately, you can't use any of your tricks here, you little brat." Brutav whispered in her ear.

Nassa tried to wrench herself away from him without drawing attention, but his grip was too tight.

"Father said I couldn't hurt you. At least not until after the wedding. Maldrig won't mind. His tastes are… different… anyway." Brutav was enjoying this.

"Let go of me." Nassa whispered through clenched teeth.

"Where would be the fun in that, cousin." Brutav continued to press his body against hers. Nassa wanted to cry. "You will learn your place one way or another." He held her wrists so tight, she could feel the bruises forming.

"May I?" Viscount Halford stood over Brutav's shoulder attempting to cut in. Brutav turned and scowled at him, but the Viscount did not leave.

"Go away, we're busy." Brutav snapped.

"The lady promised me a dance." Viscount Halford shot Nassa a sly look. Nassa felt increasingly uncomfortable with this exchange. No one ever challenged Brutav, and in public too.

"I said, go away." Brutav let go of Nassa and turned toward Volya. Volya gave him a wicked smile, sizing him up. Brutav smirked but seeing Volya's size, finally backed away turning to Nassa and giving her a look of pure contempt.

Viscount Halford watched Brutav walk away then turned and held Nassa's hand gently while putting his other hand on the small of her back. He brought her in close, but tenderly, not anything like the aggressive force Brutav had used. His hands were strong, and he used his thumb to softly rub at her bruised wrist.

"A handful that one," he commented. He looked directly at her, but Nassa couldn't help from averting her eyes. She didn't know what to say.

"Thanks for cutting in," she managed to reply.

"Truly, my pleasure." He gave her a devilish smile. She looked up at him, meeting his eyes directly for the first time. She stared deeply into his piercing gaze, wondering what it was about him that she sensed was different. This time he looked away first, seemingly uncomfortable. She couldn't help but smile.

"You have to live with that man?" He asked, clearing his throat.

"He's my cousin. I'm engaged to his brother." Nassa looked to where Voltred and her cousins were sitting.

"I see. And do they often treat you so forcefully?" Viscount Halford seemed to tense. There was anger in his voice. Nassa was unsure how to answer.

"You said you are from Baskar? What is it like? I'm afraid I haven't traveled much," she asked, changing the subject.

"Oh, it's fine. You know, all northern like. You haven't traveled? Were you born in Thessola? How did you come to live with your uncle?" Halford swung her around, following the rhythm of the song flawlessly. Nassa thought the question was awfully nosy —

"My parents died when I was a baby." Nassa replied.

"Another thing we have in common." The viscount looked deep in her eyes.

"What was the first thing?" Nassa asked.

"The first thing?" He asked distracted. He was looking at her so intensely. She couldn't look away, she was lost in his piercing gaze.

"The first thing we had in common?" She asked, dazed.

"We both found it stuffy in here." He smiled at her.

"Oh, right. How did your parents die?" She asked. He stiffened, and she regretted the question. "Never mind, sorry."

"No it's OK. I don't usually talk about it. I don't like to think about the past." He softened.

"That's number three. Things we have in common I mean." She gave him a shy smile.

"Well, look at us, practically meant to be." He winked at her. She rolled her eyes. She knew he was teasing, but she couldn't help the butterflies that suddenly took over.

"I'm marrying my cousin, remember?" Suddenly Nassa was tired. She wanted desperately to sit down. Viscount Halford must have sensed this.

"Shall we find a place to sit and talk?" He stopped dancing and began to lead her away from the ballroom floor.

Voltred intercepted them before they could find a quiet alcove.

"We are leaving." He grabbed Nassa to go. She looked back at Viscount Halford as she was dragged toward the front entry. Their eyes met. His face was a mix of curiosity and something else she could not recognize.

Chapter 20

VOLYA

His knives like limbs,
Wielded with skill,
Death at hand,
He makes his kill.

- Tales of a Thief by Pickering Fool

Volya thought about calling on the Duchess Rubela late that night. She seemed easy enough prey, and the flirting she had done throughout the night convinced him she was willing. But in the end, he decided to go back to *The Guild* instead. He paced his room, a nagging thought bothering him. This Lady Annassa, she was too young, too innocent. And as for power, she sure didn't seem powerful. Or was it all a ploy? Could she be working with Sudonia? It didn't seem likely.

He didn't like the way those awful cousins treated her. It bothered him more than he was willing to admit. The wind began to swirl around him as his frustration built. He didn't usually spend this much time thinking about a woman, unless he was in the act, and even then it was the general concept of women rather than the specific one he cared about. He needed to see Rasmere.

He made his way to Rasmere's study and knocked on the door.

"Come in," Rasmere spoke from within. Volya was relieved he was both in residence and awake.

"Volya. Sit. What did you learn," Rasmere gestured to the chair as Volya entered the room, shutting the door behind him.

"Very little. She seems very young and naive if you ask me. If she has powers, she has no tendency for them. Rasmere, I don't like the assignment. It's beneath me." Volya sat crossing his arms.

"Beneath you? Volya, this is an important assignment and if you must know, it is one very close to my heart," Rasmere spoke in his usual calm but slightly annoyed manner.

"I'm not a babysitter. I am an assassin. And it was my understanding that I was to kill those with magic, not hold their hand. I want a real fight," Volya sulked. He would never admit that he had sort of enjoyed talking with the girl. He never wanted to see her again or have anything to do with her affairs. It would be easier this way. Feelings only got in the way; he knew this from experience.

Rasmere looked at Volya for a long time, studying him. "Very well," he finally said. "I have an assignment for you, I was going to give it to a senior member, but if you want a fight, a fight you will get. But this needs to happen tonight."

"Good." Volya perked up in anticipation.

"We found him in the market place, only a few years older than you. His name is Greymor. He has earth power. We believe he was sent from Sudonia and needs to be taken out immediately. We think he is staying somewhere in the industrial district." Rasmere sat back folding his fingers together.

"I will leave right away." Volya stood to leave.

"Strap up, Volya. He is well trained." Rasmere stated thoughtfully.

Volya nodded and left the room as a messenger entered, handing Rasmere a note. Rasmere took it and shooed them both away.

An hour later Volya was perched on the rooftop of a large industrial warehouse. He looked down below, toward the street where a man was entering a local tavern. He appeared to be like any other worker, but Volya knew he was different.

Volya made sure no one was around, then hopped off the tall rooftop, bending the air to his will to slow his landing. He crossed the street and entered the tavern.

The man, Greymor, Rasmere had named him, was sitting at the bar drinking a pint. Volya sat down next to him and ordered the same.

"So, where you from?" Volya asked Greymor with a twinkle in his eye. Greymor looked up at Volya, a knowing smile forming at his lips.

"And who wants to know?" Greymor asked.

"I do." Volya downed his pint in one sip. Greymor followed suit.

"Shall we?" Volya motioned for them to move outside. "After you."

Greymor stood up slowly shaking his head and Volya followed him out the door. They rounded the corner entering an abandoned alley. Greymor slowly turned to face Volya.

"How did you find me?" Greymor asked.

"It was easy. You earth benders leave trails a mile wide." Volya shrugged then readied himself for a fight.

"Maybe I wanted to be found." Greymor moved faster than Volya could comprehend, pushing up the earth beneath Volya and knocking him on his back. Greymor chuckled.

"You know in Sudonia magic is legal. We can practice all day and all night in plain sight. You hide here like a mole. And you really think you have an advantage?" Greymor laughed.

Volya stood slowly groaning. He was caught unaware. He wouldn't let that happen again. He gathered a ball of wind in his hand and threw it at Greymor. Greymor dodged it easily.

"It's really too bad. You do realize you are killing your own kind?" Greymor continued to taunt Volya.

"You are my enemy." Volya took a deep breath. He ran as fast as he could toward Greymor, but dodged him at the last moment, jumping and flipping over him in the air. He landed behind Greymor and blew out, blasting him with a rush of air and knocking Greymor down.

The ground trembled. Volya tried to maintain his balance but couldn't, instead he used the wind to float himself above the ground. A weed grew up, snatching Volya around the ankle and pulling him back down. Another weed grabbed his other ankle, strapping Volya on the spot. He struggled but couldn't break free. He blasted Greymor with a wall of wind, but Greymor erected a boulder to block it. He hurled the boulder toward Volya, who narrowly flung it to the side with all the wind he could muster. He was getting tired.

Greymor laughed. He erected two large boulders, floating them on either side of Volya ready to crush him.

"You are young and weak."

"And you Sudonese think magic is all there is." Volya flung a dagger, hitting Greymor in the chest. A direct hit between the ribs and straight to the heart. Instant death. The boulders fell and the weeds around Volya's ankles relaxed.

Volya walked to the body.

"It's too bad. In another life we could have enjoyed more pints together." Volya closed Greymor's eyes then grabbed his dagger, wiping it on the dead man's shirt as blood began to pool. Magic or not, all men died a mortal death.

Volya was tired as he made his way back to the Hall. It had been a long night, starting with the ball and ending with a fight. But it felt good to be doing something — anything — to take his mind off things. He inwardly chided himself as his thoughts drifted once again to the porcelain skinned girl.

When he returned to the Hall. He found Rasmere still in his study. He had only been gone a couple of hours. But when he entered, he was not expecting the scene before him. Had Rasmere been crying?

"Sir?" Volya asked uncomfortable.

Rasmere looked up. There was more emotion on his face than Volya had ever seen.

"He was about your age, you know that Volya?" Rasmere slurred his words. He was clearly drunk.

"Who was?" Volya was genuinely confused. He had never seen Rasmere in this state.

"My son." Rasmere took a large swig of the bottle of whisky before him. Volya stared wide eyed, taken aback. Rasmere had a son? Volya had been living here for what, ten years? He had never heard mention of a son.

"I wasn't aware you had a son," Volya spoke, unsure how to feel. It was proving an incredibly confusing day.

"He was captured as a boy. By the Sudonese." Rasmere stared into the fire blazing in the fireplace at his side. "The messenger earlier. They finally killed him. All these years and they finally killed him. They kept him alive, so I would do their bidding. But I never killed the girl, and now they know. So they've killed my son. I thought I'd be able to bargain one day, but I was a fool."

"Who killed your son?" Volya asked.

"All this time I thought if I kept her alive, he would do the same. How ignorant am I. As soon as he heard word of her power, of course he would want her dead. There was never any hope. He strung me along this whole time. The things I've done. The blood on my hands." Rasmere held his hands up, lost in some reverie.

Volya could only nod. He had never heard Rasmere ramble on like this. It was unsettling.

"All this — All this was to get him back." Rasmere put his head in his hand. "The girl — she was to be a bargaining chip. But no more. He has forced my hand," he began to sob.

Volya really was unprepared for this. Part of him thought this would be an opportune time to kill his master and take over *The Guild*. But another part felt pity for the once great man, now fallen, a victim to his emotions. Something Volya never wanted to do.

"And what am I to do with all this?" Volya asked, not quite sure what Rasmere was blubbering on about.

Rasmere slowly looked up at Volya. "Kill the girl."

Volya nodded and left the room.

Chapter 21

NASSA

'Hurry, Hurry' they shout,
Will time be friend or foe?
The soldiers take formation,
The battlefield a sea of men.

Slithering through the ranks,
The evil one arrives,
The fate of man is at hand,
Are the stakes too high?

- The Ancient Archives, Vol I, Book 3

Nassa woke the morning after the ball with a slight headache. She had dreamt of the young man, Viscount Halford, but quickly suppressed those thoughts. She wasn't thinking clearly. The food had been too rich, and Brutav's threats had unnerved her. She had hoped once when she was married that she would be safe, but of course that was her stupid ignorance once again. She would never be safe while living with her cousins. Maldrig had no interest in her, and had even less interest in her safety. She was merely to be treated as a breeding mare. This had to be a turning point for her, she made up her mind. She resolved to run away.

The last time had been extremely unsuccessful, but now she was older and would be more prepared. There had to be some books in the library about Sudonia. Or perhaps some maps. True, it was illegal to own those sorts of books, but had she not come to the conclusion that their family was Sudonese? There must be some relics from the past left behind.

After her morning chores, she would feign cleaning the library and do some research. She would also need to store up some food, the journey had to be at least several weeks. One week, that is when she would leave. Just before she was due to be married.

She had retrieved her small dagger from the barn, but she would need more protection than that. Not only were there brigands and road thieves, but one heard tales of the menacing creatures that lurked in these woods. Not to mention, she would eventually have to make it through the border lands. Stretching the thinnest part of the continent the border was made up of the Molten Mountain range, the Eurasian pass, and the forests of Venit Vox. Before the pass stood the frontlines of the ongoing Sudo-Akkad war. She was unsure which of the three formidable locations she would pass through into Sudonia. Regardless, it would be dangerous, and she would need whatever protection she could get. There was an old sword on display in Voltred's study. Perhaps she would be able to steal it on her way out. She would think on it.

The day passed steadily by as Nassa was deep in her thoughts about the journey ahead. She didn't feel scared. For once she felt like she was doing the right thing. She was sick of being the obedient niece. It was time to find out who she really was.

After her mid-day meal, she trudged up to the library, looking for anything that would aid her in her journey. She brought her feather duster, and pretended to dust the rows of books, in case anyone came in the large room. She was unsure how the books were organized; she had never been allowed to explore the room at leisure, all the books she read over the years had been snuck to her by Ari. She quickly realized that this would be a bigger task than she imagined. There were thousands of books, and she had no idea where to begin.

Well, when one does not know where to begin, one may as well start with what is in front, she mused. She pulled out the book directly in front of her. *Arithmetic for the Learned* the title looked up at her. She dusted it off then put the book back, that one didn't sound helpful.

She continued down the first row of books, but found nothing at all that mentioned magic, Sudonia, or even a map of the world. She did find a small book on botany, however, which she pocketed. She knew quite a lot on the subject already, but in the wild it would always be good to double check.

She was standing on a step stool, reaching up to a book on the highest shelf when she sensed someone behind her. She heard a man clearing his throat.

"Nassa, can I help you with something?" She turned to see Temid starting up at her.

"Oh, sorry I didn't see you there. I was just dusting these upper shelves." She gave him her most innocent smile.

"Right," he said looking thoughtful.

"How are these books organized anyway?" Nassa asked trying to sound disinterested.

"Alphabetical order by title. Although there are sections of the greats, and those are organized by author. For example, Fillander Fortnum has his own section, as do *The Ancient Archives*. We have all twenty-three volumes," Temid said this last part with a certain amount of pride. Nassa thought it was the only time she had seen him look somewhat pleased. However, she had no idea what author or books he was referring to. Her education had truly been poor.

He must have seen her blank expression and come to the same conclusion.

"Do you know how to read, Nassa?" He asked her.

"Of course. I just rarely have the time for it." Nassa got down from her step stool and tried to busy herself. She wasn't sure where this conversation was going.

"But you never did receive a proper education," Temid seemed to be speaking more to himself. She didn't think he had meant it as a question, so Nassa remained quiet.

"I should be getting back to work." Nassa squeezed past Temid and the row of books.

"Wait, Nassa. I know my family hasn't always been warm toward you." He had the decency to look ashamed. "Is there a certain book you are looking for?"

Nassa tensed. Clearly the pretense had not fooled Temid. She weighed in her mind whether to lie, but decided she might as well take a chance. She presumed she would be taking quite a lot of risks soon.

"I'm looking for information on Sudonia." She took a deep breath pushing down her fear, and stood tall.

Temid stared at her a long while before finally answering, "In the far back corner. Top shelf. There is a false cover on the book called *A Zeitgeist of 4th century Frostlands: A Picture of Nevsky Politics*. Clearly not a book anyone would choose to read willingly." He gave her a slight smile then nodded, leaving to find a spot on the opposite side of the library, where he opened a large tome and fell deep into study.

Nassa stood there for a moment, not quite believing her luck. Temid had done her a favor. She knew the book was forbidden, as was all paraphernalia from Sudonia. Yet Temid had decided to help her. She felt a twinge of gratitude for her introverted cousin.

She rushed to the back corner, bringing the step stool with her. She held her breath as she scanned the top shelf until her eyes found the book. She was too nervous to open it there, instead tucking it in her skirt with her other stolen title.

Not wanting to take any more chances, Nassa quickly made her way up the tower and into the safety of her rooms. She sat on her bed and pulled the two books out. But before she could delve into them, there was a knock at her door. She quickly tucked the books under her mattress before Ari came strolling in.

"Nassa, dear, you have been summoned to dine with the family tonight. And you've been requested to bring your lute. What's wrong?" Ari asked noticing Nassa's startled expression.

"Oh, nothing, Ari, you just startled me. I will dress and come down," Ari nodded and left the room. Nassa wanted to at least scan the books, but she knew she would have to hurry. Voltred did not like her to be late. She quickly put on one of her worn grey dresses and then pulled the books out from under her bed.

She would look though the botany book later. She opened the title *A Zeitgeist of 4th century Frostlands: A Picture of Nevsky Politics.* Beneath the book cover there was worn leather sewn together by rough string. The pages inside felt crisp, she worried if she handled them too hard, they would flake apart. She carefully opened the book. On the title page were the words *A History of Sudonia, Volume III.* An inscription was on the top corner reading "Don't forget where your loyalties lie. — ML"

Nassa was unsure what that meant, but had to tuck the book back under her mattress. She didn't have time to read through it now. She made her way downstairs to the dining room. She brought her lute with her; it would be a night where they expected her to play. She didn't like playing for them. They enjoyed it too much, and she didn't like giving them the satisfaction. But she hardly had a choice. And she didn't want them to raise any suspicions if she challenged Voltred's orders now. Not when her freedom was hopefully so close.

Her uncle and cousins were already seated at the table. She came in, and sat down at the empty chair across from Maldrig. No one spoke to her or acknowledged she was present. Ari came in shortly serving the first course — venison with cream — and a plate of fresh steaming rolls. There was no second course tonight, but Ari did serve her famous custard with wild berry sauce. Nassa had to admit to herself that even though she did not enjoy dining with the family, the food was absolutely delicious.

When they were done, Voltred called for more wine and requested Nassa to sing. She picked up her lute by the door where she had left it and began playing a simple tune. She sang a song from her childhood, a song about saying goodbye. She thought it was appropriate for the new chapter she would begin next week.

"Very good, Nassa," Voltred said when she was finished. "Always a pleasure to hear you play and sing." He gave her a pointed stare.

"Thank you, Lord Voltred," Nassa spoke quietly averting her eyes. "May I be excused?"

"Yes, go get some rest. We have decided to move the wedding to tomorrow. You will need your beauty sleep." Voltred chuckled and smiled at Nassa who had gone white as a ghost. He was enjoying her shock.

"But the wedding was not to be for another week." Nassa stammered out. She felt lightheaded. She wondered if this is how it felt right before one fainted.

"We are moving it up. We had some news and thought, why wait?" Voltred continued to watch her with a cruel smile.

Nassa couldn't respond. She knew if she opened her mouth she would cry. Instead, she clenched her jaw, curtsied and left the room. Once she was in the hall she began running until she got to her tower. She flung open the door. There was no time to cry now, she would have to pack. She would leave tonight.

Nassa waited a few hours until she was sure Voltred, and her cousins had retired to their own chambers. She snuck down the back stairway and into the kitchens. Ari was still awake, preparing dough for tomorrow's meals. She would need to get around her somehow, Ari was no good at keeping secrets.

"Nassa, girl, you are still awake?" Ari spotted her in the doorway.

"Just hungry, Ari. I can't sleep." Nassa walked over to the old farm table where Ari was kneading dough.

"Oh, dear girl. I don't blame you. I heard the news." Ari looked like an old puppy dog, staring at Nassa with those big watery eyes.

"I wonder if you could put together a little basket for me to bring up to my room. I just need a snack for tonight, maybe something for the morning. I'm not sure there will be time to eat tomorrow." It wasn't easy for Nassa to lie to Ari. She stared at her and took a deep breath. It may be the last time she saw her.

"Very well. I will have Toc bring it up in a few. But do try and get some rest." Ari wiped her brow, leaving a mark of flour. She looked tired herself. "And Nassa?"

"Yes, Ari?" Nassa turned back to look at her as she was leaving.

"I will be there with you tomorrow. You won't go at it alone." Ari smiled at her. Nassa tried to smile back then left.

Nassa felt an ache of guilt lying to Ari, but she knew it was for the better. Tonight was her only chance. There would be no time for goodbyes.

As she was climbing the tower she saw a figure making his way down.

"Toc! What are you doing here?" Nassa asked, surprised to see Toc.

"I couldn't sleep. I came to check on you after Ari told me about the — well, you know." Toc couldn't seem to bring himself to talk about the wedding.

"Toc. I need your help." Nassa grabbed him to the side looking around to make sure no one could overhear, but they were alone in the deserted stairwell. "Toc. I'm leaving. Tonight." She saw his eyes widen in surprise.

"But Nassa — where could you go?" Toc looked stunned.

"I am going to find who I am," Nassa said with determination.

"But the forests, Nassa, there is danger everywhere," Toc said with concern.

"I will be fine. Don't worry about me Toc." But she could see the worry plain in his eyes. Maybe it was a mistake to tell him. "I need your help. Please Toc. I have to leave tonight. Ari is going to make up a small basket of food for me."

"Does Ari know?" Toc interrupted.

"No. And don't tell her," Nassa said almost too forcefully. Toc nodded reluctantly. "I need you to add some dried fish and meat to the basket. Anything you can find in the cupboards that won't rot."

"I'm coming with you." Toc took a deep breath trying to stand tall with resolve.

"You will not," Nassa spoke with as much authority as she could muster.

"Nassa, it's not safe." Toc pleaded.

"You will only weigh me down," Nassa regretted the words as she said them, but knew it was true. She saw the hurt in Toc's eyes. He nodded and left.

Nassa made it into her room and fell on her cot. She was already exhausted, but she would not give up. This time her mind was really made. No more back and forth, she needed to stick to the plan.

She packed a satchel with a few extra socks and garments. She really had very few possessions. She grabbed the two figurines that Marny and Montoc had given her so many years ago on her eighth nameday. She looked again at that mighty prince; a romantic dream that would never come true. She couldn't help but notice a certain resemblance to the young man she had met at the ball, but she quickly shook away the thought.

She placed her dagger in the satchel as well, which reminded her of the sword in Voltred's study. Slowly she made her way back down the stairs, into the main hallway and into the study. Thankfully, it was not locked.

She tiptoed across the room, holding her breath as she made her way behind Voltred's desk. She reached toward the sword on display, and grabbed it off the stand. It was much lighter than she thought, and smaller as well. It seemed almost to mold itself into her hand, her grip fit perfectly like a puzzle. She moved it around, slashing through the air. The moonlight through the large window above gleamed off the blade, sending sparkles across the room. It felt good.

The floorboards beyond the door creaked. Nassa's heart began to hammer, and she stood deathly still. But nothing happened. She waited what felt like hours, before tiptoeing back toward the hall. She peaked out, looking around, but no one was there. She tucked the sword into the belt she wore around her skirt and made her way as quickly as she could back to her tower. Not until she had shut her door did she allow herself to breathe.

A knock on the door made her jump. She quickly hid the sword under her mattress with her stolen books. Toc walked in with a basket.

"Phew. It's only you," Nassa said, relief washing over her.

"I brought what you requested." Toc put the basket down by the door. He gave a small bow and then left the room.

"Wait!" Nassa shouted to him. Toc stopped and turned his head. She ran across the room to him, kissing him on the cheek. She couldn't bare to part with her oldest friend with any animosity. "I'm going to miss you, Toc. Thank you." She gave him a sad smile.

"Anything for you, Nassa." He smiled back, but the tears in his eyes betrayed him. He left swiftly, not turning back again.

Nassa grabbed the rolls and canned goods from the basket, tying them up in a scarf and adding them to her satchel. She grabbed the books, putting the botany one in the satchel and opening *A History of Sudonia*.

The second page of the book was a map. *Thank the gods*, she thought. She would need to go north first, then east. She was contemplating her route when she thought she heard the floorboards creak again. She waited, again fear taking hold of her. But nothing happened. After several minutes she let herself relax. She must be hearing things.

She added the books to her satchel and grabbed the sword, putting it back through her belt. She grabbed her warmest cloak, threw it over her shoulders, and made her way to the door. It was time to leave.

She turned the handle and pushed. The door would not budge. Someone had locked it from the outside.

Chapter 22

VOLYA

Groans from bellow,
Battle within,
Demons creep out,
Bathed in their sin.

A blade with strength,
Lying in great fear,
When will it stop?
The darkness is near.

- Poems from the Deep, Verse 281

Volya had slept fitfully, despite his exhaustion. He was plagued with images of the girl he was to kill soaked in blood. He could not fathom why all these grown men were so afraid of her. She seemed beyond innocent; it was rather appealing he had to admit. But he could not think that way, she was to die at his hands.

She had no power that he was aware of — and he had a pretty good sense for picking out magic. It was one of the reasons he was so good at his job. But no matter how hard he thought, he couldn't figure out the connection between the girl, Lord Voltred, and Rasmere's son. So, the girl was a bargaining chip for his son. But Rasmere had kept her alive. Now he would take a life for a life. So, who was she?

She must be rather important. An orphan from Sudonia, sent to live with her uncle. There were many orphans around their ages, left over from *The Great Purge*. Volya himself was such. He would have to think on it further.

The sun was just dawning, he only had a couple hours of rest, but he got up anyway. He wasn't going to get any more sleep this night. He got on the floor and began his regular exercises that kept his body so chiseled. Then he made his way to the great dining hall to break his fast.

Halfway through eating his third boiled egg, Rasmere entered and waved him over. He would want to tell Volya the details of his mission. Volya sighed and made his way to where Rasmere stood.

"Volya, my study, now," Rasmere commanded and Volya obeyed, following him down the hall to Rasmere's study. When they entered, they both sat. There was nothing weak about Rasmere today. The vulnerability that peaked through yesterday, was now buried deep. Volya almost didn't believe he had ever seen the man cry.

"Volya. Prepare to leave. We've heard the wedding has been moved to tomorrow. I can only assume Voltred got word of my son's," Rasmere took a deep breath, "Death. They will be expecting you. She must die before the wedding night."

"Any specific instructions? What do you want me to do with the body?" Volya asked, trying not to think of those bloody images that haunted him in his sleep.

"Nothing specific. Just make sure she is dead and then report back to me. They will be leaving for the temple sometime tomorrow afternoon, it will probably be easiest to do it then. We can blame it on the road thieves. Kill anyone who stands in your way. I've left a map in your chambers. Go." Rasmere waved Volya away in dismissal. He may no longer be moping, Volya thought, but he was still in a gods-awful mood. Volya was happy to leave his miserable company.

Volya made his way back to his rooms. He spent the rest of the day preparing, and resting up for the flight. He had quite a long night so the extra rest would do him well.

He awoke early the next morning already prepared for his departure. He looked over the map, and figured it would take him a couple hours or so to make the journey, with his wind power behind him. He wouldn't want to use too much energy, however, in case the mission proved more of a fight than he imagined. It was always good to be prepared.

He dressed in all black, with a large brown overcoat and thick boots. If he was to look the part of a road thief, he may as well dress it. He wondered if the girl would look surprised to see him, if recognition would flash in her eyes as he slit her throat or stabbed her in the chest. Viscount Halford, she would think him. The man who had been kind to her, now a face of betrayal.

He strapped on his daggers, took a small swig of whiskey from his desk, and left the room.

He used the wind to guide him. Pushing and pulling on the surrounding air, Volya essentially flew across the forests below. It felt freeing, invigorating. This was all he needed in life. This was power. This was living.

He used the map to assume the route Voltred and the girl would take through the forests to the temple. There really was only one road, the manor home appeared to be in the middle of nowhere. What an isolated place to grow up, he thought. Another piece of the puzzle?

As he neared the road where he would lay in wait, he heard voices below. He landed softly several yards away from a clearing, where a small temporary encampment was set up. Several rough men grumbled and moved things around, packing up the camp. All had some form of dagger or axe strapped to their side, and all were dressed in similar style to Volya. So there really were road thieves about, Volya thought to himself with amusement.

"Beg pardon, men, I seem to be lost." Volya stepped into the clearing.

"Who ye be?" A large man with tattoos on his face stepped forward, dagger in hand.

"I mean no harm. In fact, I need your help." Volya rested against a tree, crossing his arms looking bored.

"We don't help strangers," the man said, growling. "Be gone or I'll cut you open from ear to ear." When Volya didn't move the man advanced, dagger pointed menacingly.

Volya began to laugh, taking the man by surprise. The thief paused briefly but then continued forward. When he got within reach he moved to strike, but Volya was faster. He waved the man aside with his wind, and the man flew backward several yards, hitting a tree and slumping down. Volya was unsure whether he had killed the man, but it was no matter either way. These thieves were not important enough to be alive in this world.

"Anyone else?" Volya asked looking around, calm and smiling. The men looked at each other unsure what to do.

"What do you want with us, sorcerer?" An older fellow, who had been sitting stoking the fire slowly rose. He looked worn and grey, his hair and even his skin pale with the hue. But he held himself with poise, Volya guessed this must be the leader of the pack.

"I am no sorcerer, just merely a man doing his job."
Volya held his hands up. "Like I said, I mean no harm.
Well, at least not to you."

"You are a *Guild* member." The man stated. It
wasn't a question.

"And you're not quite so dumb as your friend over
there," Volya said pointing to the tattooed man who was
still unconscious.

The old man stared at Volya but did not respond.

"There is a caravan that will be passing by the road
in the next few hours. I need you to distract them while
I find my mark, that's all." Volya shrugged his shoulders.

"And what is in it for us?" The old man asked.

"Well for one, I won't kill you," Volya spoke with
his usual self-possessed charm.

"Anything else?" The man was not as amused.

"Take whatever you want from the travelers. But
leave the girl for me." Volya's eyes gleamed with mischief.

Chapter 23

NASSA

The lion and the faun,
Not so different than you think,
One is warm with blood,
And one is want to drink.

A mighty roar,
A calming mew,
Though different are the sounds,
The way of life,
The way of death,
One life is all that rounds.

- An excerpt from The Fables of Fillander

Nassa was beyond disheartened. She had finally made a decision with conviction only for it to be stripped away. She had banged on the door crying, but no one had come. She was not able to escape her dismal fate.

Eventually she hid her supplies and fell asleep. It was not a restful night; however, anxieties and fears got the better of her and kept her tossing and turning.

She woke in the morning, puffy eyed and depressed. No one came for her in the early hours, and she was too dejected to get out of bed. But eventually she heard a key turn and Voltred opened the door.

"Ah, there you are. It is almost noonday, Nassa. We leave in one hour." He looked around the dismal room. Nassa only glared at him. Where else could she be, she had been locked in her room.

"I brought you your dress. Now get up and ready yourself, we will wait for you downstairs." Voltred draped an old, faded wedding dress on top of the cot she still lay in, and left the room, closing the door behind him. At least he hadn't noticed his sword was missing.

In time, Nassa got out of bed and got dressed. The dress was too big for her small frame, but there was nothing to be done. She stared at herself in her mirror, trying not to cry. So, this was to be her wedding day.

She choked back a sob, anger boiling inside of her. This was not fair. She had so little control over anything in her life. What bothered her the most was the person she was becoming. Not just Maldrig's wife, but a despondent, sad little thing. She could be stronger than this. She *would* be stronger than this. She was a survivor. Something needed to be done. She strapped her dagger beneath her wedding dress.

Nassa met the rest of the family in the front entryway. The men were all wearing formal tunics and coats over their breeches. Maldrig would not look at her at all but stood looking angry. He did not appear particularly happy about this union either. Brutav glared at her, but Temid managed a small nod. She remained calm and hard. She did not want to show them how vulnerable she felt.

Three carriages waited for them. She sighed in relief when she realized the men would be in one and her and Ari would be in the other. The third would contain the guards Voltred hired for the journey. The road thieves were particularly bad this season — or so Voltred claimed.

Nassa and Ari climbed in their carriage and set off to the temple. Voltred was not a faithful man, and therefore they had only been to the temple a handful of times over the years. She did remember that it was quite a long journey, around two hours through the dark and winding forests.

She sat back on her seat and sighed. Toc had not come to see her off.

"Nassa, dear, you look beautiful." Ari reached over from her seat across from Nassa. She covered Nassa's hand with her own.

"Ari, this wedding dress is ridiculous. It is too big and has been improperly stored. It is stained and yellowed. I look like a dead bride come to haunt you all." Nassa set her jaw. She couldn't laugh at her joke. It was too close to the truth.

"Oh Nassa. You exaggerate. But here, let me help you with your hair." Ari moved next to Nassa and began fussing with her hair, braiding and twirling.

They sat that way in silence for a long while, the carriage clomping along to the movement of the horses. Nassa began to drift off to sleep.

She awoke with a start as the carriage came to a stop.

"Ari, are we here already. I must have dozed off." Nassa asked.

"No, not yet, Nassa. It is too soon. I'm not sure why we've stopped." Ari pulled back the curtain on the window to look out. "I can't see anything. I'm sure we will start again soon. One of your cousins probably needed a quick relief. Not to worry." Ari smiled at Nassa trying to ease her nerves.

"I'm not worried, Ari. I do hope we get overtaken by brigands. Then this ridiculous wedding will have to be canceled," Nassa pouted.

"Nassa, now, now. I know this is not what you want. But I am going nowhere. I've a long life to live yet!" Ari stroked Nassa's hair. "I will take care of you, girl."

"Oh, Ari. I know. But it is not enough." Nassa peaked out the window. She thought she saw something moving in the brush beyond, but the forest was too dark in shadow to tell.

A thought came to Nassa. It had never occurred before that Ari may know something about her past.

"Ari, do you know anything about my birth parents?"
Nassa saw Ari stiffen.

"What makes you ask, girl?" Ari seemed reluctant to answer.

"Well, it's just that—" But Nassa didn't finish her sentence. Someone was shouting outside. "What's that?" Nassa asked.

Ari looked out the window.

"Stay back Nassa. It looks like you got your wish." Ari sounded frightened.

"Road thieves?" Nassa asked, both fear and excitement rising inside her. Ari only nodded.

There was more noise coming from outside the carriage now. She heard her uncle's distinct voice shouting, and then the clanging of metal on metal. She couldn't sit in this box and wait.

"Nassa, no!" Ari tried to grab Nassa, but she was too small and quick. She slipped past Ari and threw the carriage door open jumping out onto the road. A scene of pandemonium ensued.

Brutav, Maldrig, and Voltred had their swords out. The guards who had been at the rear, ran past Nassa to help. They were fighting off a rough looking group of men. They were too focused on the battle to notice her. She came round the other side of the carriage where Temid was fighting as well. He parried and thrust, but his skills were no match. The brutal looking man preformed an empty fade, pretending to retreat but instead lunging for Temid. The poor boy had never been as quick as his brothers, and was impaled instantly.

Nassa stared in horror as the only brother who had been nice to her bled out on the ground. More men charged at her now, and she realized she had been rather stupid to leave the carriage. She pulled the dagger out from under her skirt and flung it at the first man. It hit him right between the eyes. Her aim was true, as always. He fell.

Nassa clutched her stomach. She had never killed anyone and thought she may be sick. More men charged.

"Impressive." Nassa looked to the side. A man was staring at her from the shadows of the forest only a few yards away. He looked collected and not at all worried about the group of men who would be on top of her any second. Was he going to help her or watch her die? She looked from him to the men and was about to turn and run when a wind picked up, knocking the brigands down like an invisible wall. She looked back to the shadowed man. Nassa stared in disbelief. Did this man have magic?

Before she could think further on it, he strode confidently over to her. She gasped as she recognized him.

"It's you." She said in shock. "Viscount Halford."

"My name is Volya." He gave her a feral smile, picked her up, and flew into the air.

206

Part 3

Chapter 24

VOLYA

Creeping vines,
Swirling lines,
Extending toward the sky,

Twirling flowers,
Thorny powers,
Learning how to fly.

- Sudonese nursery rhyme, ballad 4

Volya did not necessarily have a plan. But he never really did. He liked to wing it. He watched the girl from the forest when the fighting began — sucking in a sharp breath — his memory hadn't retained her full beauty. He was surprised she came out to fight instead of remaining in the safety of her carriage. But these brigands really were a crude bunch. No finesse, no grace in their fighting. He didn't think they would last long. It didn't matter to Volya, though. He was only there for the girl.

But as he watched her, he saw some fight in her. He couldn't quite bring himself to make the kill then and there. So, he grabbed her instead. He would do the deed somewhere private. Now they were airborne. Volya concentrated on the feel of the wind, pulling and pushing them along over the forest.

The girl, Nassa, must be too shocked to fight, she instead held on to him with her dear life. If she did have magic, she sure as the hells had no clue how to use it. If she was as powerful as everyone feared, she would have had no trouble fighting off the lot of road thieves. But she hadn't. She had flung her dagger, killing one of the men, and then looked ready to vomit.

Volya stared down at her. She weighed next to nothing in his strong arms. Her skin was warm beneath his and he couldn't help but notice that her hair smelled like lilac. Gods, but she seemed too innocent for all this. Soon her blood would be on his hands.

He spied a stream and dropped them down. They were a few miles off from where he had captured her from the caravan. He didn't think they would be followed, not yet at least. He knew Lord Voltred wouldn't let her escape so easily, but Volya left no trail. Eventually he would need to produce a body, though, or Voltred would find a way to track them. Not to mention the wrath Rasmere would rain down.

The moment they touched the ground Nassa pushed him off and scrambled away.

"What in the hells was that?" She asked in a shrill panicking voice. "Who are you?" She fumbled for her dagger, but it wasn't there.

"Why I'm your guardian angel." Volya smiled and bowed gracefully. Nassa only scowled.

"You are a liar and a thief!" She shouted.

"Well, yes. I am those too," he winked at her amused by her fury. "You look cute when you are angry."

"You said your name was Viscount Halford. Who are you really?" She crouched into a Hildish fighting stance. Volya couldn't help laughing.

"My name's Volya. So, you are a Hildish fighter are you?" He raised his eyebrows. She charged him, trying to knock him over, but he was too strong. He grabbed her arms, pinning them to her sides. This was the perfect opportunity to carry out his mission.

He was contemplating slitting her throat or simply snapping her delicate neck when he was blasted away. He flew in the air several feet before coming down hard on the ground. The attack took him so much by surprise, he didn't think to defend himself in time.

He rose slowly regaining his senses. He looked up to where Nassa stood staring at him, panting, her face a mask of anger.

"Easy, tiger." Volya rubbed his neck. "So you do have some power, after all." He chuckled, winking at her again.

"Don't touch me," Nassa replied with bitterness in her voice. Volya wondered exactly what she had gone through living with Voltred and his sons. Maybe he would be doing her a kindness after all.

"What do you want with me?" She asked, fight still in her voice.

"Don't worry, Lady Annassa. I'm not here to assault you. Not like that." He softened his look.

"Like what then? How do you know who I am?" She asked him.

"I haven't decided yet," Volya responded ignoring the second question. He really hadn't decided what to do with her. It was becoming more difficult to convince himself to kill this girl. He was rather amused by her spunk. Most women wouldn't be so bold to fight him back.

"I might not have my dagger any more, but I know how to fight." Her whole body was tense.

"Relax. Just calm down, OK?" Volya came toward her, arms raised. It was like approaching a rabid dog. She wouldn't let him near, so he stopped where he was and sat on top of a fallen tree.

She must have sensed the danger was temporarily gone for she crumpled in a ball, folding her knees to her chest and began to weep. Great, Volya thought. Just what he needed. Since when had he become a magnet for people who needed to cry?

"Now what's wrong?" He asked exasperated.

"What's wrong! First, I was off to marry my awful cousin and now I've been kidnapped by a strange man who is a liar and a thief!" She managed to get that out between sobs.

"Well, it sounds like you should be thanking me then." Volya shrugged. She glared up at him wiping her eyes on the sleeves of what could only be a severely outdated wedding dress.

"That dress is horribly ugly." Volya had to point out. He regretted it immediately — it only made her start to cry again. "Shit," he said under his breath.

"What do you want from me? I have no money, nothing valuable." She looked at him through forest green eyes, red from tears.

"I was sent to... retrieve... you, but I may change my mind." Volya drummed his fingers on his chin. He had been sent to kill her actually, but he didn't need to tell her the full truth.

"Sent by whom?" Nassa asked confused. "What would anyone want with me?"

"Don't you know?" Volya questioned.

"No." She looked dejected.

"Neither do I," Volya shrugged.

"You don't know who sent you?" Nassa asked. He could see the anger in her starting to boil again. This one had a temper.

"Well, I know who sent me, although you wouldn't know him. But I don't know why you're so important." Volya picked up a rock and skipped it on the creek that ran next to them.

"I don't understand. Will you take me home?" she eventually squeaked out when she was able to regain control of her emotions.

"You want to go back to those people?" He asked with a smirk, genuinely curious.

She hesitated, staring deep into his eyes. "No. No, I don't."

"So then, where do you want to go?" Volya didn't really care, he knew he was just procrastinating. He needed to kill this girl now, but he couldn't help himself from stalling.

"Balrigard Monastery," she spoke suddenly with fierce resolve. Volya couldn't help but laugh.

"Balrigard Monastery? Are you insane?" he continued to laugh, but she seemed sincere. "Are you serious?"

"Yes. And I am going regardless of what you think or say," Nassa said.

"And if I help you?" *Shit,* Volya thought, what was he saying?

"Help me? You kidnapped me. I don't trust you," Nassa said, but he could tell she was weighing her options. If she was serious about going to Sudonia, she was not stupid enough to think going at it alone was a good idea.

"You're right about that — you shouldn't trust me," he said in earnest. "But, I will help you." He took a deep breath. This was definitely not what he had intended to happen. He would still kill her, he thought, he would just bide his time until the moment was right. But he knew there was no conviction in his thoughts.

"Why would you help me?" Nassa looked in his eyes. Volya could tell she was scared but there was something compelling about her as well. She may be innocent, but Volya could sense a hidden strength.

"Good question. Maybe I'm your knight in shining armor?" Volya gave her a half smile. She clenched her jaw, but he could see her lips twitch. He could tell she was still reluctant but after some hesitation she finally nodded.

"You've lied to me once. I'm sure you will lie to me again, Volya — if that is your real name." She narrowed her eyes at him.

"I don't doubt I will lie to you many more times. But my name really is Volya." He couldn't hide his smile.

"I don't believe anything you say." She replied with venom.

"Good." Volya said. "That would be too easy."

"And how will I know you are really taking me to Sudonia?" She asked skeptically.

"You won't." He shrugged.

"So I'm to trust you, even though you've said not to and told me you are a liar?" She asked raising her eyebrows.

"Do you have another option?" He grinned.

She stared at him for a long while, then seemed to make up her mind.

"And won't you be in trouble when you don't bring me to your keeper?" She challenged him.

"I can make my own decisions. No one owns me." He clenched his jaw.

"OK, then. For now, you can take me to the border. But first we need to go back to Voltred's manor. Do you think you can do that flying thing again? I have supplies in my room." Nassa stood ready to go. Volya was impressed by how quickly she was willing to accept him as a companion after he had just stolen her away. She must not hold grudges then, that was refreshing. Or maybe she was just a bit crazy. The scared girl from only moments before was replaced by a young woman of strength and resolve.

"Absolutely," Volya strode over to her, he looked down in her eyes as she breathed heavily. He couldn't help himself from focusing on her lips. They stood so close; he could feel her heart racing. A slow smile spread across his face. He gracefully swept her off her feet and pushed them back airborne.

Chapter 25

NASSA

The way of the world was wrought with iron,
Black and frozen wastes.
The chains and fetters locked the sun,
In a timeless rough embrace.
But, lo, a harbinger of life or death?
A crown teetering on the line,
Help has come, help is here,
The light of the world, divine.

- An excerpt from The Chronicled History of
Hilderland

This was definitely not how Nassa thought her day
would go. But she had to admit, it wasn't the worst thing
that could have happened. She did feel a pang of grief
over Temid. She had hardly known the boy, but he
helped her. Hopefully, his small acts of kindness would
be enough for the gods to take pity on him.

She held on tight to Viscount Halford's — or was it Volya's? — body. He was so strong, his broad chest warm against her side. She still was not sure what anyone could want with her or who this man was — except that he was most definitely a liar and possibly a road thief. But when he told her he would help her, she believed him. She didn't know why, and it was beyond all reason, but she felt he was telling the truth. And besides, this flying thing would be incredibly useful to get her to Sudonia.

They took off again to the skies. As frightened as she was, she had to admit it was pretty incredible. She never knew something like this was possible. Could she ever do this on her own? This time she opened her eyes. The forests sped past below her. It was different up here in the sky, a whole world she never knew existed. She smiled, turning her head to hide her grin from this stranger.

After some time, she saw the four tall towers of Voltred's manor peak through the tree line. He dropped them down at the forest line before the trees cleared opening up to the manor grounds. Nassa looked around, but there was no sign that Voltred and his men had yet returned.

"What now?" He asked her.

"See the tower on the back left of the manor? That is my room. The shutters are broken so it should be easy to get in," she spoke in a whisper just in case. He picked her back up and flew them up to her room. Luckily, it was easy for them to get in through the window, if not a little awkward.

Volya waited on the windowsill as Nassa jumped down to grab the satchel where she hid her books and supplies and the sword she stole from Voltred.

"Sort of a gloom and doom type place, isn't it?" Volya mused. Nassa shot him a glare. "Is this where you grew up?"

"Yes and no," she answered not wanting to elaborate. "Look away." She grabbed a pile of clothes and waited for Volya to turn.

"I've seen a woman's body before, you know." Volya smirked at her, still staring. She gave him a menacing scowl.

"Have you any manners at all? Look away!" she said in her most serious voice. That seemed to scare him.

"Sorry, milady. Just a bit of fun." He smiled at her and turned around. She had to be careful. She could tell he was dangerous. Nassa took a deep breath. What was she doing anyway letting this stranger come with her. She was clearly going a bit mental, but she was so desperate to make it to the monastery. This may be her only chance.

She took off the dated wedding dress, exchanging it for a plain tunic and tight trousers, pulling her boots on over them. They were her riding clothes, but she figured they would also be best suited to travel. She grabbed the sword putting it through her belt, then grabbed her cloak and satchel.

The door swung open. Nassa and Volya froze.

"Toc, you almost gave me a heart attack." Nassa tilted her head back, taking a deep breath of relief.

"Nassa, what is going on? Why aren't you at the temple? Who is *he*?" Toc strode forward protectively, pushing Nassa behind him and dropping into a Hildish fighting stance.

"Not you too?" Volya chuckled, seeing Toc assume the position. "Where did you two learn this? Hildish fighting has to be one of the silliest looking things I've ever seen."

"It won't be so silly when I push you through that window," Toc growled out, which only made Volya laugh more.

"It's all right, Toc. He is going to help me. And you—" Nassa pointed to Volya. "Shut up."

"Nassa, you cannot just go with a stranger. He looks dangerous. Please, Nassa, don't do this. What about Ari? What about me?" Toc pleaded with her, but she just shook her head.

"It will be OK, Toc. Don't tell anyone you saw us. This isn't goodbye." She hugged her friend tight. He didn't hug her back. He seemed utterly heartbroken.

Nassa had no time to think about Toc or what he was saying. She gave him a regretful smile then climbed up to the sill to Volya, who grabbed her and took off.

They left Toc standing in the window looking shocked.

They made it out just in time to see Voltred returning with his caravan. Nassa prayed to the gods that

Voltred hadn't seen them fly away. It left a nasty feeling in the pit of her stomach to think of Toc standing there and answering Voltred's questions. She shivered and tried to focus only on the feel of the air whipping her hair.

Volya landed a few miles north of the manor. Nassa could tell he was worn out. He sat down against a nearby tree, catching his breath. She imagined using his power must take a great deal out of him. She wondered how long he could go up there in the skies.

"What am I supposed to call you? Is it Viscount? Volya?" Nassa asked, sitting down on a boulder.

"I told you already — just Volya." He looked exhausted as he put his head against the trunk.

"Tell me, *Volya,*" she said pointedly, "you said someone sent you but you don't know why. Do you know where you were supposed to take me at least?"

"Does it matter? I'm not taking you there any more." He closed his eyes.

"No one ever answers my questions." She bit her lip in annoyance.

"I don't have the answers you're looking for." He spoke in shallow breaths clearly not attempting to stay awake.

"Fine. Then will you truly protect me?" She asked sincerely, stifling a yawn.

"I won't let anyone else harm you." He said. She watched him as he took a deep breath then fell asleep.

His answer would be enough for now. She lay down using her cloak as a blanket and her satchel as a pillow. It had been a long day. She quickly fell asleep as well.

Chapter 26

VOLYA

The thief in the shadows,
Dressed in black,
Sits biding his time.

No worry here,
And no fear there,
He waits to make his climb.

- Tales of a Thief by Pickering Fool

Volya woke with the dawn. He must have dozed as soon as they had landed. He knew he was running out of power when they had arrived at the manor, but he wanted to get them as far away as he could. They weren't as far as he would have liked, but it would have to do.

He gazed across to where Nassa lay bundled in her cloak. Her hair was a tangled mess, and she was lightly snoring. She must have been pretty tired herself. His hand touched the hilt of his dagger strapped in his boot.

It would be so easy to kill her in her sleep. But to kill a girl — or woman he presumed; she was after all eighteen — in her sleep seemed cowardly.

He sighed. He was going to be in some deep trouble with *The Guild*. Maybe it was best for him to be far away as well. Unless he made his kill soon.

He sat looking at her delicate frame as she breathed in and out. He had told Rasmere that a country girl would be boring, but maybe he was wrong. He sensed there was more to her than met the eye. And she definitely was not a pushover. Nor did she seem interested in him, which bothered him slightly. Most women couldn't help but fall for his charms.

Nassa began to stir.

"We should get moving," she said, all business.

"Agreed, but let's have something to eat first. What's in that pack of yours anyway?" Volya nodded to the satchel. Nassa produced two squished buns, throwing one to Volya.

"Do you think they will come looking for us?" Nassa asked.

"Most definitely." Volya took a bite out of the bun. It was delicious.

"Then we should hurry." Nassa looked concerned.

"Don't worry. I leave very little tracks. Although today I think we will have to go at it on foot. Still recovering from all that work yesterday." Volya stretched.

"Does it take a lot out of you?" Nassa asked.

"My power? Yes. Sort of like a long run I'd say," he shrugged.

"What happens when you run out?" Nassa asked, curious.

"If I use my limit, I just can't go on. I would collapse or fall asleep. If I use too much, well I suppose I would die — sort of like a heart attack. But I'll tell you now — I'm more powerful than most. It takes a lot for me to run out." He gave her a mischievous smile.

"I've never met anyone with magic. I thought they were all dead. At least in this part of the world. Do you think I could fly?" Nassa asked in a shy whisper. Volya could barely hear her.

"Depends. What kind of power do you have?" Volya asked, tilting his head. He still could not feel her power, it was odd. But he had seen it firsthand, he knew it was there. There was a lot of mystery surrounding this girl. He found it rather intriguing.

"I don't know." Nassa looked up at him, biting her lip.

"You don't know?" Volya was surprised. She didn't know what type of magic she had. "Haven't you been tested?"

"Yes, but I had no magic." Nassa shrugged.

"That's odd." Volya thought out loud. "And they tested you for all the elements?"

"I think so?" Nassa said.

"All five?" Volya asked, trying to think why her magic was so erratic.

"Five? Aren't there only four elements?" Nassa looked confused and began counting on her fingers. "Water, air, earth, fire… what am I missing?"

"Well, I guess it's not really an element." Volya considered.

"What?" Nassa looked eager to know more.

"The fifth type of magic is mind magic. It is extremely rare." Volya was skeptical but also a bit excited.

"How do you test for that?" She asked Volya, intrigued.

"I'm not really sure. I don't know anyone who has it." Volya ran his fingers through his hair. Could she really have mind magic? He had never heard, let alone met anyone who possessed the remarkable gift. He knew she had power but not which kind. But only royal blood could have mind magic. *Could that mean she was Sudonese royalty*, he thought with a shock. It would explain a lot though.

"What does it mean to have mind magic, anyway? What do you control? Minds?" Nassa looked confused.

"Well, no. Not exactly. Sort of like how I have wind power — I can use wind to change my surroundings, to push and pull and to manipulate. Mind magic can use the mind to change one's surroundings, to manipulate the world through one's mind." Volya thought there was probably a much better explanation, but couldn't quite figure out how to put it, especially to one who clearly knew so little about power.

"Does that mean a mind mage can do anything?" Nassa asked sounding eager.

"Well, not exactly. In theory one could pretty much do what all the other elements can do since you can use your mind to bend the elements to your will. But in practice I'm not sure. I've never known anyone to have it. But I've heard stories, and most with mind magic still have limitations." Volya finished eating his bun, musing what this could mean.

Nassa looked thoughtful. "I wonder—" she said to herself but didn't finish. Volya thought it an awful waste that no one had ever taught her powers, and yet if she had known how to use them sooner, she may have been killed as a child. What was the point of having magic, really, it only got you killed. Unless of course, you were like Volya and worked for the underground. Hypocrisy at its finest. Volya snorted to himself.

"I think maybe I have fire magic. When I was a kid, I sort of caused an…explosion. Can you teach me to use it?" Nassa asked reluctantly. Volya thought about it. He was supposed to be killing this girl. She was supposed to be a threat. And now he was contemplating teaching her how to use her powers. What was wrong with him?

"I can try." Volya smiled wickedly.

Nassa beamed.

"You look much more pleasant with a smile on your face, you know," Volya couldn't help telling her, smiling himself. Her smile quickly faded. "Ah well, but a fleeting moment. Back to doom and gloom Lady Annassa. Raised in her doom and gloom tower."

"I am not all doom and gloom," Nassa said defensively.

"Well, I see a timid country girl who never smiles." Volya laughed casually. But the girl only looked hurt. *Oh, crap*, Volya thought. She was far too sensitive. "Don't be so sensitive, girl." Volya rolled his eyes.

"Well, all I see is a cocky *boy*, who thinks too highly of himself because he can do some silly tricks." Her face was turning red with anger.

"Ouch, you got me there," Volya replied but couldn't help laughing.

"You are maddening!" She stood up and began to storm off.

"And where do you think you are going?" Volya asked, entertained.

"Away from you," Nassa continued to march away.

"That is all fine and good, but you are heading south. We need to get moving north," Volya continued to sit, watching her. She slowly turned around, her hands clenched into fists. She came back in his direction, grabbed her coat and satchel, and stormed off in the opposite direction.

Volya grabbed the few things he brought, stood up and followed her, chuckling quietly to himself.

Chapter 27

NASSA

The drums beat in the dark,
The very heart of battle,
Pumping in tune,
Veins drawn to the darkness of the fight.

The Ancient Archives, Vol II, Book 1

This man was truly irritating, Nassa thought as she trudged through the woods. She did realize he was useful, especially when it came to finding direction, a skill she so lacked — but she would never admit it to him. One day on the road and she already had no idea what she was doing or where she was going.

She continued to huff and pout the remainder of the morning. She took the lead out of pride, but Volya would clear his throat whenever she began drifting in the wrong direction. At least he had the decency to stay mostly quiet and relatively distanced.

As the day wore on, she knew they would need to stop for their noontime meal. Her bad mood was wearing off with the physical exertion of the trek as well as her natural inclination against grudges. When Volya tripped over a root, subsequently falling on his face, Nassa had to laugh and admit to herself that she was no longer upset.

"I swear that root was not there," Volya said annoyed.

"I don't know how a root could just appear, Viscount Volya." Although in the back of her mind she did wonder if she had somehow caused it.

"Not Viscount Volya. Just Volya." Volya got himself up and sat down on the very root which caused his downfall. He put down the small pack he carried. Nassa followed suit and dropped her satchel, taking off her cloak and sitting on a log. Her legs were tired, and her feet were sore.

"I guess we may as well stop here for our noon meal," Nassa said. She handed them each another roll and some dried beef.

"So you are talking to me now, Lady Annassa?" Volya asked, eyebrows raised.

"Not Lady Annassa. Just Nassa." She gave him a sly sideways look. He grinned. "When will you start teaching me how to use my magic?" She asked.

"Have you always been so demanding?" Volya chuckled. She didn't respond. "OK. How about after we eat?"

Nassa nodded. She was both fascinated and anxious by the possibility of understanding her own power. Would she finally feel the weight lifted? She had suppressed her magic for so long, often denying to herself that she even possessed a gift. In fact it had never felt like a gift at all, but a burden. That is until now. Now that she had met someone else who possessed such power, she didn't feel quite so alone or ashamed.

But would this explain it all — having mind magic? It made sense, it was the only power she had not been tested for. Had Montoc known? Or had he forgotten that fifth element as well?

They spent the rest of their small meal in silence. She was still very skeptical of Volya — if that was even his real name. She knew he was hiding something, and she knew there was more to his kidnapping story — which hadn't quite turned into a kidnapping at all — he was too quick to help her. But for now she would use him to get to Sudonia, while he seemed willing. Although what was in it for him, she did not know. Maybe she would just go ahead and ask.

"What's in all this for you, anyway?" She asked him suspiciously.

"You mean why would I want to take a pretty girl across the country into danger?" Volya asked, a sparkle in his eye.

"Yes, that is exactly what I mean." She rolled her eyes. He was irritating.

"Well for one, I get to hold you awfully close when we are airborne, and I've always enjoyed a woman in my arms." Volya winked.

"I'm sure you have." Nassa sighed, annoyed. *Did he ever take anything seriously?* She wondered.

"And two, my boss is probably pretty mad at me about right now, so a little distance will be just fine."

"Then why do it?" Nassa asked. Volya seemed very thoughtful at this question. Almost irritated. He didn't answer her.

"Anyway, now is as good a time as any to start practicing. Come on, get up. Not really sure how we are going to do this, but we may as well try!" He got up rubbing his hands together and motioned for her to stand in front of him.

"Now this is how I learned," he said. She wasn't really sure what that meant, but before she could guess a ball of wind came hurtling toward her hitting her in the chest and knocking the wind out of her. She buckled over.

"What the hell's Volya! A little warning." Nassa sputtered out, trying to catch her breath.

"I did warn you." He looked amused. "Come on get back up."

She struggled to her feet but got up. She had been wearing her tangled hair loose, but now she tied it back with a small strip of leather. She moved her weight from foot to foot, more prepared now for an attack.

"What am I supposed to do?" She asked in nervous anticipation.

"Well, usually you think about a certain element and just sort of react. For you, maybe just focus your mind?" Volya stood tall looking bored. She couldn't help but find him handsome. But the gods knew how many women had fallen for his charms. She would not be one of them. And it bothered her that he found her pain so amusing.

She waited and waited but another assault never came.

"Aren't you going to hurl something at me again?" She asked, irked, standing up straight.

"I think it is better if you aren't anticipating it." Volya's eyes gleamed. A gale came from behind knocking her off her feet. He held his lips pursed trying not to laugh. She wanted to wipe the smirk off his face.

He walked over to her and grabbed her hand helping her up. She punched him in the arm.

"Stupid irritating thief. That's what you are." Nassa gave him a nasty glare.

"Ow." He rubbed his arm chuckling, eyes twinkling.

"This doesn't seem to be working," Nassa said.

"You can't give up after two tries! Besides, we have plenty of time. It will take a week or so to get to Sudonia — even with taking to the skies for parts of it." He raised his eyebrows at her. "Anyway, you are doing it all wrong. Stop thinking so much. What made your magic come out in the past?"

She hesitated, unsure how much she should tell him. But she wanted to learn how to use her magic — she needed to learn. It was a desire that came deep within her, almost as if it was a part of her very soul. Now that she knew it was possible — and she wasn't alone — she couldn't look back.

"Well it's only happened three times. Once, as a child when my parents died. Once, when I was—" She looked up at him embarrassed, feeling her cheeks go red. "When I was in danger. And the third time with you, yesterday — also in danger I might add."

"OK so it seems to come out when you are in danger, or maybe overtaken by emotions." Volya paced in thought. "You will need to learn to control that. First lesson I learned is to get rid of anything or anyone that brings any emotion out."

"That sounds rather lonely and depressing," Nassa had to comment.

"It's not. It's freeing." He stopped pacing and looked at her. He was deathly serious. Too serious. For the first time Nassa saw a glimpse into a broken side of him. Maybe his life hadn't been so easy either.

"I think that's enough for now. We should probably keep moving," Nassa said.

Chapter 28

VOLYA

To the demon who cries in the dark,
I beg come to the call of my hark,
On the eve which I fled,
Away from the dead,
I saw wonder alight with a spark.

- Poems from the Deep, Verse 24

They spent the next several days making their way north. Volya and Nassa had fallen into a familiar routine, waking upon dawn, breaking their fast, preforming a few exercises, then continuing their journey, either walking our taking to the skies, depending on Volya's energy. He didn't want to use up too much power in case they ran into any danger along the way. He would need some reserves to fight off any threats.

Each day they would break for a mid-day meal and Volya would try to help Nassa learn her powers. But so far, it wasn't working. Volya couldn't figure out where they were going wrong. Although he still couldn't sense her powers, he knew they were in there, he had seen it himself. Maybe he was wrong about the mind magic, but he couldn't form any other explanation for her odd gifts. He was determined to find the key to unlock her power. Although after that, he wasn't sure what to do.

In the evenings they would set up camp, he would make them a small fire, Nassa would divvy up their rations, and they would fall asleep quickly from exhaustion.

Volya continued to procrastinate his mission. He told himself he would still kill her. Although now he started to think that banishing her to Sudonia would be as good as dead anyway. Perhaps that is what he should do — just take her to Sudonia and leave her there for good. He shivered at the thought. Sudonia — the land of magic. The country that had so brutally killed his parents. The very place that had caused the rock of hate in his heart.

What was it about this girl, anyway, he couldn't help but wonder. Why was he so easily agreeing to do her will? He knew mind magic could not actually control minds, although it would be easier to accept that as a reason for his newfound inclination to charity. That would be preferable to his possible development of a conscience, but he knew it wasn't possible. Maybe she reminded him of some past life where he was a kinder and more merciful person — if that boy even still existed. He wasn't sure why it was just so hard to kill her. It had never been a problem for him before. For the first time in years he was reminded of Mara, her throat slit, dead eyes staring up at him. He shook away the image.

What was happening? He needed to get control of himself. They were becoming too familiar with each other. There was a reason he did not make friends. Friends only held him back. He should never have agreed to this, he should have killed her outright. Now he felt he was in a predicament. Serves him right for his ridiculous behavior. He was only prolonging the inevitable. He just couldn't bring himself to kill the poor girl in cold blood.

"We are almost out of supplies," Nassa told him as they stopped for their midday meal, breaking him out of his reverie. They had made it through the forest the day before and were now traveling through The Plains, miles of rocky outcroppings where the air was dry, and the sun was hot. They would have to decide soon if they were to go north toward the Molten Mountains or East through the Forests of Venit Vox.

"I figured as much," Volya said. "I'm surprised they lasted this long."

"What should we do?" Nassa questioned him. He hoped she wasn't coming to depend on him. That would only bring up more unwanted complications, pressuring him further to go through with the killing.

"There is a village close by. We will go there and restock. I need a rest today, but I'll be able to get us airborne tomorrow. I'll go set some traps. Do you know how to forage?" He asked.

"I do. Although it doesn't look like there is a whole lot of vegetation out here. I can try though." She took her last bite of hardtack.

"There isn't much life out here at all. Hopefully, I will be able to trap a rabbit, or else we may be eating snake and lizard." Volya chuckled as he saw the look of disgust on Nassa's face. "Well, we best get to work. I think we might as well stop here for the day. We are making good time, and no one seems to be following us yet."

Volya set down his belongings and gathered a few sticks and rocks, designating a place where they would make a fire. He took out some twine from his small pack, and set off to make traps. He glanced at Nassa, who was putting down her satchel and grabbing a scarf, tying it into a makeshift sack. She looked up at him their eyes meeting for a second but then she looked away and continued on her way. He was left feeling bothered by her stare.

Volya knew Nassa was wary of him. He didn't blame her. She still looked over her shoulder when he walked behind her and would steal dubious glances when she thought he wasn't looking. When they were airborne, she would hold on to him tightly, but her body was rigid and tense. But slowly each day, she was beginning to relax. They had grown more comfortable with each other, and she had become a little less suspicious.

He walked a few minutes outside their camp then began to set up traps. He used his last couple pieces of dried meat to tie around the strings that would set the makeshift contraption into motion. Although he was a city boy, he had gone on several missions as an apprentice all around Akkadia, and he knew how to run a camp, how to make a fire, and how to set a trap. It had all been part of his training. Survival.

He was just finishing his final trap as he heard a scream from beyond the other side of camp. *What had that girl gotten herself into,* he thought. She probably tripped and fell into a hole, there were a lot of those out here among all these rocks. He started to run and then decided what the hells, and threw himself into the air.

It took him a minute to get his bearings. He found the camp easy enough, but Nassa was nowhere to be seen. He knew she had gone out foraging eastward, so he headed in that direction. He scanned the rocks, and listened closely for any more screaming, but heard nothing. He continued on until he thought he heard a low growl and turned toward the sound. Finally, he spied her. Nassa had fallen on her back and was inching slowly backwards toward a rock wall. In front of her was a large and feral dog. Volya landed down next to Nassa, the ferocious beast snarling in front of them both, drool dripping from its large fangs.

"Easy boy," Volya spoke softly putting his hands up. "Nassa, stand up slowly and grab on to my back."

He crouched down, trying to make it easy for Nassa, but she seemed frozen.

"Nassa, get on my back now," he spoke again trying to sound calm not to spook Nassa or the dog. The beast continued to snarl and began inching closer. Still Nassa sat unmoving. Volya stirred up a wind to keep the animal at bay, but the beast was strong, and began to push through.

"Nassa, now!" Volya shouted as the beast lunged at them. When Nassa didn't move, Volya pushed her out of the way. *Damned girl!* he thought. The dog lashed on to his arm, fangs puncturing his skin. Volya used his other arm to shove the beast with wind, but the beast's teeth held firm. The wind only pushed the dog, causing his fangs to rip through Volya's flesh. Shit.

Nassa finally seemed to come to. She jumped up and grabbed a large rock. She began to hammer the beast with it. Instead of injuring him, however, she only seemed to entice him. Thankfully, he let go of Volya's arm, but unfortunately lunged for Nassa. This time she did not freeze in fear. Instead, a powerful blast sent the beast flying backward. Nassa had finally used her power. *But what kind?* He wondered. He once again couldn't quite tell. She had pushed back the beast just as she'd pushed him, but it didn't feel like wind power.

The beast groaned and thrashed around before finding it's bearings and popping back up on its four muscular legs. It began to charge at the two of them, but there was enough distance now that Volya was able to grab Nassa with his one good arm and fling them into the air. They left the creature barking and jumping below.

"That was close," Volya whispered into Nassa's hair as the wind whipped at them. Nassa flung her arms around Volya's neck. She buried her face into his chest. Volya smiled and held her tight, putting his cheek against the top of her head.

Chapter 29

NASSA

My blood runs red,
Alas I feel well,
I had fear in my veins,
Of the color of darkness.

- The Ancient Archives, Vol IX, Book 2

They quickly got back to camp but Nassa was still shaking. Part of her bubbled with excited amazement that she had used her magic and part of her was wrought with the shock that they had almost died.

Volya started a fire, but Nassa was aware that the beast was not very far off.

"Don't you think that thing will come after us?" Nassa asked trying to keep her voice steady.

"Hopefully, it won't want to come near us for a while," Volya said, stoking the flames with his one good arm. The fire began to crackle, licking at the twigs. "But you're right, I will take us a bit farther away, I just don't want to use too much energy if that thing comes back, and we need to fight it off."

"What was that anyway?" Nassa asked, taking a deep breath.

"A *bogri*. They are wild dogs, usually they just roam the marshes, but this one must have strayed north." Volya finished with his fire and came to sit down close next to Nassa. She was aware of him not quite touching her, but she could feel the heat of his thigh, where it was only an inch or so away from her own.

"Are you hurt?" She asked, glancing to the arm that hung limp at his side.

"Just a scratch." Volya smiled, but Nassa could see the pain in his eyes.

"Here let me bandage it." Nassa ripped a few pieces off the hem of her tunic. She boiled the last of their water in a small foldable pot Toc had the foresight to slip in her satchel for her.

She began to clean his wounds gently. He winced. There were five large bite marks that ripped through his skin, but as far as she could see, no serious damage. She wrapped the bandage around his muscular forearm then sat back down. She looked up, he was staring at her with a look she couldn't place.

"There that looks better." She smiled. "Can your magic heal you?"

"No, although I do seem to get better slightly quicker than most." He looked at her tenderly then and brought his hand down on top of hers. "Thank you,

Nassa," he spoke genuinely. Nassa thought it was the first sincere thing she had ever heard him say. She held her breath at the feel of his hand gently placed on top of hers. It was so warm and heavy and strong, but nice. She hoped he couldn't hear her heart racing.

"For what? All I did was rip a couple rags." She quickly pulled her hand out from under his. "Besides, you came and saved me, I should be thanking you."

"Well, you're welcome then," he said reverting back to his indifferent charm.

"How do you know so much about the world, Volya?" Nassa asked. He was not much older than her, but he seemed to know much more than she. Truly she felt sheltered at this moment. If only she had had some sort of education, maybe things would seem easier.

Volya shrugged, "It was all part of my training."

"Training for what?"

Volya stoked the fire and didn't answer.

"Will you tell me who you are, Volya?" Nassa looked at him askew. She knew he had to be some sort of conman. But she couldn't figure out where she fit into the puzzle. And she wasn't sure why, or even if, he was helping her now.

"Nothing, never mind." Volya shot her a sideways glance and stood up. "Well, you clearly didn't forage much, I laid some traps but I'm not too hopeful. Maybe we should try to make it to that town tonight instead. Besides, if that thing comes back, I'm not sure how helpful I'll be all wrapped up."

"Is there an inn? Oh, but we are almost out of money, we will need it for the supplies," Nassa sighed.

"I have a little we could use, and yes there should be an inn, but we will have to share a room." He gave her a wicked grin.

"Oh, wipe that look off your face. You will be sleeping on the floor." Nassa attempted light humor, but the thought of sharing a room with him did make her heart jump. Volya laughed.

"I wouldn't dream of taking advantage of you. If I had wanted to, I already would have. Anyway, you are not my type." Volya stood up and began stomping out the fire. Nassa was offended.

"First of all, no, you could not have — even if you wanted to. I am very powerful don't forget. And you are not my type either." Nassa stood as well, gathering her things.

"Yes, I'm sure your type is the kind of weak halfling that bows and scrapes to your every need. Not a real man like me. Anyway, you are too high maintenance," Volya looked amused. Nassa was furious.

"High maintenance! I am not. I haven't bathed in half a week, I'm eating food that tastes like a boot, and I haven't complained at all along the way!" Nassa was so angry she walked over to him and kicked him in the shin. Then she started to punch him in the chest.

Volya curled up laughing as if she was tickling him. "OK, OK. You're not high maintenance." She stopped hitting him, somewhat satisfied. "Just bossy," Volya continued to laugh at her.

"Ugh!" Nassa threw her head back, exasperated.

"Nassa." Volya suddenly sounded serious.

"What now?" Nassa looked up at him, but he was looking past her. Suddenly she was filled with foreboding. All amusement had gone from his face. She looked over her shoulder to see a pack of *bogri* rushing toward them, teeth bared.

She turned back to Volya, flinging her arms around his neck. He used his good arm to get a firm grip around her waist, pressing their bodies close together, and catapulted into the air.

Chapter 30

VOLYA

A liar or a thief,
Which one is stranger?
A liar and a thief,
Now there's the real danger.

- Tales of a Thief by Pickering Fool

Volya was acutely aware of how tired he was as he navigated Nassa and himself through the sky. He had been hoping for a restful afternoon and a leisurely flight to town in the morning, but alas plans had changed as they so often do. It was exactly why he never made plans, he reminded himself. If they didn't make it to the town soon, he would risk running out of power.

Nassa held on tight, but Volya's arm was growing tired. He was strong but holding someone with one arm for hours was not an easy feat.

"There!" Nassa shouted, pointing out. "I see light in the distance."

Volya looked out and saw what she was pointing at. Good timing, too, as the sun was beginning to set. Volya decided to land them now, and walk the rest of the way. They were only a mile or two out, and the *bogri* were long gone. They would make it to the town by nightfall and he would reserve the small amount of power he had left until he was able to sleep.

They landed down, and it was all Volya could do not to fall asleep then and there. Nassa looked at him with questioning eyes.

"Can you make it to town? You look exhausted. Are you all right?" She asked him.

"I'm fine." He took a deep breath, steadying himself and then began to walk. "It shouldn't be too far from here, but I should save some reserves. I will need a good sleep tonight."

Nassa nodded at him and followed. The sun was setting over The Plains. It was a beautiful swirl of reds, golds, and pinks, with a line of green on the horizon. Volya breathed in the fresh air. He preferred it out here in the open to the stuffiness of congested Thessola City. He smiled. This was definitely not his plan, but he had to admit it wasn't so bad. Nassa was not like all the other girls he had met. For the first time in his adult life he wasn't necessarily eager to escape from her. Not a good thing, though, since he was supposed to kill her.

"What are you smiling at?" Nassa asked him.

"Oh nothing. You're just different from most girls." He winked at her. She scowled.

"Yeah and you are not so well mannered as most boys." She trudged forward, looking annoyed.

"And what good have manners ever done for you? I never said I was a gentleman." He replied playfully.

"Oh really, *Viscount Halford?*" She mocked.

"OK, maybe I did. But I don't like to play by the rules." He caught up to her, pushing her gently and running ahead.

"What was that for!" Nassa exclaimed, faltering but keeping upright. Volya just chuckled.

They went relatively quickly considering how tired they both were. Soon the lights in the city came near and they made their way to the edge of the village. The small town was built in a large rift in The Plains, presumably for shelter from the wind. The huts were made out of clay bricks and thatched roofs. A few larger adobe buildings stood in the middle. They made their way through the streets toward the center, where the homes opened up to a square with a large well. From here several other streets branched off in different directions. A marketplace lay on the northern side of the square, where people were still going about their business even though it was getting quite dark.

Nassa and Volya approached a cart where a middle-aged mustached man was selling spiced wine.

"Where is the nearest inn?" Volya asked him while rifling through his pocket for a few coins.

"Just up that road and to the left." The man replied with a suspicious look, taking Volya's coin and handing him two cups of the sweet-smelling spiced wine. Volya nodded, took the wine then turned, handing a cup to Nassa. She took a sip and began coughing.

"It's only a little spiced wine, Nassa," Volya said suppressing a grin. She glared back at him.

"I'm not used to drinking much." Nassa took another sip and made a face.

Volya grabbed her arm and lead them down the road to the inn.

"I can walk on my own," Nassa said, shaking him off. Volya didn't respond.

She really was a testy one, Volya thought. And she wasn't responding to his charms like most women did. He pretended he didn't care, but at the back of his mind it bothered him.

They made their way up the street and then rounded a corner. The inn was up ahead, a group of rough looking men standing outside the door. A lamp flickered with firelight above the door where a sign hung saying "Doober's Inn." The place seemed dirty and worn, and Volya thought maybe they should have camped outside the village after all.

"Get behind me and stay close," Volya told Nassa, pushing her behind him. He glared at the men as they entered the inn. A few whistled and jeered as Nassa walked by. Volya clenched his jaw. Not worth the fight. Well, maybe they would be if he weren't so tired and if his arm wasn't still so sore.

The front room of the inn also served as a tavern. The floors were worn wood and the circular tables that were spread throughout appeared dusty and overused. Volya made his way to the bar where a portly woman stood pouring ale from various taps.

"We need a room and two pints. What's the fare tonight?" Volya asked.

She gave him a once-over before answering. "Rabbit stew. Take the room top of the stairs. Two marks each," she continued to eye Volya suspiciously.

"We only have three marks." He told her ,feeling in his pocket for the remaining funds.

"Well then I guess you're out of luck. Get out of here." She scowled and turned.

"Wait." Nassa stepped out in front of Volya. *Gods what was she up to.* Volya sighed.

"I can sing for our food." She told the woman. The woman eyed her skeptically.

"I won't be paying you, but if you can get anything out of the customers, you're welcome to it. The stage is over there." She pointed to a corner where a small step stool sat. *Not much of a stage,* Volya thought.

"Nassa, you don't have to do this." He grabbed her arm as she walked over to the "stage."

"Trust me. I can sing." She gave him a mischievous smile.

Volya found a tattered booth, where he could keep close enough to Nassa if any trouble ensued. He watched as Nassa took a deep breath then stood on the stool, turning to face the room. She looked nervous as she wrung her hands, but slowly she closed her eyes and began to sing.

The room was loud but as Nassa's voice carried, everyone stilled. Volya caught his breath. She was right — she could sing. He had never heard anything so beautiful, so truly devastatingly beautiful. He couldn't look away. His heart pounded and for a moment he forgot everything. Every horrible thing that had ever happened, every awful thing he had done. For one moment he was at peace.

When Nassa finished, the tavern erupted in applause. Several patrons threw marks on the floor at her feet. She gave Volya a beaming grin. He couldn't smile back. He didn't know what to think.

Nassa handed Volya the four marks. He walked over to the woman, handing her the money, daring her to question him. She poured them two pints. He grabbed the drinks, served in some sort of dirty looking clay cup, and steered Nassa back toward the corner booth.

A cockroach scurried across the floor. Volya came down on it with a hard stomp, squishing it and spilling its juices across the ground. "Well, it may not be the most luxurious of places," Volya said, looking up at Nassa.

"No, I wouldn't say so," Nassa replied looking somewhat sick, but sitting down and taking a sip of her ale.

"You weren't lying. You really can sing." Volya said.

"I told you so — I'm not the one who is a liar."
She smiled.

Volya couldn't argue there, and for the first time he had no words. They drank in silence as they waited for the stew. When it arrived, Volya thought *rabbit stew* was a rather optimistic name for it. The broth was thick and black with an assortment of unknown materials floating throughout. They both reluctantly began eating. Luckily, they were both extremely hungry or else it would have been hard to get through.

Volya was really feeling the extent of his exhaustion, it became difficult to sit there with eyes open any more, and he yawned trying to keep from nodding off.

"Let's get up to the room," he said and stood slowly. Nassa got up and followed.

"Thanks." He nodded to the woman as they passed her to the staircase. "The mushrooms in the soup were particularly delicious."

"I didn't put any mushrooms in the stew." The woman scowled at him. Volya felt a tad nauseous. He wasn't entirely sure exactly what he just ate. He turned to Nassa who began to giggle. He narrowed his eyes at her.

"What?" She asked trying to hide her smile but doing a poor job of it.

"You think it's funny?" He asked.

"Kind of," she replied pressing her lips together keeping a laugh at bay.

He rolled his eyes at her and continued up the stairs to their room. Once inside, they both looked around at the sad sight before them. The room was bare save for a bed tilting down with only three legs and a small chest of drawers. The sheets were stained and messy, as if someone had just left the room and no one had bothered to clean it.

"I suggest we sleep on top of our coats," Volya spoke slowly. This time Nassa couldn't help herself from laughing. Volya looked at her, wanting to be annoyed, but at the sight of her bright face, he couldn't help but laughing too. He was so tired, and everything seemed too ridiculous.

"I think I can fix this for you." He walked over to the bed and used his remaining strength to kick out the other three legs, breaking them off. The bed now essentially lay on the floor, but at least it was straight. He kicked the broken pieces of wood aside and put his coat in a ball, lying down on the floor.

"Wait — don't," Nassa said as he was about to put his head down.

"Nassa I really need to sleep," Volya said so tired he no longer cared about the surroundings. Besides, he had slept in much worse.

"That floor will give you a disease. You can sleep on the bed with me, just put your head on the other side — and don't touch me." Nassa scooted over her coat and turned toward the wall. Volya was too tired to argue with her over it, so he grabbed his coat, lay it on the bed, and promptly fell asleep.

The next morning Volya was awoken by the piercing light coming through the broken window. He had slept so soundly he momentarily forgot where he was. That is until Nassa kicked him in the face.

"Ugh," he groaned holding his cheek where Nassa struck him with her heel.

"Oops, sorry," Nassa said sitting up and stretching.

"Damn woman." Volya muttered under his breath. This is why he never spent the night with a girl. At least not the sleeping part of it.

"I heard that," Nassa said, and kicked him again. Volya sat up and brought his legs around on the floor. He looked over at Nassa where she sat with her knees up stretching her neck. She raised her eyebrows at him, challenging him to object to her kicking again.

He looked at her intently. Her eyes were so large and innocent hidden under those lush eyelashes and her lips were so plump and rose colored. *Shit.* He once again chided himself for not killing her sooner. He had had so many opportunities but instead continued on this stupid trek across Akkadia to Sudonia. Her singing had stirred something in him he thought lost — and wanted lost. He could no longer delay. Today. He would finish it once and for all today before they made their way out of the town. Then he would go back to Thessola City and forget this ever happened.

"Why are you staring at me like that?" Nassa asked him.

"You stink," he replied rubbing his neck and standing up.

"Well, I've hardly had an opportunity to wash this last week! You smell too, by the way, and you snore." Nassa shot back at him.

"You've been snoring all week." Volya responded with a half-smile.

"I have not!" Nassa replied looking indignant.

"Anyway, get up. We have lots to do today. You go restock our food; I've got a couple errands to run. I'll meet you at the edge of town mid-day and we will decide which direction to go from there." Volya shook his coat out and put it on. Nassa did the same.

"How's your arm?" She asked him.

"Much better. See?" He moved his arm around for her. It was still sore, and would probably leave a scar, but it wasn't too bad. It wouldn't stop him from doing what he needed to do. Nassa nodded, seemingly pleased with his rapid healing. They left their small room and went downstairs.

After a quick breakfast of barely edible runny eggs and boiled oats, Volya left Nassa and headed toward the town center. He was glad to be rid of the girl for a while. Being so close to her for so long had muddled his judgement. He needed a minute alone.

He made his way back to the town center. He passed merchants and folks about their morning business. No one seemed to pay much attention to him, even though he wasn't dressed in the normal garb of their kind. He made it to the well, taking a drink and washing his face. He ran water through his hair and looked up into the bosom of a young lady. He brought his eyes farther up, looking into a pair of bright blue eyes. The woman smiled at him coyly. He gave her a wicked grin back.

"And how do you do?" Volya asked her.

"Foll'w me, good s'r," she spoke flirtatiously with a thick mid-Akkad accent. Volya had a brief flash of Nassa's face before shaking it away and following the pretty girl. He should have asked her more questions, he should have been more suspicious about this woman approaching him out of nowhere, but instead he only had one thought on his mind — and that was to get Nassa out of his.

She led him down a deserted street. The sun beat hot above them, and he could feel sweat already forming at his brow. He looked around his surroundings so he would remember how to get back, but they hadn't gone very far before the woman knocked on a dilapidated wooden door, then entered pulling him in behind her. Volya walked into a dim hallway and looked around.

The hallway was unfurnished with dark clay walls. There was single lamp at the end lighting the whole of the corridor. He tried to allow time for his eyes to adjust to the faint light, after having come from the bright sunlit streets. He thought he saw movement at his side and turned to look, when he felt a brief blinding pain, and everything went black.

When he came to, he was not sure how much time had passed. Would Nassa already be waiting for him? He sat up squeezing his eyes at the throbbing headache. He rubbed the back of his head where he had been struck.

"Feeling better?" Volya heard a male voice coming from behind him. He blinked his eyes, getting used to the light and looked around. They were in a small room; he was laying on a rough-hewn wooden table placed in the center. He turned to see the voice.

"Ah, Tremore." Volya greeted the man. He recognized him instantly, one of Rasmere's thugs. Well, it was only a matter of time before someone caught up to them.

"How's your head?" The ugly man asked with a smirk.

"It's not the first time I've been hit today, so don't go feeling too special," Volya joked. Tremore did not smile.

"Rasmere is not pleased with you," Tremore growled.

"Go figure," Volya replied.

"I'm not happy to come out to this gods-forsaken place either," Tremore said dangerously.

"Then go home," Volya continued to rub his head, bored by this unexpected turn of events.

"Volya, you've always been a little shit. I won't be sad to see you die." Tremore barred his teeth coming close to Volya.

"Tremore, your bark is bigger than your bite. Scurry home before you regret it." Volya smiled at him.

"Where is the girl?" Tremore asked, fists clenched.

"Don't worry about her, tell Rasmere I am taking care of it." Volya shrugged.

"She should have been dead days ago. Now, I'll kill you both. I won't chicken out like a milksop. What is wrong with you? Did you want your way with her first? You've always been a cocky bastard." Tremore licked his lips.

Volya had had enough. Nassa would be waiting, and he would kill her himself. He didn't need this oaf telling him what to do or doing his job. Volya stood up, wincing against the pain in his skull. It made the throb from his arm wound seem paltry in comparison.

"Out of my way," Volya spoke quietly but with venom.

"Or what?" Tremore replied.

"Or this." Volya blew a wind below Tremore's feet, knocking him flat on his back. Tremore looked up at him startled, but unable to move quick enough to combat Volya's skill.

Volya took out a small knife from his belt and plunged it into Tremore's heart.

Chapter 31

NASSA

A spider spins its web,
With sparkling silver thread,
The morning sun shines bright,
But one will soon be dead.

The trap is set,
The fly is caught,
Life meets end,
Was it for naught?

- Sudonese Nursery Rhyme, Ballad 8

Nassa spent the morning walking the village town and buying up supplies for their trip with the extra coin she made singing in the tavern. She was uncertain when they would make it to another town, so she made sure they would have enough hardtack and dried meats for at least a week. Her satchel slowly got heavier and heavier. She had shoved Voltred's sword in there as well, seeing as she had no idea how to use it, and didn't want it bringing her any trouble.

She was fascinated with the small town, which to her did not feel quite so small at all. As a child, she had barely left Montoc's cottage, and then when she had moved to Voltred's estates, she had been so sheltered.

People busied about their day, going from shop to shop, just as she was doing. There were merchants lining the market square, where she heard and felt the hustle and bustle of buying and selling wares. The men and women here were clothed differently than the bright colored silks of Thessola city. Instead, they wore rough spun variations of brown and orange tunics over thick boots, perfect for the dry and dusty life of the plains.

She smiled to herself as she observed the movement of the village. It felt alive, and it made her feel alive too. She enjoyed being among the people. There was a crowd gathering at the other end of the square. The mass of people was slowly pushed like a tide toward the commotion, and Nassa was taken along with it. She pulled up the hood of her cloak, trying to blend in even though her clothing stood out. When she arrived at the scene of the commotion, she inhaled a gasp.

There was a young boy tied between two posts. Both his wrists and his ankles were fastened with rope, stretching him out into an x shape between the large wooden poles. He was naked except for a small cloth tied around his waist. Blood ran down his forehead, where Nassa could see he had clearly been beaten to a pulp. He couldn't be more than twelve years old.

"This boy," began a man dressed in all black, standing beside the boy. "Has been tried and found guilty of using magic."

Nassa stared in horror as she felt a pit in the bottom of her stomach. She knew they killed those who used magic, in fact she had seen it done before when she was young, but even so the sight both terrified and disgusted her. How could they do that to someone so young? And why didn't this young boy use his powers to escape? And yet Nassa had done the same her whole life she realized with a start.

The executioner turned around and began fumbling with something. When he stood tall, Nassa saw that it was a lit torch.

"Any last words?" The executioner asked the young boy.

The boy grunted but looked as though he was trying to say something. Someone from the crowd threw a stone at the boy, making several of those around Nassa laugh.

"What's that boy?" The executioner leered at him.

"I'm not ashamed." The boy managed to choke out as loudly as he must be able. The executioner sneered then lit the pile of wood and kindling that Nassa just now noticed was piled below the boy's stretched out body.

She wanted to scream, she wanted to do anything she could to save the boy, but she didn't know what. She cursed herself for having no control or knowledge of how to use her power. What was the point of magic if she couldn't even use it to help others. She felt weak and disgusted. She turned and ran away, feeling like a coward.

She ran through alleys and streets, making her way to the edge of town where she would meet Volya. She wanted desperately to get away from this town and the people, who only a short time earlier she had admired.

She glanced back over her shoulder, feeling as though someone may be following her, when she suddenly bumped into something and fell forcibly to the ground. She looked up to see a gritty man smiling down at her.

"'Ello, miss." The man smiled at her with yellow teeth and hunger in his eyes. Nassa felt a pang of fear as she looked up at the man whose leering grin reminded her only too closely of Brutav. She began to back away on the ground, but her back hit against the side of the building. She looked around but the small street was deserted. Her heart beat wildly.

"And what do we have here. A lady in distress?" The man chuckled to himself. His face was smeared with dirt and his clothes had holes. She could smell the sour odor of his body.

"Go away, mister. I am due to meet someone, he will be looking for me," she tried to speak with authority and lingering threat, but the man did not seem afraid of her words. He chuckled and got down on his knees, grabbing each one of Nassa's wrists with his own large hands. Nassa began to struggle and twist out of his grip, but he was too strong.

"Sweet as a rose," he whispered in her ear as he smelled her hair.

Nassa's heart was beating furiously but she tried to calm her mind. She took several deep breaths and focused.

She blew a deep breath out, trying to push the man away, hoping her power would boil to the surface. But nothing happened.

The man started to bite at her ear, nipping her neck, and Nassa screamed and struggled, but no one came. She kicked at him furiously, but he didn't seem to feel the pain, numb with his lust.

"No," Nassa said under her breath, trying once again to focus. She had been in this position before and she had somehow fought back with her power. But she had no idea what she had done then, or how to make it happen again. The man pinned her down with his greasy body as he tried fumbling with the laces of her dress.

"I said no," this time Nassa spoke calmly. The man looked up into her eyes, and Nassa saw a small glimpse of fear reflected back. He stumbled off of her clutching at his chest.

Nassa sat there breathing heavily, holding the small dagger, now wet with the man's blood. The man stared at her in shock looking from the knife to his chest where she had stabbed him. He fell to the side, dead, eyes still open in shock.

Nassa tried to stand up but was shaking uncontrollably. For the second time, she had killed a man.

"Nassa, what in the hells…" Nassa looked up to see Volya coming around the corner. He began to run, rushing forward.

"I—" She began but couldn't find the words. "He tried to—" She wasn't sure how to explain.

Volya's look hardened and Nassa could see the anger writ clearly on his brow. He helped her up and brought her close, putting his arms around her and hugging her tight. Nassa closed her eyes against his chest, feeling slightly better.

"You did good, Nassa," he whispered in her hair, but Nassa could feel his body tense. "We need to go." He pushed her away, searching her eyes. Nassa nodded and began to stumble away from the body.

Volya lingered behind, staring down at the dead man, then kicked him with all his might. "Dirty bastard." Nassa heard Volya whisper through clenched teeth as he spit on the body.

"Let's go," he said returning to her and grabbing her arm, steering her toward the edge of the village.

Luckily, it seemed the whole of the village had been distracted by the execution, so there was no one to stop them as they made their way to the edge of the town. Volya picked her up and flew them into the air.

They landed several miles out of the city, so that they could regroup and make a plan.

"Are you OK?" Volya asked as they settled down beside a small stream.

"I'm fine." Nassa said, not wholly convinced she was. Volya gave her a sideways glance indicating he didn't believe her either.

"Did that man hurt you?" He asked.

"No, I stopped him before he could," she replied quietly.

"Good." Volya clenched his jaw. Nassa saw the fury in his eyes.

"We should wash in the stream, but then we need to decide which route to take. I want to get far away from this gods-damned town." Volya walked down where the stream was, splashing water on his face.

"How do you do it, Volya?" Nassa asked.

"Do what?" Volya looked up at her from where he crouched by the bank.

"Use your magic without fear?" She looked into his eyes.

"Nassa, this is not a friendly world. It is a harsh world and the ones like you and me — us with power — it is even more unkind. But fear... it is OK to be afraid, Nassa. But you need to be strong in the face of fear. Don't let it rule you." He looked at her sincerely with those piercing eyes. Nassa took a deep breath. She had fought and won. Volya was right. She needed to be strong. Strong just like her name, *Annassa*.

She had killed a man for the second time that week. But she knew she was defending herself. Although thinking of the blade piercing flesh made her slightly nauseous, she was surprisingly OK. She knew she did what she had to do. She had done it all on her own. And there was a sense of pride in that.

She nodded to Volya, and he nodded back to her. She took a deep breath. She wouldn't let some awful man bring her down.

A while later, after they both shook off the bad memories of the village, Volya stood and pulled the shirt off his back. Nassa watched as he moved with predatory grace. His body was powerful and brawny, and her heart leapt as she saw strength in the movement of his bare muscles. He was distractingly handsome. He glanced back at her as he began to remove his trousers and she felt her cheeks burn. She looked away quickly, trying to busy herself in removing her satchel.

"You should come join me," Volya shouted to her as he began splashing around in the watering hole.

"No, thank you," Nassa replied still trying to look away. Although she couldn't see below the murky water, she knew he was naked beneath the surface, and the knowledge made her blush uncontrollably.

"I must tell you, though, you really are starting to smell." He chuckled, trying to splash water in her direction.

"I will bathe after you, thank you very much. When you go to collect the wood for the fire." Nassa stood, wiping the dirt from her tunic out of nervousness.

"Suit yourself," he said ducking his head under the surface. He emerged from the water, his hair dripping and rivulets cascading down his rugged chest. Nassa looked away before she could see farther down his athletic torso.

"Have you ever seen a naked man before?" Volya asked her chuckling to himself.

"No, and I don't intend to start right now," Nassa replied flushing.

"You may like what you see." Volya spoke with humor in his voice. Nassa was too nervous to respond. "You can turn around now, Nassa. I'm quite well covered."

Nassa turned slowly to see him standing before her. His trousers were back on, but his chest remained bare. She took a quick intake of breath.

"Like what you see?" He asked with a grin.

"Oh stop." Nassa said too seriously, making Volya laugh. "Now leave, so I can bathe."

"If you're sure you don't want me to join you?" he said again with a wink.

"No!" Nassa exclaimed.

"Relax, I'm only teasing. I'll be gone long enough to give you some privacy. Don't you worry milady." Volya put his shirt back on and gave Nassa a little bow. She did not find it amusing.

When Volya was out of sight, Nassa looked around, making sure Volya was really gone, before she stripped bare and jumped in the cool water. It felt heavenly on her dirty skin, and she swam luxuriously relishing the feel of being cleansed. She tried to not only wash off the dirt, but to wash off her past. She wanted to start anew, leaving behind the hurt and pain, the losses that she had suffered. This would be a new chapter in her life.

When she finally emerged, she felt absolved, the fear no longer weighing her down. She would be strong, and she would learn how to use her power. Someone needed to fight for those who couldn't. Her thoughts drifted to Volya, the pain she had seen in his eyes, but also the secrets. She would need to figure out who he worked for and what he wanted with her, but first she needed him to get her to Sudonia. She knew she couldn't do it alone. And somewhere in the back of her mind she didn't hate his company — although she would never admit that to him.

She had to decide which path to take. Going through the Molten Mountains would lead them quickly to Belrigard Monastary according to her map, but they would have to pass the front lines of the war. Not to mention cross dangerously cold and treacherous mountains. The forests of Venit Vox would lead them past Montoc's cottage, and she wasn't sure if she could handle returning there. Plus, the forests were rumored to have many deadly perils. They would come out of the Venit Vox uncomfortably close to the capital of Sudonia. She only knew the rumors of the horrors that went on there, and she was not quick to pass so closely to the danger. But the Molten Mountains were unknown, and the unknown had always frightened her.

"Have you decided which path you want to take?" Volya asked as he came back with an arm full of kindling.

"Yes," Nassa sighed. In the end there only seemed to be one way.

"Molten Mountains or the Venit Vox?" Volya asked.

"The Forests of Venit Vox." Nassa took a deep breath, *strength.*

Chapter 32

VOLYA

A spider and a thief,
Both one and the same,
Cunning and sly,
Neither are tame.

- Tales of a Thief by Pickering Fool

Tonight. It had to be tonight. He had never had a problem killing before, what was it about this girl, he thought to himself for the hundredth time. The swim in the watering hole had been divine, and when Nassa had jumped in he had to use every muscle in his body to restrain himself from watching her. But his morals — morals he didn't think he had — shone through and got the better of him. The timing was not the best to develop a conscience, he thought to himself. Any other girl and he would have jumped in the pool after her, seducing her on the spot, temporarily filling the void he carried deep within his soul.

But somehow Nassa was different. He still boiled with anger about the man in the alley. If only he had been there moments sooner, he would have liked to kill that man himself, and slowly at that. But Nassa had proven she was not quite as weak as she seemed — even without using any power.

They had continued on a little further after their noonday meal. Volya wanted to get away from the open expanse of The Plains. They stopped where the trees began to thicken once again, but did not quite make their way into the Venit Vox yet. Although Volya had explored farther north and south, he had never ventured this far east close to the border — at least not since he escaped from his hometown as a boy.

It would take them a few days to get through the Venit Vox. He told Nassa they would make the journey mostly by foot so that Volya could preserve his energy for the dangers that lurked throughout. He had no doubt they would need to do some fighting at some point. The Forests of Venit Vox had a dangerous reputation for a reason. But what was he thinking? He didn't really need to plan, since he would kill her tonight and then make the return journey back to Thessola City.

Volya looked over to where Nassa was laying out her coat, readying for bed. She bit her lip as she worked, pushing her flowing hair out of her face. He ran his eyes down her body, imagining the curves below her loose tunic. He shook his mind clear. Stop, he thought to himself. He needed to kill her tonight, not fantasize about her.

He sighed and began sharpening his blade. Nassa looked up at him then with playful eyes.

"Should we get some practice in before bed?" She asked him eagerly.

"You sure are in a good mood for gutting a man only a few hours ago," Volya regretted saying it as he watched Nassa's face fall. "I'm only joking, Nassa."

"Sorry, I forgot momentarily how much I hated you," she replied bitterly. "You did kidnap me after all."

"I would hardly call it kidnapping any more, seeing as I am helping you now," Volya replied.

"Yes, but the real question is 'Why?'" Nassa said under her breath.

"All right, let's go," Volya ignored her comment, getting to his feet. "You want some practice, let's see if we can figure it out. I noticed you did not use your magic against the brute."

"I tried. It just didn't work," Nassa said.

"Well, lucky for you, a knife works just as well." Volya smiled with amusement.

"True," Nassa replied with a shrug. Volya was impressed by how Nassa had handled the whole thing. Most women he knew would have swooned to even think about using a knife on someone. But Nassa had proven she had an inner strength and common sense that was not usually a characteristic of her class. It would be a waste to see her dead. Volya wondered again if leaving her in Sudonia would be a better solution. The thought gave him a strange comfort but also made him feel weak.

"I've decided something," Nassa said as she stood facing Volya a good ten feet away.

"Yeah, what's that?" Volya asked stirring up a wind around the forest floor, preparing to hurl it at Nassa. His head still pounded violently, and his forearm wasn't so much better, but he figured the best way to heal was to ignore the pain.

"I really want to learn to use my magic," Nassa said with fervor.

"Didn't you already decide that?" Volya asked, not paying much attention to her. He hurled a ball of wind at her, but she dodged it. Volya looked up in surprise.

"Sort of. For so long I wanted to suppress it. Then I was curious. But now I really want to use it. I don't want to be weak any longer." Volya looked at her quizzically, thinking that was an odd thing to say.

"What do you mean?" He asked hurling another ball at her. To Volya's continued surprise, she dodged it again.

"I mean, I saw a boy hanged today for having power. It was wrong. He didn't even try to use his power to fight. And I just watched, like a coward," she said it quietly, almost under her breath. Her cheeks grew red with embarrassment. Volya stared at her a long while. He didn't understand this girl. Why would she want to help complete strangers.

"It is just the way it is here. We kill those with magic. They test them young before they know how to control it. Makes it easier to kill them — they can't fight back. There was nothing you could have done to save that boy." Volya narrowed his eyes at her.

"I don't know. I just had this feeling — like I should be doing something more." Nassa looked to him with pleading eyes, wanting him to understand, but he could not. Those with magic had Sudonese blood. And he hated the Sudonese for what they had done to his family. He even hated himself, he realized with a twinge of anger. And he should hate Nassa, too. Instead, he was here teaching her power. Why did everything turn upside down when he was in her presence?

"The Sudonese are evil, Nassa. They have been killing our people for decades. It is only right we kill them back," Volya spoke more harshly than he meant.

"Volya, *we* are from Sudonia." Nassa stared at him deeply. She was right. They were. He couldn't explain it, but his whole life he had hated the Sudonese. Even though he was one of them. Even though he and his group of assassins all were from the dreaded place. But they didn't count, he tried to convince himself. They didn't count because they were eliminating the threat. Looking at Nassa, he knew he couldn't hate her either. Maybe there were just exceptions? He pushed the thoughts away, he had held on to his anger for so long, he was not ready to let it go.

275

"We are different, we don't count." Volya stirred the wind up, forming a small tornado around Nassa. It danced and swirled around her body, whipping her hair. Volya took a deep breath, she looked beautiful and fierce.

"We are not all so different." Nassa glared at him. The wind around her began to bend, flattening into a disc of spiraling air around her feet. Volya watched it move, then looked up into her eyes. She had a look of wild resolve. This was not Volya's doing.

His lips parted in awe, as she controlled the wind, sending it hurtling back at Volya, knocking him off his feet. He stayed there a moment unable to move. She could control the wind.

He heard Nassa squeal.

"I did it." She ran over to him helping him up and hugging him, jumping up and down. He was caught off guard but didn't push her away. Slowly he brought his arms around her and lifted her body, twirling her around.

"Nassa, that was—"

"Amazing!" she finished for him.

Volya put her down slowly, their bodies still touching as she slid down, their skin only separated by a few layers of cloth. He could feel the heat radiating off of her body. His breathing became shallow. She stared up at him, searching his eyes. Her arms were still around his neck. They were so, so close. He looked down at her parted lips.

She turned her head. "I can't believe I did it." Color rose to her cheeks. She sounded relieved but nervous. He let go of her.

"Do you know what this means, Nassa?" Volya asked seriously.

"That maybe I will learn to control my power after all!" Nassa spoke with excitement.

"No, Nassa. You controlled the wind. And I've seen you do that push thing — not really sure what element that is. And you told me you had used fire magic. Nassa, if you can control more than one element, then we were right. You most certainly have mind magic." Volya stared down at her, enjoying the astonished look on her face.

"Do you think I can control all the elements?" Nassa asked wide-eyed.

"Yes, Nassa, I do." Volya smiled back at her. But his jaw tightened.

For the first time he realized Rasmere might be right — this girl may be a greater threat than he ever realized. *She is royal.* Now more than ever, he needed to act before it was too late.

Chapter 33

NASSA

Through darkness they fought,
A beast coming forth,
With guise of a friend,
They met with their death.

- The Ancient Archives, Vol IV, Book 1

Nassa stood there stunned. She knew she had magic. And ever since the day her parents had died, she had known she was powerful. But she didn't like to think about that day. In fact, she tried so hard *every day* not to think about it. But with the release of her power, the memories came flooding back. Her parents — burned to death, dead in the locked stall. Her childish self, desperately trying to get through the flames to them. And the eruption from deep within her core, fire exploding but not burning. She took a deep breath steadying herself.

She meant what she told Volya. She had made up her mind. She would learn her powers. She would become *Strength*. It was her namesake. She felt it in her very soul. Maybe that resolve was why she was finally able to will her power. Maybe she had broken down a barrier she didn't even know was there. She would grow strong, the problem was — she had no idea how.

She looked up at Volya who stood there smiling at her. But the smile did not reach his eyes. Something dark lay beneath his stare. Some emotion she didn't recognize. She still knew so little about him. But nonetheless she felt a certain comfort in his presence. She felt somehow safe.

"I want to thank you," she told him shyly looking down at her toes.

"For what?" He seemed taken aback at that remark.

"For helping me. And for saving my life. More than once." She quirked her lips in a half smile, looking up into his eyes.

"It's nothing. You saved yourself most of the time," he replied, jaw tight. He looked annoyed by her sincerity.

"Well, never mind then, if you won't accept my gratitude." She scoffed at him and turned, moving away. They had still been standing so close.

"Nassa, it's not that—"He grabbed her arm and pulled her back toward him. His fingers lay around the bare skin of her arm. He held her tight, but not with force. His touch was warm. Her heart dropped. "It's just that…"

He didn't finish his thought. Nassa realized she wasn't breathing and let out a shuddering sigh. His body pressed up against hers and she could feel his powerful muscles against her chest. His warm breath mixed with her own as the world around them grew silent.

He lifted his hand to her face, trailing a finger down the length of her jaw. Her eyes fluttered closed at the sensation and her body trembled. She instinctually raised her chin, lifting herself to him. He continued to trace her jaw with his finger, bringing it down to trail the shape of her lips. He moved his face to hers, dragging his strong hand through her hair and cupping the back of her head. Her body tensed in expectation.

From the corner of her eye she saw his other hand move to the dagger at his belt and pull it free. She pulled away, looking at him confused. She saw a look of guilt in his eyes, then felt a sting at her neck and the world went dark.

Chapter 34

VOLYA

Demons, demons everywhere,
Haunting, haunting,
Best beware.

Moans and groans,
And screeching nails,
Hide away,
Leave no trails.

- Poems from the Deep, Verse 113

Volya wanted her. He couldn't help himself; he was after all a healthy man. She stood there in front of him, and he could hardly breathe with the ache of his desire. She lifted herself to him, and he could feel his passion rising.

But he knew that something had to be done. For the last ten years he had tried to rid Sudonia of their power. He couldn't possibly deliver this girl into their hands now. She may one day be their most powerful weapon.

He understood that now. And if she had mind magic that meant she was of royal blood. The same royal family who had started *The Great Purge*. The royal family whose ongoing wars had led to the death of his parents. And yet, they had wanted her dead too…

He grabbed his dagger, distracting her with soothing strokes as he prepared to slit her throat. She looked at him, a look of pure confusion in her eyes as he brought the dagger upwards.

But then something stung at his own throat and the world went black.

When he awoke, the world was dark and he was lying in a hut, wrists tied together with a rough shining material he didn't recognize. Nassa lay next to him, wrists also tied, but her chest still rose and fell with sleep. *Shit*. She was still alive. She looked so peaceful. He almost regretted that he ever tried to kill her.

He tried to move to the entrance of the hut quietly, so he would not wake her. He inched along the dirt floor then stuck his head out of the crude opening. The land beyond was dark but he made out rows of similar huts.

They appeared to be deep in the forests now, so whoever had found them had clearly moved them within the Venit Vox itself. The large trees grew up hundreds of feet, obscuring the night, making it impossible to see the sky or stars. He wondered if this part of the world was always dark, even during the day. Vines hung from the trees, and he thought he made out bridges strung above them between the large trunks.

Who were these people? Although a few brave souls did reside in the Venit Vox, he knew of no cities or tribes who occupied these parts. There was one main thoroughfare and a small town, but nothing he ever heard of to match this place. He was utterly confused, but as no one seemed to be out and about, he figured it must be the middle of the night, and he would have to wait until morning for answers.

He scooted back into his original spot, laying back down, but unable to get comfortable on the rough floor with his hands still tied together. He sighed. He passed the rest of the night in and out of fitful sleep.

A few hours later, he turned over to see a dim light coming from the entrance of the hut. He looked to Nassa; she began to stir turning over, then slowly opened her eyes.

It took her a moment but once she had her bearings she began to struggle and panic.

"Where are we? Why can't I move? What happened?" she spoke quickly jerking around, trying to free her hands.

"Calm down," Volya spoke with a calm and cool voice.

"How can you say that?" But she took a deep breath and quieted. She looked at him suspiciously.

"You tried to kill me." Panic and shock grew in her eyes as Volya saw the realization dawn. She scrambled away from him, her body tense as if for a fight.

"Nassa, let me explain," Volya spoke pleading. He did not like the way she looked at him now. Like he was an animal, a monster.

"You were always going to kill me, weren't you? Was that the plan the whole time? Was that why you were going to kidnap me in the first place?" Nassa asked voice rising with anger and fear.

"Yes." Volya decided honesty was best. He took a deep breath.

"Why?" she spoke in barely a whisper, the look of betrayal in her eyes ran deep.

"The man I work for, he wanted you dead. You were supposed to be a bargaining chip for his son, but they killed him. After that he wanted you dead as well." He brought his hand to his face, rubbing his temples.

"Who are 'they'?" Nassa said with frustration.

"Sudonia." Volya put simply.

"But what would Sudonia want with me? Who do they think I am?" Nassa asked, confusion plain on her face.

"Your uncle is somehow involved." Volya shot her a sideways glance, not sure how she would react.

Nassa just sat there, her cheeks hot with anger. She looked furious but not surprised.

"I don't understand." She finally got out.

"Neither do I," Volya said sincerely. "I am just a tool, Nassa."

"You are just a coward. You are not your own man, at all," Nassa spoke with spite and Volya felt the blow as if she had knocked the wind out of him.

He could only nod back.

"Why didn't you just kill me right away, why play this whole thing out? A true coward through and through," she practically growled.

"You're right," Volya spoke dejectedly. She *was* right. He was a coward. He should have killed her from the get-go. He couldn't explain to her that he just couldn't do it — he couldn't even explain it to himself. His brain wanted one thing but his heart another. This girl, this silly slip of a thing, she would finally be the one to break him apart. After so many years of pushing away emotion, he couldn't do it any more. He was tired.

He must have looked really pathetic for she seemed to soften, taking a moments pity on him. Although that did not make him feel any better at all.

"Where are we?" She asked through clenched teeth, anger still searing in her eyes.

"I'm not sure. Somewhere in the Venit Vox," Volya replied.

"When we get out of here are you just going to try to kill me again?" She had anger in her voice and perhaps resentment, but Volya was surprised to note she did not sound afraid.

"Nassa, you don't understand." Volya closed his eyes in frustration.

"Then explain it to me." Nassa brought her knees in close to her body, hugging them tight with her tied hands.

Volya took a deep breath. He might as well tell her everything. It would be a relief actually.

"When I was a child, I lived on the border lands just North of here — right near the war front. My parents were killed — murdered — right in front of my eyes. I barely escaped myself. Sudonia did that. Our own people. I fled, and made it to Thessola City. I was a street urchin, that is until I met *The Guild of Thieves*. They took me in and taught me all I know. I work for them now. I hate Sudonia, Nassa. They killed my family, took my life away. They cannot have your power."

Nassa had been listening intently. She stared at him now with such a penetrating gaze but did not speak. They were silent a long time.

"I knew you were a coward. Only a coward kills his own people instead of trying to solve the problem." Nassa looked at him with acid in her gaze.

"There is no other path for me, Nassa." Volya hung his head.

"There could be." She seemed so sure of herself in that moment, but Volya only shook his head. He stared at her, anger now rising in him as well. He knew she could never understand.

At that moment, a strange looking man — or was it a creature — poked its head through the hut's entrance. His skin looked rougher than a man's and was pale yet tinged with purple. Or was that just the dim light reflecting off his features? His eyes were slightly farther apart than one would expect, and rounder too. They were the deepest shade of blue Volya had ever seen. His ears were elongated, almost pointed, but then again that could just be the odd angle at which he poked his head through the rough doorway.

"Come with me. I don to bring yon to elder council," the man or whatever it was said with a strange and thick accent. Volya and Nassa looked at each other — there was betrayal, there was anger, there was bitter indignation. But somehow beyond all odds there was a sense of companionship; they were still in this mess together.

Chapter 35

NASSA

In the arms of a mother,
The baby is cooed,
But here comes the fox,
Looking for food.

- Sudonese Nursery Rhyme, Ballad 22

Nassa felt broken. She hadn't realized she had come to trust Volya — but she had. And now this. He betrayed her. He meant to kill her. But... he hadn't. Did that count for something? Would he have gone through with it if they hadn't been abducted? She pushed the thoughts away. She was furious. She had never felt so lonely in her life. Not after all the years up in her tower, serving Voltred's family, all the years of solitude and isolated work. Then at least she had had Ari and Toc. They seemed loyal, but were they? Was anyone really? She didn't think she could trust anyone ever again. She looked over to Volya with bitter resentment on her face. He had done this to her.

She had no time to think further on it, however, as a strange man had spoken to them through the doorway. She had to admit, she was rather curious despite the fact that they were tied up and clearly prisoners of a sort. She didn't feel particularly in danger even though she was with an assassin and thief on one side, and a strange creature was speaking to her from the other. She found it curious indeed that she felt no fear, but perhaps she just didn't feel anything any more. Even though she was furious at Volya for attempting to murder her, she found she was not afraid of death itself. In fact, she almost welcomed the idea. Would it really be so bad to die? It may be a relief. But then again, she had just decided to learn her powers, to be strong. *How little faith to give up so easily,* she thought.

Nassa looked at Volya. He looked dejected — almost as broken as she felt, but she couldn't bring herself to feel any sympathy for him. He had after all tried to kill her. But he had also delayed, he had also taught her power, and taken care of her the past week. She didn't know what to think. She shook off the thoughts before she was overcome with emotion. Volya stood and ducked out of the doorway and Nassa followed.

They walked on across the forest floor, thick with layers of soft mulch. Small, thatched huts, like the one they had awoken in, stood in lines crowding the forest floor. She didn't see any more of the creatures.

She looked ahead trying to make out exactly what the man was. He was smaller than a normal human, and his skin was shaded almost purple, but that could just be the lighting. The whole entire village — if that is what she could call this place — was lit with a strange purple aura. The light filtered in high above the tree line, but the forest canopy was so dense, it was impossible to see the sky.

As she looked up, she saw more of the thatched huts built into and around the incredibly large tree trunks. They looked almost like the beehives that Nassa had seen growing up close to the forest. They were connected together by a network of bridges made of vines from the trees. Nassa had to admit the whole place was quite magical.

"Where are we?" she whispered to Volya momentarily forgetting her anger as she was overtaken by awe.

"I don't know," Volya whispered back, also looking around in a state of wonderment.

"I should have figured," Nassa whispered under her breath. Volya shot her a sideways glance letting her know he had clearly heard.

They continued following the strange little creature for some time, weaving their way through the multitude of huts. Eventually they came to an open space, where the huts gave way to a large fire pit.

"Do you think they plan to burn us?" Volya whispered with amusement.

"Do you take anything seriously?" Nassa scowled back at him.

"I am being serious," Volya shot back. Nassa rolled her eyes. He truly was obnoxious.

She didn't think they would burn them, she figured they would have already killed them if they had wanted her dead. Although that thought made her immediately think back to Volya. Why had he waited so long to kill her?

Although she had very little control over her powers, she knew Volya was strong, and felt pretty confident that the two of them could easily get out of this situation if they wanted to. She just wasn't sure if she wanted to join forces with him at all.

"Sit," the man creature said, indicating a rough tree branch that stood facing the firepit. Looking around there were rows of similar logs set in circles around the center. This must be where the creatures meet, she thought with fascination.

The little man thing left them sitting there for some time. Nassa refused to look at or even speak to Volya. She could feel his glances though, she could tell he periodically was staring at her.

"Nassa, I—" He began.

"I don't want to hear it," she snapped back.

Before Volya could try again, a loud horn was blown, piercing the air. Volya and Nassa both looked up to see where it was coming from, but neither could spot the culprit.

Footsteps approached, first one, then many, then what sounded like hundreds. Nassa looked to Volya then, slightly alarmed, but he seemed poised, as if he was readying for a fight.

Abruptly, hundreds of the little creatures came filtering in through the layers of huts around them. Most were men like the one who had led them, all wearing similar rough spun tunics, tied at the waist. Others were women, who appeared to be taller than the men, more similar to Nassa's own height. The women did not have the same purplish tinge, instead there was something almost green about them. Their hair was long and braided with flowers strewn throughout. They wore tight trousers and flowing tunics with puffed out sleeves. They were beautiful.

"I may like this place after all," Volya whispered to Nassa with a grin. She gave him her most venomous glare. He somehow was able to remain so calm through everything. As if nothing anyone could do truly bothered him. She hated him for his selfishness.

One woman — the tallest of them all and with the longest hair by far, strode to the center of the circle. As the other creatures took their seats Nassa's heart began to beat quicker and quicker. They were all staring at Nassa and Volya with large deep eyes. Old eyes, Nassa thought. These were not young creatures.

The woman said something in their native tongue and the others began to laugh. Volya gave Nassa a sideways glance. Nassa gave him a wary look back. She truly had no idea what was going on. Her sheltered life had changed so much in so short a time.

"Guests," the woman spoke directly to Volya and Nassa in a thick accent.

"Guests or prisoners?" Volya whispered out the side of his mouth to Nassa. The woman's lips quirked up in not quite a smile.

"We welcome you to, Finderlind." She nodded to Nassa and Volya each in turn. *Finderlind.* Nassa thought in shock and wonder. The land of the fairy elves?

"An interesting welcome," Volya replied holding up his tied hands for the woman to see.

"Ah yes. Well, we didn't want you to escape before we could talk. Couldn't have you using those powers now, could we?" She smiled but her eyes looked serious. She motioned for a man to come over, and he did so quickly, bowing as he pulled out a rough metal tool. Nassa realized with a start that this man was a servant. Were all the men here servants? He bent down and cut the strings loose around Volya's wrists and then Nassa's.

Nassa hadn't realized that the strange material around her wrists had been blocking her power, but now that they were off it felt as though a great weight was lifted from her. Nassa, newly attuned to her powers, hadn't even tried to use them to escape, she thought with frustration in hindsight. She wondered if Volya had tried to use his.

Volya breathed out and a wind whipped through the crowd. "Ah, better." He gave the woman a wicked smile. *Was he flirting with her?* Nassa thought to herself in astonishment. Does he know no shame? She felt her stomach knotting.

"Are you fairy elves?" Nassa couldn't help but asking. The woman looked at her with amusement.

"My name is Shantara. I am the queen here among my people. You may call us fairy elves; we call ourselves the Rodehendra." She gave Nassa a sly look. "We have been waiting for you."

Nassa looked sideways at Volya. He was staring back at her looking amused by the whole thing. Infuriating.

"How did you know I would come?" Nassa asked in true wonder.

"Our people are gifted with foresight. Although the paths are not always correct. You humans change your minds so quickly," she smirked.

"What do you want with me?" Nassa started to feel slightly anxious. Here were more creatures who seemed to know more about her than she did. Everyone in the whole world seemed to know more about her than she did. It made her feel like less of a person and more of an object. She didn't like the feeling.

"I will introduce you to our people first. Then you will come with me, and we will speak with privacy." She nodded down to Nassa, who nodded back.

"Rodehendra," she spoke to the creatures surrounding them. They all shouted what Nassa assumed was a 'here, here' in their native tongue. "These are our guests. Treat them as such," she said a few more lines in her native tongue, that Nassa and Volya could not understand. The creatures shouted back some sort of agreement and then all began to file away.

Shantara led Nassa and Volya to a hut on the other side of the fire. It was larger than most, so Nassa assumed it was the hut reserved for the queen. Upon entering, it definitely was larger than the one in which they had slept. It was furnished too, with rich carpets layered on the ground. There was a table made of beautiful wood of a kind Nassa had never seen.

"Sit children," Shantara motioned to them. They both sat. "What answers are you looking for?"

"Who am I? Why are we here?" Nassa asked quietly.

"As to why you are here, well, we found you two at the edge of the forest. We've been waiting for you. We took you before any harm could be done and brought you here. To Finderlind." Shantara gave Volya a pointed look, then sat as well. "And as to who you are, and why we felt a need to protect you? Well, it is a long tale indeed."

Nassa looked at Volya , who had the dignity at least to look somewhat shame faced. So, the fairy elves had protected Nassa from him.

"We have time. Tell us the tale," Nassa spoke with a somewhat demanding tone, but she had waited so long for answers.

"I will start at the beginning. There was a prophecy. The King — the King of Sudonia — he is a selfish man. A man driven by power and greed. He wants nothing to come between him and his rule, not even his own children. When he was younger, he began a quest for eternal life. This is not possible of course, but some live longer — some such as our own people," Shantara paused to make sure they were keeping up. Nassa nodded for her to continue. Volya looked somewhat bored.

"He sought us out, befriending our people at first. The shaman of our village, she gave him a prophecy. Then he killed her. He killed many of our kind before we were able to stop his magic." Shantara closed her eyes, emotions surfacing.

"Do you know it?" Nassa asked.

"The prophecy?" she questioned back.

"Yes." Nassa was sitting on the edge of her seat. She had a profound sense that this was important.

"Yes, I know it." Shantara stared deep into Nassa's eyes.

"And will you tell it to me?" Nassa asked back with just as much depth.

She looked around cautiously. "I will."

Nassa waited.

"Of bastard born — no virgin she,
The cause will come from far,
The son will rule father's land
And mend the broken scar.
With power reigning down on all,

The son will find a way,
The king will see his doom enthroned,
His neck the son will slay."

Shantara finished taking a deep breath.

"And what does it mean?" Nassa asked slightly bewildered.

"It means that the King of Sudonia will be killed by his own son. A bastard-born child that is." Shantara gave Nassa an unusual look tilting her head to the side.

"That's why the king started *The Great Purge*," Nassa said with an intake of breath, the pieces fitting together.

"Exactly. After the King heard the prophecy he began *The Great Purge*, killing all the children of his land for years. He didn't want to take any chance that one of his bastards would live to kill him." Shantara's eyes looked weary. Nassa wondered how old she truly was.

"But — why kill all the children if it is only his son that will kill him?"

"The king had many bastard children. He didn't - doesn't — want any of them to live. Besides, prophecies are not always as they seem."

"So, he killed all those innocents, and even his own children…"

"Not the legitimate ones — they still rule with him at the capital." She paused and looked deeply into Nassa. "And not those who slipped through his fingers." She smiled at Nassa then, a mischievous smile that made Nassa's heart pound.

Chapter 36

VOLYA

A thief in the night,
A thief in the day,
What separates them?
One cannot say.
In night there is darkness,
And light in the day,
But the thief's heart is black,
As he enters the fray.

- Tales of a Thief by Pickering Fool

Volya's mind was racing although he was trying his best to look bored. He had never heard this prophecy, and although he didn't doubt its origins, he got the distinct impression that this woman — if that is what you called a fairy elf — was leaving something out.

If this prophecy was to be believed, then the King of Sudonia would finally meet his demise at his own son's hand. That made Volya want to smile. But where did Nassa fit into this all.

He looked at her, the puzzlement written clearly on her face.

"What have I got to do with any of this?" Nassa asked Shantara, mirroring Volya's thoughts.

"Do you know what the King's power is?" Shantara asked Nassa smiling.

Volya suddenly caught his breath. He felt like he had been hit with a boulder. It all made so much sense, how could he not have seen it before? Nassa, the obscure niece from nowhere. Nassa, the bargaining chip. Nassa, the one they feared. Nassa, the mind magician with royal blood — but she was not just any royal.

"Mind magic," Volya whispered, answering for her. His eyes looked up at Nassa and he saw that she was afraid. She hadn't known what she was — who she was.

Nassa jerked her head in his direction. "What did you say?"

"Mind magic, Nassa. I knew you must have royal bloodlines but I didn't realize until now — the King's power is mind magic." He looked at her again, letting the information sink in. "Nassa, the King of Sudonia is your Father."

Nassa stood abruptly, knocking over her chair. She looked confused and overwhelmed, dizzy almost. Volya stood up and grabbed on to her arm, steadying her.

"Nassa, are you OK?" Volya asked, real concern tinging his voice.

She only nodded in return. Volya grabbed her chair, righting it, and sat Nassa back down. "Sit, Nassa." Volya sat back down as well but still held on to her arm. He couldn't help himself; he liked the feel of her skin under his. He felt stronger this way and hoped she would too.

He was slightly in shock as well. Here he was the whole time, with the King of Sudonia's daughter. His most hated enemy. And yet, the look of utter discomposure on Nassa's face stirred something inside him. He wanted to protect her, even as he had known he should kill her. But this prophecy — did it change everything? Was she actually the solution to all their problems? Could she be the one to kill the king?

"But I am a woman," Nassa spoke as if she could hear Volya's thoughts.

"Yes, Nassa. But still, you may be our only hope." Shantara gave her a hopeful smile.

"The prophecy says a son will kill the king. I am useless," Nassa barely managed to speak, still in shock of who she really was.

"Nassa," Shantara spoke slowly. "There are no other mind magicians left in the world. The king has killed them all."

"But—" Nassa began. Volya could see the world spinning in her eyes. Was she truly the only mind magician left besides the King? Volya's mind hardened. He couldn't possibly kill her. If he killed her, there may be no one left powerful enough to fight the King. But if she were to side with her father — there would be no stopping the might of Sudonia then.

Volya shut his eyes. He made a vow then and there. He would protect the girl. He would give everything he had — his life included — to keep Sudonia from getting their hands on her. *The Guild* be damned.

When he opened his eyes, Shantara was looking back and forth between Nassa and Volya, a knowing smile on her lips.

"What?" Volya asked her annoyed.

"Oh, nothing," Shantara replied with a grin.

"I have to get out of here," Nassa said suddenly. She stood quickly, making her way to the entrance of the queen's hut.

"Nassa, wait." Volya stood up as well, planning to follow her. He felt a sharp slap at his wrists and looked down. Then he looked up to Nassa, who let out a short scream.

The queen was now standing smiling at them, whip in hand. "You didn't think we could possibly let someone so valuable go?"

She held the small whip at her side, made of the same material that she had just lashed around their wrists. *Hells,* Volya thought.

Chapter 37

NASSA

A snake in the grass,
A hawk in the sky,
On belly one crawls,
One soaring up high.

- An excerpt from the Fables of Fillander

Nassa stared down at her wrists. So, the fairy elves wanted to keep her captive. They wanted to use her, just as everyone had been trying to use her, her whole life. But now at least she finally understood why. She wasn't sure what to think of everything that had happened. The past day had been complete with multiple betrayals and too much information for her to sort through. But a small part of her, a small hole that had always resided inside her, closed up. A tiny piece of the puzzle completed. She knew who her father was.

That isn't to say she was happy about who her father was. The very prospect was completely unbelievable and almost disturbing. Was she a princess? No. She was a bastard. Unwanted even in birth. Her father had killed thousands of children just to kill her. Or an unknown brother she supposed, not her. All those deaths still felt like her fault. But she had power in her veins. Power in her blood.

She thought back to Voltred. He had wanted her for breeding, for the power in her blood. Now it made some sense. Voltred must be the King's brother. The King's powerless brother. Did the King know what Voltred was up to? Had he banned him to Akkadia? Or did Voltred leave on his own? Or perhaps Voltred was a spy. There were still so many unanswered questions.

Nassa and Volya were led back to the hut that they had awoken in that morning. The fairy elf men brought in meals periodically, but the day passed quickly with Nassa in a fog of thought. Volya didn't attempt to talk to her either, he seemed quite lost in his thoughts as well.

"I need to escape," Nassa said suddenly looking at Volya.

"Nassa, we need to talk," Volya said, urgency in his eyes.

"Not now, Volya. I need to get out of here. I need to get to Balrigard Monastary now more than ever." Nassa thought back to the note Marny had left her all those years ago. *Find Master Perigreen.* She would find him, and he would help her. There was no one else she could trust, but she had to trust Marny. Marny had died for her, she was sure of it now more than ever.

"Nassa, I want to help you." Volya looked at her candidly.

"Yesterday, you wanted to kill me," Nassa spoke plainly.

"Nassa, I did. But you have to understand. I could not let Sudonia get your power. I still cannot. But maybe you can be trained. I can teach you, Nassa, how to fight." She could see the zeal in his eyes, and the truth behind his words.

"You only want to use me, Volya. Just like everyone else. You only care about yourself." Nassa looked at him with contempt.

"No, Nassa. It's not that," Volya implored.

"It is, Volya. I am not some hero. I just want answers. I'd like to learn my powers. Maybe I will help a few people along the way. But nothing more. I will not help you in your personal war against the world," Nassa spoke passionately, the anger that had been building throughout her day coming out in her words.

"I am fighting against evil, Nassa. You yourself said you wanted to help those who couldn't help themselves," Volya retorted, anger now filling his voice as well.

"You kill your own people in the name of justice?" Nassa spit out at him, her temper beginning to boil over.

"It is justice. You think Sudonia hasn't killed thousands of innocents? You think they care about you? Look what they did to you. These people have no mercy. They deserve to die." Volya looked at her with outrage.

"Do you even pause to think about those you kill?" Nassa stared up at him, they had been moving closer together in their fury.

"I did with you." Volya was now standing directly in front of Nassa. He was breathing hard, and so was she. She could feel his hot breath on her, she could almost touch his panting chest. Despite all her resentment against him, she couldn't resist the pull she felt to get closer. She kicked him in the shin as hard as she could.

"That's for trying to kill me," She shouted at him. She turned to move away but he took his bound hands and quickly slipped them over her head, pulling her close in an embrace.

"I deserved that," he said through clenched teeth, even as he held her close. She tried to worm her way out of his grip, but he was strong, and she was tired. She didn't want to admit it to herself, but it felt good to be held; she was so, so lonely.

"Nassa," he said her name quietly and she stopped trying to wiggle away. She looked up at him. There was so much she could see in those piercing eyes. He was filled with a deep loneliness just as she was. There was anger there too, plenty of it, and something else. Desire.

Nassa's chest tightened, her own desire coming unbidden. But she was lost in his eyes and could not look away. He bent down to her slowly at first, then brought his lips down on her hard. He was not gentle, but he was not forceful either. He was passionate. It was an angry kiss, and a kiss filled with suffering and longing. Nassa resisted at first, but then melted into him, parting her lips.

It wasn't enough, she wanted more. But she pulled away, ducking under his bound hands. She could see the frustration in his furrowed brow. He looked up at her with hunger in his eyes, but with their hands tied there was no more they could do. She moved away from him. She shouldn't have let him do that. But it felt so good. She still hated him, she had to remind herself.

"Why did you do that?" She asked her anger coming back.

"You wanted me to," he said flatly.

"I did not." She clenched her jaw.

"Say what you want." He shrugged and then sat on the floor.

"You can't just do whatever you want!" Nassa shouted at him in frustration.

"I didn't. I did what you wanted." Volya lay on his back putting his bound hands across his chest. Nassa's whole body shook with anger.

"Ugh!" She couldn't put her anger into words, which only made it worse. She closed her eyes trying to regain control of her temper. She needed to escape, she needed to get out of this place. These shackles on her wrists were making her want to scream. Volya did not seem eager to help them escape, so she would come up with a plan on her own and then go her own way. She thought she had needed Volya for protection, but she would continue to practice her powers and she would get strong so she could protect herself. Luckily, she still had her satchel, the sword, and the book containing the map of Sudonia. She would use it to go to Balrigard Monastary. There she would start her new life.

She lay down on the bare floor and curled up into a ball, turning her back toward Volya. She may as well try and get some rest.

She was just nodding off when Volya decided, annoyingly she may add, to begin speaking again.

"Nassa—" He started before she interrupted him.

"I was almost asleep." She ground out with indignation.

"I think I have a plan." Nassa sat up and looked at him with surprise. He smiled at her.

"What is it?" She asked.

"Well, we can't use our powers, which is not ideal. But I do have these." He reached into his pocket, pulling the odd metal contraption the fairy elf man had used to break the magical twine tying their wrists.

Nassa stared at him dumbfounded.

"You've had those the whole time?" Nassa asked half maddened with fury and half relieved.

Volya nodded with a boyish grin.

"Are you a complete fool? What were you waiting for?" Nassa practically shouted.

"Well, a few things really. First, I just wanted to watch you squirm. You look cute when you are irritated, and I find it particularly satisfying when you are bothered." He winked at her. She clenched her jaw. "And second, I thought it best to wait until it was dark."

"But what if the man noticed they were gone?" She asked confounded.

"Well, then we would have to come up with another way to escape," he shrugged. Nassa couldn't even start with him.

"How did you manage to get them?" Nassa asked, still stunned but beginning to regain her composure. They would be able to escape, she thought with relief.

"I am a member of *The Guild*, you know. Or was at least. Always was the best pickpocket in town." He gave her a wide grin.

"The cockiest too, I'm sure," Nassa replied. "Well, what are you waiting for?" Nassa brought up her wrists bringing them to him.

He handed her the tool so she could cut his ties first. She handed them back and Volya went to cut hers as well. At the last second he pulled back.

"Hmm, this is an interesting situation," he mused out loud.

"Cut the ties, Volya." Nassa insisted with irritation.

"But should I? This could be fun." He gave her a wicked smile.

"Are you still planning on killing me? Now would be a good time." Nassa clenched her jaw.

"I'm not going to kill you anymore. But I won't let Sudonia have your power either." Volya rubbed his chin.

"Volya, untie me now." Nassa could feel her temper rising again. Was he really going to leave her in these cuffs? She may have to kill *him* now.

Volya hesitated, then winked, and cut the ties. Nassa punched him hard in his good arm. She thought about hitting him where he was still bandaged, but she found she wasn't so cruel, even with all her hatred.

"Ouch." Volya laughed rubbing his arm. "It was just a little fun, Nassa. Trust me, there are some very enjoyable things I could do to you all tied up." He smirked.

"I don't trust you," said Nassa.

"You're so serious all the time, Nassa." Volya sighed.

"Well, yes, I do take attempted murder pretty seriously." Nassa glared at him.

"Well, you need to get over it, we are past that now. If it makes you feel better, I don't think I would have gone through with it." Volya stretched his arms high above his head, moving them back and forth.

"Are we past that? If I recall it was only yesterday," Nassa spoke with contempt.

Volya laughed and put his arm around her, using his other hand to mess her hair. "Let's get going." Nassa swatted him away. But she grabbed her satchel and followed him out of the hut, nonetheless.

She wasn't sure why she followed him exactly. She should have gone her own way. She knew she should. Volya had proved himself to be a liar, a thief, and a murderer. But there was such a strong pull to stay with him, it was as if she couldn't help herself. And although she hated him, she couldn't help but feel the lingering effects of his kiss.

They wove their way through the huts, going the opposite direction than they had when they met the queen. Volya quieted their steps with his wind powers, and thankfully no one seemed to be out and about while the sun was down. It was curious in fact. Nassa knew there were hundreds of them, yet they had only seen all the creatures when the queen had summoned them, except for the man who had collected them.

They made it to the edge of the huts without incident. Either the fairy elves had way too much trust in their magic rope, or else something was amiss. They hadn't even had a guard at their door.

"Does this seem too easy?" Nassa whispered to Volya.

"I was thinking the same thing," Volya whispered back.

They slipped past the last row of huts. No wonder they had not seen any of the fairy elves. All of them stood before them now, a barrier between Nassa and a strange shimmering wall of light purple. As Nassa looked at the wall, she realized it was in fact not quite a wall but a kind of force field. It seemed to raise up past the canopy of the forests, forming a dome over their entire settlement. This must be what protected the fairy elves from being seen and found by outsiders. No wonder so many thought of them as mythical creatures, they must be impossible to find. Unless you were captured by them of course.

"We cannot let you leave," Shantara spoke to Nassa.

"Why not?" Nassa asked standing her ground. The men stood in ranks behind Shantara, crude looking spears in their hands.

"We need to study your power, to look for ways to fight against the King of Sudonia. It is a simple thing," Shantara spoke with a measured calmness.

"I'm not what you think I am. I'm no fighter, just a plain girl. I cannot give you what you want. I don't even know how to use my powers." Nassa pleaded with her and looked to Volya. He gave her a slight frown, maybe she shouldn't have told them that.

"You are too dangerous in their hands," Shantara said simply.

"On that we agree," Volya spoke quietly so only Nassa could hear. She scowled at him. Was no one on her side?

"I am leaving," she said stubbornly and walked forward. The line of the men stuck out their spears. "Really? And you call yourself fair, yet you enslave your men?"

"They are the lesser species of Rodehendra." Shantara did not take her eyes off of Nassa.

"I find that hard to believe. You are just like them all. All rulers take what they want, they take and take from their own people, stuffing their own pockets. All you do is provide yourself with power and leave your people miserable." Nassa spat at her trying to decide how she was going to get past the men.

"You think you know so much of the world for so very little you have seen of it," Shantara replied. Nassa felt the truth in the insult. She may be sheltered, but she had seen what greed for power does to people and it was never good.

"Move aside," Nassa commanded. The men looked around hesitantly but did not move.

"They will only obey me," Shantara explained.

"Do you want me as your ally or your enemy?" Nassa looked sharply at Shantara as she asked.

"I want you as a tool," Shantara spoke and Nassa could see the greed in her eyes.

"Wrong answer, Queenie. She doesn't take well to being used. Trust me, I've tried myself," Volya said from behind Nassa, giving her a wink.

He was right. It was the wrong answer. Even Volya must understand now that Nassa was sick of being used by others. She was angry, but more than that she was fiercely determined. The world looked at her as a weapon of some sorts. Something they could take for themselves and hone. But she wasn't a weak vessel to be used. She was Annassa. *Strength.*

She held on to that thought as she closed her eyes, taking a deep breath in. She imagined what she wanted. She opened her eyes, looked at Shantara, and pushed.

Shantara flew into the air several yards, landing on her back. She clearly had not been prepared for Nassa to use her magic.

The men charged forward with their spears, but Volya was quicker. He used his powers, blowing wind and knocking the spears away from Nassa, keeping the men at bay. Shantara still lay there frozen, Nassa didn't think she was dead, that had not been her intention, however, Shantara did not move.

The men attacked. Nassa and Volya were surrounded, but they had the benefit of their powers. Volya hit one with a bolt of wind, as he punched another in the gut. Nassa ducked as a man came, with spear ramming toward her. She stuck out her leg, sweeping it underneath, and the man went sprawling.

She concentrated her power again, focusing her mind. Fire. She used her hands now, gracefully sweeping a semi-circle in the air, and to her amazement fire appeared. They turned their backs on the flames as Nassa and Volya looked to the men in ranks before them.

"We need to get through that wall, Volya. Pick me up, do your flying thing," Nassa told him. He nodded and grabbed her. They flew straight at the wall, but whatever it was made of would not let them through. They bounced off, falling to the ground with a thud.

It took a moment to recover from the fall, but soon Nassa and Volya were back on their feet. They turned around, relieved to be past the ranks of the fairy elf men, but still stuck within the walls of Finderlind.

Shantara slowly stood, rubbing her head. She looked strong and regal and stared at Nassa with what almost looked like respect.

"You cannot make it through the wall. It is impervious to magic." She stated with a smile. "But it is nice to see that you do know how to use your magic." Barely, Nassa thought with regret.

Nassa only stared back at her.

"Capture them," Shantara ordered her men. They regained their bearings and began to approach, spears raised.

"Do you still have those metal things?" Nassa whispered to Volya as it struck her that they had been able to cut magic before. Volya nodded and grinned.

"Well, be quick about it," Nassa told him, trying to keep the panic out of her voice, as the men came closer. Volya took out the metal tool, piercing the shimmering wall. He grunted as he used all his strength to cut a rough opening. Nassa stared at Shantara whose eyes grew in consternation.

"Get them!" Shantara shouted. The men charged quickly now. But it was too late. Volya had pushed Nassa through the crude hole he made. She looked back at the purple barrier, now on the other side, but she couldn't see anything but forest. The hole had closed with Volya still in Finderlind.

Chapter 38

VOLYA

And when the thief comes,
His pockets are full,
His eyes still a'gleaming,
The greed of a troll.

- Tales of a Thief by Pickering Fool

Hells. Volya thought for the second time that day. The opening had been too small, there was no way they would both have fit through in time. He had pushed her pretty forcefully, hopefully she would not be too irritated — she had quite a temper that one. His shin still hurt where she kicked him early, but he supposed he deserved it, it only added to all the other injuries he had accumulated protecting her. Now he needed to stall so Nassa could get as far from here as possible, he would catch up with her eventually, he hoped. He knew he wouldn't be able to fight them off forever, but he was sure he could last a pretty long time. Especially with his powers strong from disuse.

He turned back toward the oncoming men, smiling, ready for a fight. He blasted wind at them, flying himself into the air and flipping over a few close by. There were hundreds of them, but they were smaller than him, and had no power that he was aware of. They continued to come after him and he continued to mow them down with a powerful wind. He kept trying to turn and make another opening in the barrier, but they were giving him no break. *This is getting annoying,* he thought.

Suddenly he was thrown off his feet as two of the men jumped on top of him. One of them pierced the flesh on his bad arm with a spear before Volya was able to throw them off again. He got back to his feet, feeling a bit lightheaded, before a stinging sensation whipped at his ankles and he fell back down. He looked up to see Shantara holding her whip, the whip that had just bound his feet together with the magic rope.

"Stupid, boy," she said, and flicked the whip at his hands, binding them as well. "No one buys you as the noble gentlemen, you fool." She spat out; anger pooled in her blue eyes.

"You are just an old bitter hag." Volya quipped back. Her eyes narrowed at his not-so-clever insult. It was all he could think of at the moment though, as he was quite frustrated lying here on his back tied up. "Why don't you go after her then? Are you afraid to leave the comfort of your hidden land?" He meant it as an insult, but he saw the fear in her eyes. These creatures were deathly afraid of the outside world, he saw it plainly written on her face.

"Take him away," Shantara instructed the men. "But first take the *torthrill*. The men came and grabbed the metal tool away from his trouser pockets. They grabbed his ankles, dragging him through the forest mulch. They deposited him back in the same hut he had recently occupied with Nassa.

He looked around. He had to admit to himself that he missed Nassa's presence even though he wished he didn't. He didn't want her to have such an effect on him, but he just couldn't help it. He was drawn to her. Nassa had crawled under his skin somehow and she was still there. He smiled to himself, though, recalling their kiss. It had been different than any other kiss before with any other woman. Somehow it had made him feel alive. Made him feel like maybe he had a purpose in life. And for the first time ever, he realized, he did have a purpose. He would protect Nassa from the grips of Sudonia. But first he had to get out of this gods forsaken place away from these annoying little pests.

He fell asleep quicker than he thought possible, bound as he was. He must have been particularly tired after the fight. When he woke, the dim light was poking through.

A head appeared in the doorway.

"I enter?" the face spoke in heavily accented Akkadian. The woman entered. She was beautiful, with pale skin tinged with green and long flowing blond curls. Her overly large eyes shone a deep purple, reminding Volya that she was not quite human.

"Can I help you?" Volya asked giving her a charming grin, not quite able to keep the seductive note out of his voice in the face of such beauty.

"You help me? No, I help you." She walked over to where he was now sitting up intently. "You need woman? I sent to keep you warm." She sat down on his lap.

Volya felt her warmth and saw the willingness in her eyes. These creatures were truly fascinating. Women had always been willing to bed him, he had never had much issue there, but the hospitality of these creatures was amusing. And even for him — being a prisoner and all.

"And do you creatures seduce all your prisoners?" He asked with a smile bending down to her as she stroked his chest and looked up at him with those big eyes.

"You entice me." She batted her eyes up at him. "I am here to give welcome."

"Welcoming a prisoner? You folk do have strange traditions." Volya laughed as she brought her arms up around his neck. "You realize I am still all tied together."

"We welcome you as guest. We want you to stay here. You help us," she began to kiss his neck. He took a deep breath and closed his eyes against his growing lust. But when he did, all he saw was Nassa. He pushed the fairy elf away.

"Will you untie me so we can enjoy this a little more?" He asked with a lecherous grin.

"I not supposed to untie," she replied as she began to unbutton his shirt and kiss his chest.

"I promise, it will be much more enjoyable for both of us," he said trying to keep his voice light hearted and flirty.

"No, I get in trouble then." She looked up at him all seriousness in her eyes.

Volya sighed, "Very well then."

He lifted his bound hands together swinging back. He brought the strength of his force down on her head, knocking her out. He looked down at her, it was unpleasant to hit a woman and it left a bad taste in his mouth. But really, she was quite annoying. And he needed to escape.

He poked his head out of the hut, looking for guards. Sure enough, this time they had been smart enough to post a man at his door.

"Excuse me," Volya said to the man. "The lady in here needs some help." The man nodded. Volya waited until the man had come fully in the hut.

"What did you do to—" The man began to question, but Volya knocked him out before he could finish. He almost felt bad for these little creatures. They were an interesting and unique race, but really not very clever. And not very good fighters either, it was remarkable that they hadn't gone extinct.

He wound his way awkwardly through the huts, sticking to the shadows and quieting his steps. It wasn't easy to get around with his feet still bound, but he managed to shuffle on without making too much noise. He peered out where the fire pit stood, but no one was around. He made his way over toward the queen's hut.

He crept to the side of the door, crouching down and peering in, trying not to be seen. The queen was sitting at her table with her back to Volya. Perfect.

He snuck in slowly, hoping she would not turn around before he was close enough. Thankfully, she did not. He came up behind her, slipping his arms quickly around her head and tugging, strangling her. He brought his head close by and whispered in her ear.

"You underestimated me," he spoke softly. "Who is the fool now?" He brought his forehead down on the top of her head, head butting her and knocking her unconscious.

He searched around the room looking for the tool, but found nothing. A thought occurred to him, and he began riffling through Shantara's pockets until he found what he was looking for. He grabbed the odd tool and brought it down to his legs, awkwardly cutting the tie. Ah, that felt good, he thought, stretching his legs.

Cutting the cord at his wrists proved to be much more difficult with bound hands. But after some time, he managed. He twirled his wrists in appreciation of their freedom then pocketed the metal device.

He poked his head out and looked around. No one was out and about on the ground, but when he looked up he saw a few of the fairy elves crossing bridges above him. He snuck out of the hut, using his powers to quiet his steps. It was much faster moving without being bound. He made it back to the shimmering wall without incident this time. He cut a rough opening like before, this time stepping through himself. He was free. He breathed in the fresh air of freedom then leapt into the sky. Time to find Nassa.

Chapter 39

NASSA

The fight began,
Beast versus man,
The battlefields red,
Blood thicker than water.

- The Ancient Archives, Vol II, Book 3

When Nassa had escaped Finderlind, she ran. She wasn't sure where she was going, she didn't even know which direction she was traveling in, but she knew she needed to get as far away as possible. She felt uneasy without Volya with her for protection, but she would just have to get over that. She had used her powers again on her own, bringing them forward purposefully, and she had to confess she was proud of herself. She still had a long way to go, but she didn't feel quite as helpless as she used to.

She spent the night curled up in a ball against a tree. She was hungry and cold, but sleep came, nonetheless.

She thought of Volya as she drifted off, it wasn't lost on her that he had sacrificed himself for her freedom. He had betrayed her, but he had also saved her. She would sort through that all later.

When Nassa awoke, she was surprised to recognize where she was. She must be pretty close to the Sudonese border then. Montoc's old cottage was only a short way beyond. She recognized the hill in the distance, she could see the other side of it from the home she lived in as a girl. Her stomach flipped at the prospect of going there again. She never thought she would go back.

She was still half a day away, so she decided that once she made it to the cottage she would stay there the night — if it wasn't occupied. The thought made her extremely anxious knowing past memories were bound to resurface. But at the same time, she was so close she could feel the land. She needed to see for herself what had become of it.

Around midday she glimpsed the lane leading to the cottage in the distance. She crept up the bank to cross the main road. No one was anywhere to be seen, but it still made her nervous to be so exposed on the thoroughfare. She looked from side to side then ran across to the lane that would lead her back to her childhood.

She walked slowly down the road. Weeds were sprouting through cracks in the packed dirt, it didn't appear that anyone had been this way in a long time. She rounded the bend where the stables used to be, and her heart dropped. The vegetation that had overgrown the rest of the property was absent here. It looked like a large circular gap, where the stables had burned on that horrible day long ago. It hadn't changed at all — it mirrored the empty space inside her. Her eyes began to water.

She crossed the once bustling stable yard and made her way down to the creek. Three patches of flowers stood, the flowers blooming with strength and vigor. Nassa fell to her knees and began to weep. She touched the dirt, watching the small droplets coalesce where her tears fell.

"Oh Marny, oh Papa." She cried bringing her hands to her face. And Alago too, she thought, the faithful stable master from Hilderland. Oh, how she missed them.

"Miss, are you all right?" Nassa leapt to her feet at the touch on her shoulder. She had thought she was alone, but someone must have snuck up on her while she was distracted by her grief. Her heart was racing as she turned to face the newcomer.

"I'm fine. Who are you?" She stood there; the startled expression written plainly all over her face. A tall man stood in front of her. He was strong with a powerful nose and slicked back greying hair.

"I'm just a friendly visitor. I used to know the man who lived here." He gave her a kind smile, but there was something else in his look that made Nassa uneasy.

"You knew Montoc?" Nassa asked with surprise.

"He was my… friend," the man said.

"Your friend?" Nassa asked with suspicion before she could contain herself.

"And who was he to you, dear?" The man asked with eyebrows raised.

"He was my Fa—" Nassa caught herself. "He was also my friend."

"Then we have that in common. Shall we go inside and talk?" he motioned with his hand for her to lead the way. Nassa hesitated. A feeling of dread came over her. She definitely did not trust this man. But she didn't see much other choice than to talk with him briefly while she composed herself and came up with a plan. She nodded slowly then began to walk in the direction of the cottage.

They walked in silence, Nassa stealing glances at the man every few steps, making sure he didn't advance on her in any way. She tried keeping part of her mind focused just in case she needed to bring her magic forward at any moment. She wished she could do Volya's flying trick, which would really come in handy. If she ever saw him again, she would force him to teach her. Well, maybe not, she shook off the thought. He only wanted to teach her to use her as a weapon.

They came through the final bit of woods into the clearing containing Montoc's cottage. Nassa's breath caught, and she momentarily stopped in her tracks. She had such fond memories of the place. Fond memories and awful ones too. It had been so long since she had seen her old home, feelings of nostalgia surfaced, almost overwhelming her.

The cottage looked like it had not been touched since that horrible day when she had left, ten years prior. The door was swinging partly open, broken off one set of hinges. Weeds and vines had been the sole occupant, growing on the surfaces and in between cracks in the worn mortar of the walls. The roof of the chicken coup, adjacent to the cottage had fallen in, the little sanctuary where she had spent her mornings collecting eggs and sweeping the mess. On the other side of the cottage, Marny's garden had been overwhelmed by weeds and native plants, no longer a lush plethora of fresh fruits and vegetables. Nassa wiped away a tear.

She went to the door, opening it as it screeched at her in protest. She thought for a moment it may fall completely off its hinges, but it managed to hold itself together. Entering the cottage was surreal. It was exactly the same and yet so very different. The furniture was precisely as it had been left, there was even wood still in the fireplace, although it looked now to be the nest of some sort of vermin. A thick layer of dust and grime covered the dining table and chairs, but Nassa walked over, blowing away as much as she could which sent her into a coughing fit.

The man followed her in, ducking across the threshold. He pulled out a chair, shaking it off while covering his mouth, then sat. Nassa did the same, but she supposed they would still be awfully dirty when they decided to stand back up.

"What brings you here?" The man asked, looking at her with unfeigned interest.

"I—" Nassa hesitated unsure what to tell the man. She hoped for a quick conversation and then to have him moving on his way. "I was just passing by, and thought I would call upon Montoc. It's been a while since I've seen him. But unfortunately, it seems as though he has moved," Nassa tried to lie smoothly but it sounded hollow even to her own ears.

"And what brought upon those tears?" He asked her. Shoot. She forgot he had seen her crying, did he know Montoc was buried there? *No,* she thought to herself, no one else knew that except Toc.

"I thought momentarily I was lost, but how silly of me." She tried to laugh it off nonchalantly, but she could tell he knew she was lying.

"Hm," was all that he said in reply.

"And what brings you here?" She asked smiling trying to play the innocent.

"I'm looking for someone," he stated not taking his eyes off her.

"And who is it you are looking for?" Nassa asked trying to keep her voice even.

"A girl. About your age. She used to live here." He smiled at her knowingly. Nassa's heart dropped into her stomach. No, it dropped all the way into her toes.

She stood up. "I'm sorry, but I really cannot help you there. In fact, it is getting late, and I should be going."

Unfortunately, Nassa had sat in the chair by the fire furthest from the door. The man sat across from her, blocking the entrance. She would have to pass him to get out. She stood there stuck, but he remained seated.

"It doesn't look like anyone has lived here in a long time." The man stated. Nassa began to inch her way toward the door. "Take that fire, for example." He nodded to the fire, which to Nassa's horror, burst to life.

Nassa's eyes went wide. This man had fire power. Her face went pale as she tried to figure out any way out of the cottage.

"Who are you?" Nassa asked in a whisper.

"A friend of a friend." He smiled at her, this time there was a menacing gleam in his eye. "You've managed to lose the boy, I see."

"I don't know what you are talking about." Nassa tried to move past him to the door, but he stopped her with his arm.

"Not quite so fast. There is unsettled business between us." He stood slowly towering over Nassa. She couldn't wait any longer. She didn't want to be trapped in here. She kicked him in the groin with her full force then ran out the door, taking advantage of his momentary incapacitated state.

She ran as fast as she could across the clearing to the small lane. She kept going, not looking back even though she knew he would chase her. She made it all the way to the old stable site before she skidded to a halt as a wall of fire burst before her.

She turned around to see the man stalking toward her leisurely, the fire now at her back.

"What do you want with me! Who are you?" she shouted at the man.

"My name is Rasmere, head of *The Guild of Thieves*. And like I said, Lady Annassa, we have unfinished business." He looked confident and wolfish. *The Guild of Thieves — he must be the one who sent Volya to kill her*, Nassa thought. The one who wanted her dead. He swaggered toward her and Nassa could tell where Volya had learned some of his mannerisms.

"He is like you, you know?" she spoke through clenched teeth. She tightened her firsts readying for a fight she knew she was under qualified for.

Rasmere laughed. "Volya, you mean? Well, I did teach him all I know. He proved to be quite incompetent though in the end," he said motioning to her. Nassa felt her anger beginning to rise.

"Then I take it back, he is a better man then you." Nassa growled.

"Is that what he did then? Win you with his charms? Don't feel too special, girl, he does it with all the ladies. He has a new girl in love with him every week. He doesn't care about any of them. You'll find men like him — they only care about themselves." He smirked. Nassa felt a knot in her stomach. She knew he was trying to rile her up, but it was working.

Nassa had enough. She didn't want to talk to this man any longer. She took a deep breath, steadying herself and opening her mind. Before she could manage to do anything productive, however, he hurled a ball of fire directly at her. She dodged, rolling to the floor, before another ball came flying from the other direction. That one narrowly missed her as he continued to throw ball after ball. The wall of fire was still behind her, and she found that she had nowhere to run. She continued to dodge the fireballs, trying to summon her magic, but unable to do so without having the time to focus her mind.

A particularly large ball of fire came hurtling after her and she turned, running and leaping through the wall of flame. She somehow made it through with only her tunic in flames as she dropped to the ground rolling around putting them out. It wasn't lost on her that she now stood on the scar of earth where Marny and Papa had gone up in flames all those years ago. Perhaps it was a fitting way to go, she would meet the gods in the same place they had, and in the same way. Maybe they were waiting for her now, just on the other side of life.

Instinct took over, however, and she continued to run down toward the stream as Rasmere strode confidently through his flames, the curtains of fire easily parting for him.

Nassa was almost to the stream, but it was too late. Rasmere gathered his strength, throwing a mountain of flame at her.

This time she was unable to dodge it. She felt the fires raining down on her with a vengeance. She took a deep breath. She would see Marny and Papa soon — with that thought, the fire hit her.

Chapter 40

VOLYA

When demons do feast,
With moan and a groan,
The munching and crunching,
Of teeth on a bone.

- Poems from the Deep, Verse 56

Volya had no idea which direction Nassa had run off in. He knew she would have *wanted* to go toward Sudonia, but he also knew from experience that she had a very poor sense of direction. He was at least half a day behind her, but if he was airborne he could catch up quickly. The only problem was, airborne he would not be able to see her tracks.

He sighed and made his way back to the forest floor. He didn't like being so close back to Finderlind, but there was no other way, he needed to start from the beginning. When he got back to the ground, he saw her tracks right away, she had not tried to hide them, he thought with a sigh. She clearly hadn't been thinking straight, but luckily it didn't appear anyone had followed her.

He followed her tracks all morning long, moving as quickly as he could hoping he would catch up with her. He used his wind power to cover both their tracks. It wouldn't perfectly get rid of their trail, but it would be good enough for anyone but the best hunters.

After a couple of hours he got to the spot where she must have slept, he could see the markings of sleep indented clearly up against the moss-covered tree. He hoped that meant he was only a few hours behind. Hopefully, she had slept long, and therefore wasn't much further ahead. It was still not quite mid-day. He took a short break, catching his breath and drinking some water he had in his pack. Nassa had taken the food, but that should be no matter, he would catch up to her, he was sure of it.

He continued to follow her, using his wind now to speed up, anxious to overtake her, a building sense of foreboding growing inside him. She had to be near, he moved so much faster than she could.

It was afternoon when he finally made it to the main thoroughfare, one of the only ones that ran through the Venit Vox. He was near the border, then. He knew this road to be infamous for its danger, but now it looked deserted. He quickly crossed and followed Nassa's tracks down a small lane.

After going for what felt like hours but what was actually probably only tens of minutes, Volya came across a wide opening where the luscious forests cleared. It was not a natural looking place. What could have happened here to have caused such a desolate scar in the earth? He knew Nassa must be close. He almost thought he could feel her presence.

"Volya." Volya whipped around at the sound of his name to see the last person he was expecting — Rasmere. His heart practically stopped beating in his chest, apprehension searing in his veins.

"Where is Nassa?" Volya asked not masking the concern in his voice.

"She's gone Volya, I killed her. I did what you could not." Rasmere gave Volya a curious look.

Volya felt his heart ripping apart. He wanted to run away, to hide away from here, this horrible place. He had only just made his decision. He was going to protect her. And already he had failed miserably.

"I don't believe you," Volya said, feeling the blood drain from his face.

"I told you, Volya, emotions only hinder you. Look at yourself. You act as if you cared for the girl." Rasmere narrowed his eyes. Volya couldn't respond. Rasmere tilted his head at him and smirked. "You did care for her, didn't you? I never thought I would see the day." Rasmere chuckled to himself.

"You will pay for this." Volya managed to get out through gritted teeth.

"You cannot beat me, Volya. I taught you everything. I know your strengths. And especially your weaknesses," Rasmere sighed.

"You did not teach me everything. You honed me into a monster. I let you kill Mara, and all my brothers. And now I let you kill Nassa. You will not get away with it this time." Volya felt the tension rising inside him, about to burst.

"Volya, do not be so self-righteous. You wanted them all dead too. You wanted power for yourself. Pride Volya, I have always told you it would be your downfall." Rasmere smirked. Volya couldn't take it another moment longer.

Volya attacked then, years of pain and hurt rushing forward in his movements. This man had caused the deaths of Mara and all his band of brothers, he had killed anyone and everything that ever mattered. And Volya had let him. He hated himself for it, but he hated the man in front of him too. And now Nassa. It was his only purpose, and the only job he had ever decided on for himself — and he had failed abysmally.

He shot at Rasmere with spear after spear of wind. Wind so sharp and piercing it could kill a man if it hit the right spot — but he kept missing the right spot, he thought with frustration. He didn't let up though, he kept going, not caring if his strength failed him, not caring about anything except the hatred he had eating him up inside.

Rasmere shot back with flame, but Volya didn't care. He didn't care if Rasmere killed him. He didn't care if he burned up in painful flames, his soul was already scorched. Wind and fire bounced back and forth, a true parry of the elements. But slowly, inch by inch Volya crept toward Rasmere. He was stronger than him now, he realized with irony. But his strength hadn't helped when it mattered.

"Volya, give up, it is a lost cause!" Rasmere shouted above the whirl of flame and wind when Volya was only a few feet away.

"Never. I will kill you for what you did." Volya sneered back, venom in his words.

"She is not worth it Volya. She needed to die. You know it as well as I," Rasmere spoke with strain in his voice trying to hold Volya at bay.

Volya tore a dagger from his side, throwing it and piercing it in Rasmere's shoulder. Rasmere let out a cry and his fire began to falter.

"There is another way. We could have protected her, used her against the King," Volya shouted anger and hurt making his eyes water.

"He killed my son, my child! So, I killed his," Rasmere spat.

"That is what he wanted! Don't you see he wanted his children dead. You did what he wanted the whole time," Volya shouted. His anger and pain had overtaken him, his mind was only on one thing — vengeance. He breathed in deeply then blew out a wind with such devastating force. Rasmere was knocked off his feet and his flames went out. Volya could see his wind shaking the trees in the distance.

"It was more than that Volya! Don't you understand anything? We've been killing our people for years — the King has been forcing my hand for years to kill anyone with magic — anyone who got away during *The Great Purge*. He won't take any chance — leave no bastard living. All those dead children, Volya, so many years ago. You think that was sport? Many of them were refugees like you." Rasmere shouted over the noise of the wind, unable to get up.

"That was all for the king?" Volya paused, soaking in this information. "You mean you have been working for him this whole time?"

"He made me. He knew he could get me to do anything while dangling my son's life in front of me. But I didn't kill her — I thought we could trade once we knew she had power. A child for a child. I was wrong."

"You've been working for the King." Volya said again, anger rising. The one man he hated more than anything else. The man he found responsible for his parents death. The man responsible for so many innocent deaths. "And now you've killed Nassa for revenge. But who will avenge her?" Volya could no longer tamper his anger.

"She's dead, Volya, it is over," Rasmere spoke. Volya saw in Rasmere's eyes that he knew he was about to meet his end. He was not angry, however, but looked relieved.

"It isn't over until Sudonia pays. And until you pay." Volya looked into Rasmere's eyes as he brought his hands down, using the strength of his wind power to twist Rasmere's head, breaking his neck. It was a quick death — the only mercy Volya let this man have — this man who had been his mentor, who had been like a father.

Volya fell to his knees and wept for the first time since his parent's death. He wept bitterly for his own sardonic life. He wept for Rasmere who deserved death but yet had been kind to Volya in his own way. He wept for everyone he had killed. He wept for all those he had seen die — Mara, his brothers. But most of all he wept for Nassa, the only girl who had ever made him feel like he could be more.

THE END OF BOOK 1

EPILOGUE

Old road, again we meet,
Is it the end or full circle?
My feet are weary,
The day drags on,
Let us rest now, before the dawn.

- The Ancient Archives, Vol I, Book 1

Master Perigreen woke in the middle of the night to a loud and obnoxious knocking. *Who could be here at this hour*, he thought with a panic. He was an old man now. Older than even the Headmaster — and the Headmaster looked to be straight out of the crypt. Master Perigreen thought he would die years ago, but the gods had taken pity on him, or maybe they had a wicked sense of humor.

Now here he was, limping slowly to the front gates of the monastery. The stone floors felt cold under his bare feet. In fact, his whole body felt chilled to the bone. It was always cold here in Northern Sudonia. He sighed, bringing his lantern up and opening the small hatch in the doorway to peer out into the night. It was snowing, he realized with a groan.

He brought the lantern out farther, looking into the darkness. A small, hooded figure stood before the gate.

"Who goes there?" Master Perigreen sneered.

"Help." It was a small and young voice, he realized with a shock. The voice of a girl.

He quickly unlatched the lock which tied the handles of the monastery gates together. He used all his strength to pull open the massive doors, heavy with inlaid iron. The girl stumbled forward, her breathing ragged. She took one step inside and then collapsed.